THE
HIDDEN
SIDE
OF
THE
MOON

MW00472913

THE HIDDEN SIDE OF THE MOON

STORIES BY

JOANNA RUSS

ST. MARTIN'S PRESS · New York

Grateful acknowledgment is made for permission to reprint the following:

"The Clichés from Outer Space" appeared in *Women's Studies International Forum* 7:2, 1984. Copyright © 1984 by Pergamon Press. A shorter version appeared in *The Witch and the Chameleon* April 1, 1975.

"Come Closer" appeared in *The Magazine of Horror* 2:4, August 1965. Copyright © 1965 by Health Knowledge Inc.

"Elf Hill" appeared in *The Magazine of Fantasy and Science Fiction* 63:5 (378) November 1982. Copyright © 1982 by Mercury Press, Inc.

"Existence" appeared in *Epoch* 1975 (New York: Putnams). Copyright © 1975 by Robert Silverberg and Roger Elwood.

"The Experimenter" appeared in *Galaxy* 26:9, October 1975. Copyright © 1975 by UPD Publishing Corporation.

"Foul Fowl" appeared in *The Little Magazine* 5:1, Spring 1971. Copyright © 1971 by The Little Magazine.

"How Dorothy Kept Away the Spring" appeared in *The Magazine of Fantasy and Science Fiction* 52:2 (309) February 1977. Copyright © 1977 by Mercury Press, Inc. Reassigned to Joanna Russ in 1981.

"'I Had Vacantly Crumpled It into My Pocket . . . But My God, Eliot, It was a Photograph from Life!'" appeared in *The Magazine of Fantasy and Science Fiction* 27:2 (159) August 1964. Copyright © 1964 by Mercury Press, Inc. Reassigned to Joanna Russ in 1981.

"It's Important to Believe" appeared in *Sinister Wisdom* 14, 1980. Copyright © 1980 by Sinister Wisdom.

Continued on page 230.

THE HIDDEN SIDE OF THE MOON. Copyright © 1987 by Joanna Russ. All rights reserved. Printed in the United States of America. No part of this book may be used or reproduced in any manner whatsoever without written permission except in the case of brief quotations embodied in critical articles or reviews. For information, address St. Martin's Press, 175 Fifth Avenue, New York, N.Y. 10010.

Design by Janet Tingey

Library of Congress Cataloging-in-Publication Data

Russ, Joanna, 1937–
  The hidden side of the moon.

  I. Title.
PS3568.U763H5   1987   813'.54   87-16275
ISBN 0-312-01105-9

First Edition
10 9 8 7 6 5 4 3 2 1

CONTENTS

THE
HIDDEN
SIDE
OF
THE
MOON

THE LITTLE
DIRTY GIRL

Dear———,

Do you like cats? I never asked you. There are all sorts of cats: elegant, sinuous cats, clunky, heavy-breathing cats, skinny, desperate cats, meatloaf-shaped cats, waddling, dumb cats, big slobs of cats who step heavily and groan whenever they try to fit themselves (and they never do fit) under something or in between something or past something.

I'm allergic to all of them. You'd think they'd know it. But as I take my therapeutic walks around the neighborhood (still aching and effortful after ten months, though when questioned, my doctor replies, with the blank, baffled innocence of those Martian children so abstractedly brilliant they've never learned to communicate about merely human matters with anyone, *that my back will get better*) cats venture from alleyways, slip out from under parked cars, bound up cellars steps, prick up their ears and flash out of gardens, all lifting up their little faces, wreathing themselves around my feet, crying *Dependency! Dependency!* and showing their elegantly needly little teeth, which they never use save in yearning appeal to my goodness. They have perfect confidence in me. If I try to startle them by hissing, making loud noises, or clapping my hands sharply, they merely stare in interested fashion and scratch themselves with their hind legs: how nice. I've perfected a method of lifting kitties on

1

the toe of my shoe and giving them a short ride through the air (this is supposed to be alarming); they merely come running back for more.

And the children! I don't dislike children. Yes I do. No I don't, but I feel horribly awkward with them. So of course I keep meeting them on my walks this summer: alabaster little boys with angelic fair hair and sky-colored eyes (this section of Seattle is Scandinavian and the Northwest gets very little sun) come up to me and volunteer such compelling information as:

"*I'm* going to my friend's house."

"I'm going to the store."

"My name is Markie."

"I wasn't really scared of that big dog; I was just *startled*."

"People leave a lot of broken glass around here."

The littler ones confide; the bigger ones warn of the world's dangers: dogs, cuts, blackberry bushes that might've been sprayed. One came up to me once—what do they see in a tall, shuffling, professional, intellectual woman of forty?—and said, after a moment's thought:

"Do you like frogs?"

What could I do? I said yes, so a shirt-pocket that jumped and said *rivit* was opened to disclose Mervyn, an exquisite little being the color of wet, mottled sea-sand, all webbed feet and amber eyes, who was then transferred to my palm where he sat and blinked. Mervyn was a toad, actually; he's barely an inch long and can be found all over Seattle, usually upside down under a rock. I'm sure he (or she) is the Beloved Toad and Todkins and Todlekrancz Virginia Woolf used in her letters to Emma Vaughan.

And the girls? O they don't approach tall, middle-aged women. Little girls are told not to talk to strangers. And the little girls of Seattle (at least in my neighborhood) are as obedient and feminine as any in the world; to the jeans and tee-shirts of Liberation they (or more likely their parents) add hair-ribbons, baby-sized pocketbooks, fancy pins, pink shoes, even toe polish.

The liveliest of them I ever saw was a little person of five, coasting downhill in a red wagon, her cheeks pink with excitement, one ponytail of yellow hair undone, her white tee-shirt askew, who gave a decorous little squeak of joy at the sheer speed of it. I saw and smiled; pink-cheeks saw and shrieked again, more loudly and confidently this time, then looked away, embarrassed, jumped quickly out of her wagon, and hauled it energetically up the hill.

Except for the very littlest, how neat, how clean, how carefully dressed they are! with long, straight hair that the older ones (I know this) still iron under waxed paper.

The little, dirty girl was different.

She came up to me in the supermarket. I've hired someone to do most of my shopping, as I can't carry much, but I'd gone in for some little thing, as I often do. It's a relief to get off the hard bed and away from the standing desk or the abbreviated kitchen stools I've scattered around the house (one foot up and one foot down); in fact it's simply such a relief—

Well, the little, dirty girl *was* dirty; she was the dirtiest eight-year-old I've ever seen. Her black hair was a long tangle. Her shoes were down-at-heel, the laces broken, her white (or rather grey) socks belling limply out over her ankles. Her nose was running. Her pink dress, so ancient that it showed her knees, was limp and wrinkled and the knees themselves had been recently skinned. She look as if she had slid halfway down Volunteer Park's steepest dirtiest hill on her panties and then rolled end-over-end the rest of the way. Besides all this, there were snot-and-tear-marks on her face (which was reddened and sallow and looked as if she'd been crying) and she looked—well, what can I say? *Neglected.* Not poor, though someone had dressed her rather eccentrically, not physically unhealthy or underfed, but messy, left alone, ignored, kicked out, bedraggled, like a cat caught in a thunderstorm.

She looked (as I said) tear-stained, and yet came up to my shopping cart with perfect composure and kept me calm company for a minute or so. Then she pointed to a box of Milky Way candy bars on a shelf above my head, saying "I like those," in a deep, gravelly voice that suggested a bad cold.

I ignored the hint. No, that's wrong, it wasn't a hint; it was merely a social, adult remark, self-contained and perfectly emotionless, as if she had long ago given up expecting that telling any-one she wanted something would result in getting it. Since my illness I have developed a fascination with the sheer, elastic wealth of children's bodies, the exhaustless, energetic health they don't know they have and which I so acutely and utterly miss, but I wasn't for an instant tempted to feel this way about the Little Dirty Girl. She had been through too much. She had Resources. If she showed no fear of me, it wasn't because she trusted me but be-cause she trusted nothing. She had no expectations and no hopes. Nonetheless she attached herself to me and my shopping cart and accompanied me down two more aisles, and there seemed to be hope in that. So I made the opening, social, adult remark:

"What's your name?"

"A. R." Those are the initials on my handbag. I looked at her sharply but she stared levelly back, unembarrassed, self-con-tained, unexpressive.

"I don't believe that," I said finally.

"I could tell you lots of things you wouldn't believe," said the Little Dirty Girl.

She followed me up to the cashier and as I was putting out my small packages one by one by one, I saw her lay out on the counter a Milky Way bar and a nickel, the latter fetched from somewhere in that short-skirted, cap-sleeved dress. The cashier, a middle-aged woman, looked at me and I back at her, I laid out two dimes next to the nickel. She really did want it! As I was going into the logis-tics of How Many Short Trips from the Cart to the Car and How Many Long Ones from the Car to the Kitchen, the Little Dirty Girl spoke: "I can carry that." (Gravelly and solemn.)

She added hoarsely, "I bet I live near you."

"Well, *I* bet you don't," I said.

She didn't answer, but followed me to the parking lot, one pro-prietary hand on the cart, and when I unlocked my car door, she darted past me and started carrying packages from the cart to the front seat. I can't move fast enough to escape these children. She sat there calmly as I got in. Then she said, wiping her nose on the back of her hand:

"I'll help you take your stuff out when you get home."

Now I know that sort of needy offer and I don't like it. Here was a Little Dirty Girl offering to help me, and smelling in close quarters as if she hadn't changed her underwear for days: demandingness, neediness, more annoyance. Then she said in her flat, crow's voice: "I'll do it and go away. I won't bother you."

Well, what can you do? My heart misgave me. I started the car and we drove the five minutes to my house in silence, whereupon she grabbed all the packages at once (to be useful) and some slipped back on the car seat; I think this embarrassed her. But she got my things up the stairs to the porch in only two trips and put them on the unpainted porch rocker, from where I could pick them up one by one, and there we stood.

Why speechless? Was it honesty? I wanted to thank her, to act decent, to make that sallow face smile. I wanted to tell her to go away, that I wouldn't let her in, that I'd lock the door. But all I could think of to say was, "What's your name really?" and the wild thing said stubbornly, "A. R." and when I said, "No, really," she cried "*A. R.!*" and facing me with her eyes screwed up, shouted something unintelligible, passionate and resentful, and was off up the street. I saw her small figure turning down one of the cross-streets that meets mine at the top of the hill. Seattle is grey and against the massed storm clouds to the north her pink dress stood out vividly. She was going to get rained on. Of course.

I turned to unlock my front door and a chunky, slow, old cat, a black-and-white tom called Williamson who lives two houses down, came stiffly out from behind an azalea bush, looked slit-eyed (bored) about him, noticed me (his pupils dilated with instant interest) and bounded across the parking strip to my feet. Williamson is a banker-cat, not really portly or dignified but simply too lazy and unwieldy to bother about anything much. Either something scares him and he huffs under the nearest car or he scrounges. Like all kitties he bumbled around my ankles, making steam-engine noises. I never feed him. I don't pet him or talk to him. I even try not to look at him. I shoved him aside with one foot and opened the front door; Williamson backed off, raised his fat, jowled face and began the old cry: *Mrawr! Mrawr!* I booted him ungently off the porch before he could trot into my house with me, and as he slowly prepared to attack the steps (he never quite makes it) locked myself in. And the Little Dirty Girl's last words came suddenly clear:

I'll be back.

Another cat. There are too many in this story but I can't help it. The Little Dirty Girl was trying to coax the neighbor's superbly elegant half-Siamese out from under my car a few days later, an animal tiger-marked on paws and tail and as haughty-and-mysterious-looking as all cats are supposed to be, though it's really only the long Siamese body and small head. Ma'amselle (her name) still occasionally leaps on to my dining room windowsill and stares in (the people who lived here before me used to feed her). I was coming back from a walk, the Little Dirty Girl was on her knees, and Ma'amselle was under the car; when the Little Dirty Girl saw me she stood up, and Ma'amselle flashed Egyptianly through the laurel hedge and was gone. Someone had washed the Little Dirty Girl's pink dress (though a few days back, I'm afraid) and made a half-hearted attempt to braid her hair: there were barrettes and elastic somewhere in the tangle. Her cold seemed better. When it rains in August our summer can change very suddenly to early fall, and this was a chilly day; the Little Dirty Girl had nothing but her mud-puddle-marked dress between her thin skin and the Seattle air. Her cold seemed better, though, and her cheeks were pink with stooping. She said, in the voice of a little girl this time and not a raven, "She had *blue* eyes."

"She's Siamese," I said "What's your name?"

"A. R."

"Now look, I don't—"

"*It's A. R.!*" She was getting loud and stolid again. She stood there with her skinny, scabbed knees showing from under her dress and shivered in the unconscious way kids do who are used to it; I've seen children do it on the Lower East Side in New York because they had no winter coat (in January). I said, "You come in." She followed me up the steps—warily, I think—but when we got inside her expression changed, it changed utterly; she clasped her hands and said with radiant joy, "Oh, they're *beautiful!*"

These were my astronomical photographs. I gave her my book of microphotographs (cells, crystals, hailstones) and went into the kitchen to put up water for tea; when I got back she'd dropped the book on my old brown-leather couch and was walking about with her hands clasped in front of her and that same look of radiant joy on her face. I live in an ordinary, shabby frame house that has four rooms and a finished attic; the only unusual thing about it is the number of books and pictures crammed in every which way among the (mostly second-hand) furniture. There are Woolworth frames for the pictures and cement-block bookcases for the books; nonetheless the Little Dirty Girl was as awed as if she'd found Aladdin's Cave.

She said, "It's so . . . sophisticated!"

Well, there's no withstanding that. Even if you think: what do kids know? She followed me into the kitchen where I gave her a glass of milk and a peach (she sipped and nibbled). She thought the few straggling rose bushes she could see in the back garden were wonderful. She loved my old brown refrigerator; she said, "It's so big! And such a color!" Then she said anxiously, "Can I see the upstairs?" and got excited over the attic eaves which were also "so big" (wallboard and dirty pink paint) to the point that she had to run and stand under one side and then run across the attic and stand under the other. She liked the "view" from the bedroom (the neighbor's laurel hedge and a glimpse of someone else's roof) but my study (books, a desk, a glimpse of the water) moved her so deeply and painfully that she only stood still in the center of the room, struggling with emotion, her hands again clasped in front of her. Finally she burst out, "It's so . . . *swanky!*" Here my kettle screamed and when I got back she had gotten bold enough to touch the electric typewriter (she jumped when it turned itself on) and then walked about slowly, touching the books with the tips of her fingers. She was brave and pushed the tabs on the desk lamp (though not hard enough to turn it on) and boldly picked up my little mailing scale. As she did so, I saw that there were buttons missing from the back of her dress; I said, "A. R., come here."

She dropped the scale with a crash. "I didn't mean it!" Sulky again.

"It's not that; it's your buttons," I said, and hauled her to the study closet where I keep a Band-Aid box full of extras; two were a reasonable match: little, flat-topped, pearlized pink things you can hardly find anymore. I sewed them on to her, not that it helped much, and the tangles of her hair kept falling back and catching. What a forest of lost barrettes and snarls of old rubber bands! I lifted it all a little grimly, remembering the pain of combing out. She sat flatly, all adoration gone:

"You can't comb my hair against my will; you're too weak."

"I wasn't going to," I said.

"That's what *you* say," the L.D.G. pointed out.

"If I try, you can stop me," I said. After a moment she turned around, flopped down on my typing chair, and bent her head. So I fetched my old hairbrush (which I haven't used for years) and did what I could with the upper layers, managing even to smooth out some of the lower ones, though there were places near her neck nearly as matted and tangled as felt; I finally had to cut some pieces out with my nail scissors.

L.D.G. didn't shriek (as I used to, insisting my cries were far more artistic than those of the opera singers on the radio on Sundays) but finally asked for the comb herself and winced silently until she was decently braided, with rubber bands on the ends. We put the rescued barrettes in her shirt pocket. Without that cloud of hair her sallow face and pitch-ball eyes looked bigger, and oddly enough, younger; she was no more a wandering Fury with the voice of a Northwest-coast raven but a reasonably human (though draggly) little girl.

I said, "You look nice."

She got up, went into the bathroom, and looked at herself in the mirror. Then she said calmly, "No, I don't. I look conventional."

"Conventional?" said I. She came out of the bathroom, flipping back her new braids.

"Yes, I must go."

And as I was wondering at her tact (for anything after this would have been an anti-climax):

"But I shall return."

"That's fine," I said, "but I want to have grown-up manners with you, A. R. Don't ever come before ten in the morning or if my car isn't here or if you can hear my typewriter going. In fact, I think you had better call me on the telephone first, the way other people do."

She shook her head sweetly. She was at the front door before I could follow her, peering out. It was raining again. I saw that she was about to step out into it and cried "Wait, A. R.!" hurrying as fast as I could down the cellar steps to the garage, from where I could get easily to my car. I got from the back seat the green plastic poncho I always keep there and she didn't protest when I dumped it over her and put the hood over her head, though the poncho was much too big and even dragged on the ground in the front and back. She said only, "Oh, it's swanky. Is it from the Army?" So I had the satisfaction of seeing her move up the hill as a small, green tent instead of a wet, pink draggle. Though with her tea-party manners she hadn't really eaten anything; the milk and peach were untouched. Was it wariness? Or did she just not like milk and peaches? Remembering our first encounter, I wrote on the pad by the telephone, which is my shopping list:

Milky Way Bars

And then:

1 doz.

She came back. She never did telephone in advance. It was all right, though; she had the happy faculty of somehow turning up when I wasn't working and wasn't busy and was thinking of her. But how often is an invalid busy or working? We went on walks or stayed home and on these occasions the business about the Milky Ways turned out to be a brilliant guess, for never have I met a child with such a passion for junk food. A. R.'s formal, disciplined politeness in front of milk or fruit was like a cat's in front of the mass-produced stuff; faced with jam, honey, or marmalade, the very ends of her braids crisped and she attacked like a cat flinging itself on a fish; I finally had to hide my own supplies in self-defense. Then on relatively good days it was ice cream or Sara Lee cake, and on bad ones Twinkies or Mallomars, Hostess cupcakes, Three Musketeers bars, marshmallow cream, maraschino chocolates, Turkish taffy, saltwater taffy, or—somewhat less horribly—Doritos, reconstituted potato chips, corn chips, pretzels (fat or thin), barbecued corn chips, or onion-flavored corn chips, anything like that. She refused nuts and hated peanut butter. She also talked continuously while eating, largely in polysyllables, which made me nervous as I perpetually expected her to choke, but she never did. She got no fatter. To get her out of the house and so away from food, I took her to an old-fashioned five-and-ten nearby and bought her shoelaces. Then I took her down to watch the local ship-canal bridge open up (to let a sailboat through) and we cheered. I took her to a department store (just to look; "I know consumerism is against your principles," she said with priggish and mystifying accuracy) and bought her a pin shaped like a ladybug. She refused to go to the zoo ("An animal jail!") but allowed as the rose gardens ("A plant *hotel*") were both pleasant and educational. A ride on the zoo merry-go-round excited her to the point of screaming and running around dizzily in circles for half an hour afterwards, which embarrassed me—but then no one paid the slightest attention; I suppose shrieky little girls had happened there before, though the feminine youth of Seattle, in its Mary Jane shoes and pink pocketbooks, rather pointedly ignored her. The waterfall in the downtown park, on the contrary, sobered her up; this is a park built right on top of a crossing over one of the city's highways and is usually full of office-workers; a walkway leads not only up to but actually behind the waterfall. A. R. wandered among the beds of bright flowers and passed, stooping, behind the water, trying to stick her hand in the falls; she came out saying:

"It looks like an old man's beard," (pointing to one of the ragged Skid Row men who was sleeping on the grass in the rare,

Northern sunlight). Then she said, "No, it looks like a lady's dress without any seams."

Once, feeling we had become friends enough for it, I ran her a bath and put her clothes through the basement washer-dryer; her splashings and yellings in the bathroom were terrific and afterwards she flashed nude about the house, hanging out of windows, embellishing her strange, raucous shouts with violent jerkings and boundings-about that I think were meant for dancing. She even ran out the back door naked and had circled the house before I—voiceless with calling, *"A. R., come back here!"*—had presence of mind enough to lock both the front and back doors after she had dashed in and before she could get out again to make the entire *tour de Seattle* in her jaybird suit. Then I had to get her back into that tired pink dress, which (when I ironed it) had finally given up completely, despite the dryer, and sagged into two sizes too big for her.

Unless A. R. was youthifying.

I got her into her too-large pink dress, her baggy underwear, her too-large shoes, her new pink socks (which I had bought for her) and said:

"A. R., where do you live?"

Crisp and shining, the Little Clean Girl replied, "My dear, you always ask me that."

"And you never answer," said I.

"O yes I do," said the Little Clean Girl. "I live up the hill and under the hill and over the hill and behind the hill."

"That's no answer," said I.

"Wupf merble," said she (through a Mars Bar) and then, more intelligibly, "If you knew, you wouldn't want me."

"I would so!" I said.

L.D.G.—now L.C.G.—regarded me thoughtfully. She scratched her ear, getting, I noticed, chocolate in her hair. (She was a fast worker.) She said, "You want to know. You think you ought to know. You think you have a right. When I leave you'll wait until I'm out of sight and then you'll follow me in the car. You'll sneak by the curb way behind me so I won't notice you. You'll wait until

I climb the steps of a house—like that big yellow house with the fuchsias in the yard where you think I live and you'll watch me go in. And then you'll ring the bell and when the lady comes to the door you'll say, 'Your little daughter and I have become friends,' but the lady will say, 'I haven't got any little daughter,' and then you'll know I fooled you. And you'll get scared. So don't try."

Well, she had me dead to rights. Something very like that had been in my head. Her face was preternaturally grave. She said, "You think I'm too small. I'm not.

"You think I'll get sick if I keep on eating like this. I won't.

"You think if you bought a whole department store for me, it would be enough. It wouldn't."

"I won't—well, I can't get a whole department store for you," I said. She said, "I know." Then she got up and tucked the box of Mars Bars under one arm, throwing over the other my green plastic poncho, which she always carried about with her now.

"I'll get you anything you want," I said; "No, not what you want, A. R., but anything you really, truly need."

"You can't," said the Little Dirty Girl.

"I'll try."

She crossed the living room to the front door, dragging the poncho across the rug, not paying the slightest attention to the astronomical photographs that had so enchanted her before. Too young now, I suppose. I said, "A. R., I'll try. Truly I will." She seemed to consider it a moment, her small head to one side. Then she said briskly, "I'll be back," and was out the front door.

And I did not—would not—could not—did not dare to follow her.

Was this the moment I decided I was dealing with a ghost? No, long before. Little by little, I suppose. Her clothes were a dead giveaway, for one thing: always the same and the kind no child had worn since the end of the Second World War. Then there was the book I had given her on her first visit, which had somehow closed and straightened itself on the coffee table, another I had lent her later (the poems of Edna Millay) which had mysteriously been there a day afterwards, the eerie invisibility of a naked little girl hanging out of my windows and yelling; the inconspicuousness of a little twirling girl nobody noticed spinning round and shrieking outside the merry-go-round, a dozen half-conscious glimpses I'd had, every time I'd got in or out of my car, of the poncho lying on the back seat where I always keep it, folded as always, the very dust on it undisturbed. And her unchildlike cleverness in never revealing either her name or where she lived. And as surely as A. R. had been a biggish eight when we had met weeks ago, just as surely she was now a smallish, very unmistakable, unnaturally knowledgeable five.

But she was such a *nice* little ghost. And so solid! Ghosts don't run up your grocery bills, do they? Or trample Cheez Doodles into your carpet or leave gum under your kitchen chair, large smears of chocolate on the surface of the table (A. R. had), and an exceptionally dirty ring around the inside of the bathtub? Along with three (count 'em, three) large, dirty, sopping-wet bath towels on the bathroom floor? If A. R.'s social and intellectual life had a tendency to become intangible when looked at carefully, everything connected with her digestive system and her bodily dirt stuck around amazingly; there was the state of the bathroom, the dishes in the sink (many more than mine), and the ironing board still up in the study for the ironing of A. R.'s dress (with the spray starch container still set up on one end and the scorch mark where she'd decided to play with the iron). If she was a ghost, she was a good one and I liked her and wanted her back. Whatever help she needed from me in resolving her ancient Seattle tragedy (ancient ever since nineteen-forty-two) she could have. I wondered for a moment if she were connected with the house, but the people before me—the original owners—hadn't had children. And the house itself hadn't even been built until the mid-fifties; nothing in the neighborhood had. Unless both they and I were being haunted by the children we hadn't had; could I write them a pychothera-peutic letter about it? ("Dear Mrs. X., How is your inner space?") I went into the bathroom and discovered that A. R. had relieved herself interestingly in the toilet and had then not flushed it, hardly what I would call poetical behavior on the part of some-body's unconscious. So *I* flushed it. I picked up the towels one by one and dragged them to the laundry basket in the bedroom. If the Little Dirty Girl was a ghost, she was obviously a bodily-dirt-and-needs ghost traumatized in life by never having been given a proper bath or allowed to eat marshmallows until she got sick. Maybe this was it and now she could rest (scrubbed and full of Mars Bars) in peace. But I hoped not. I was nervous; I had made a promise ("I'll give you what you need") that few of us can make to anyone, a frightening promise to make to anyone. Still, I hoped. And she was a businesslike little ghost. She would come back.

For she, too, had promised.

Autumn came. I didn't see the Little Dirty Girl. School started and I spent days trying to teach freshmen and freshwomen not to write like Rod McKuen (neither of us really knowing why they shouldn't, actually) while advanced students pursued me down the halls with thousand-page trilogies, demands for independent study, and other unspeakables. As a friend of ours said once, everyone will continue to pile responsibility on a woman and everything and everyone must be served except oneself; I've been a flogged horse professionally long enough to know that and meanwhile the dishes stay in the sink and the kindly wife-elves do *not* come out of the woodwork at night and do them. I was exercising two hours a day and sleeping ten; the Little Dirty Girl seemed to have vanished with the summer.

Then one day there was a freak spell of summer weather and that evening a thunderstorm. This is a very rare thing in Seattle. The storm didn't last, of course, but it seemed to bring right after it the first of the winter rains: cold, drenching, ominous. I was grading papers that evening when someone knocked at my door; I thought I'd left the garage light on and my neighbor'd come out to tell me, so I yelled "Just a minute, please!" dropped my pen, wondered whether I should pick it up, decided the hell with it, and went (exasperated) to the door.

It was the Little Dirty Girl. She was as wet as I've ever seen a human being be and had a bad cough (my poncho must've gone heaven knows where) and water squelching in her shoes. She was shivering violently and her fingers were blue—it could not have been more than fifty degrees out—and her long, baggy dress clung to her with water running off it; there was a puddle already forming around her feet on the rug. Her teeth were chattering. She stood there shivering and glowering miserably at me, from time to time emitting that deep, painful chest cough you sometimes hear in adults who smoke too much. I thought of hot baths, towels, electric blankets, aspirin—can ghosts get pneumonia? "For God's sake, get your clothes off!" I said, but A. R. stepped back against the door, shivering, and wrapped her starved arms in her long, wet skirt.

"No!" she said, in a deep voice more like a crow's than ever. "Like this!"

"Like what?" said I helplessly, thinking of my back and how incapable I was of dragging a resistant five-year-old anywhere.

"You hate me!" croaked A. R. venomously; "You starve me! You do! You won't let me eat anything!"

Then she edged past me, still coughing, her dark eyes ringed with blue, her skin mottled with bruises, and her whole body shaking with cold and anger, like a little mask of Medusa. She screamed.

"You want to clean me up because you don't like me!

"You like me clean because you don't like me dirty!

"You hate me so you won't give me what I need!

"You won't give me what I need and I'm dying!

"I'm dying! I'm dying!

"I'M DYING!"

She was interrupted by coughing. I said "A. R.—" and she screamed again, her whole body bending convulsively, the cords in her neck standing out. Her scream was choked by phlegm and she beat herself with her fists; then wrapping her arms in her wet skirt through another bout of coughing, she said in gasps:

"I couldn't get into your house to use the bathroom, so I had to shit in my pants.

"I had to stay out in the rain; I got cold.

"All I can get is from you and you won't give it."

"Then tell me what you need!" I said, and A. R. raised her horrid little face to mine, a picture of venomous, uncontrolled misery, of sheer, demanding starvation.

"You," she whispered.

So that was it. I thought of the pleading cats, whose open mouths *(Dependency! Dependency!)* reveal needle teeth which can rip off your thumb; I imagined the Little Dirty Girl sinking her teeth into my chest if I so much as touched her. Not touched for bathing or combing or putting on shoelaces, you understand, but for touching only. I saw—I don't know what: her skin ash-grey, the bones of her little skull coming through her skin worse and worse every moment—and I knew she would kill me if she didn't get what she wanted, though she was suffering far worse than I was and was more innocent—a demon child is still a child, with a child's needs, after all. I got down on one knee, so as to be nearer her size, and saying only, "My back—be careful of my back," held out my arms so that the terror of the ages could walk into them. She was truly grey now, her bones very prominent. She was starving to death. She was dying. She gave the cough of a cadaver breathing its last, a phlegmy wheeze with a dreadful rattle in it, and then the Little Dirty Girl walked right into my arms.

And began to cry. I felt her crying right up from her belly. She was cold and stinky and extremely dirty and afflicted with the most surprising hiccough. I rocked her back and forth and mumbled I don't know what, but what I meant was that I thought she was fine, that all of her was fine: her shit, her piss, her sweat, her tears, her scabby knees, the snot on her face, her cough, her dirty panties, her bruises, her desperation, her anger, her whims— all of her was wonderful, I loved all of her, and I would do my best to take good care of her, all of her, forever and forever and then a day.

She bawled. She howled. She pinched me hard. She yelled, "Why did it take you so long!" She fussed violently over her panties and said she had been humiliated, though it turned out, when

I got her to the bathroom, that she was making an awfully big fuss over a very little brown stain. I put the panties to soak in the kitchen sink and the Little Dirty Girl likewise in a hot tub with vast mounds of rose-scented bubble bath which turned up from somewhere, though I knew perfectly well I hadn't bought any in years. We had a shrieky, tickly, soapy, toe-grabby sort of a bath, a *very* wet one during which I got soaked. (I told her about my back and she was careful.) We sang to the loofah. We threw water at the bathroom tiles. We lost the soap. We came out warm in a huge towel (I'd swear mine aren't that big) and screamed gaily again, to exercise our lungs, from which the last bit of cough had disappeared. We said, "Oh, floof! there goes the soap." We speculated loudly (and at length) on the possible subjective emotional life of the porcelain sink, American variety, and (rather to my surprise) sang snatches of *The Messiah* as follows:

Every malted
Shall be exalted!

and:

Behold and see
Behold and see
If there were e'er pajama
Like to this pajama!

and so on.

My last memory of the evening is of tucking the Little Dirty Girl into one side of my bed (in my pajamas, which had to be rolled up and pinned even to stay on her) and then climbing into the other side myself. The bed was wider than usual, I suppose. She said sleepily, "Can I stay?" and I (also sleepily) "Forever."

But in the morning she was gone.

Her clothes lasted a little longer, which worried me, as I had visions of A. R. committing flashery around and about the neighborhood, but in a few days they too had faded into mist or the elemental particles of time or whatever ghosts and ghost-clothes are made of. The last thing I saw of hers was a shoe with a new heel (oh yes, I had gotten them fixed) which rolled out from under the couch and lasted a whole day before it became—I forget what, the shadow of one of the ornamental tea-cups on the mantel, I think.

And so there was no more five-year-old A. R. beating on the door and demanding to be let in on rainy nights. But that's not the end of the story.

As you know, I've never gotten along with my mother. I've always supposed that neither of us knew why. In my childhood she had vague, long-drawn-out symptoms which I associated with early menopause (I was a late baby); then she put me through school, which was a strain on her librarian's budget and a strain on my sense of independence and my sense of guilt, and always there was her timidity, her fears of everything under the sun, her terrified, preoccupied air of always being somewhere else, and what I can only call her furtiveness, the feeling I've always had of some secret life going on in her which I could never ask about or share. Add to this my father's death somewhere in pre-history (I was two) and then that ghastly behavior psychologists call The Game of Happy Families—I mean the perpetual, absolute insistence on How Happy We All Were that even aunts, uncles, and cousins rushed to heap on my already bitter and most unhappy shoulders, and you'll have some idea of what's been going on for the last I-don't-know-how-many years.

Well, this is the woman who came to visit a few weeks later. I wanted to dodge her. I had been dodging academic committees and students and proper bedtimes; why couldn't I dodge my mother? So I decided that *this time I would be openly angry* (I'd been doing that in school, too).

Only there was nothing to be angry about, this time.

Maybe it was the weather. It was one of those clear, still times we sometimes have in October: warm, the leaves not down yet, that in-and-out sunshine coming through the clouds, and the northern sun so low that the masses of orange pyracantha berries on people's brick walls and the walls themselves, or anything that color, flame indescribably. My mother got in from the airport in a taxi (I still can't drive far) and we walked about a bit, and then I took her to Kent and Hallby's downtown, that expensive, old-fashioned place that's all mirrors and sawdust floors and old-fashioned white tablecloths and waiters (also waitresses now) with floor-length aprons. It was very self-indulgent of me. But she had been so much better—or I had been—it doesn't matter. She was seventy and if she wanted to be fussy and furtive and act like a thin, old guinea hen with secret despatches from the C.I.A. (I've called her worse things) I felt she had the right. Besides, that was no worse than my flogging myself through five women's work and endless depressions, beating the old plough horse day after day for weeks and months and years—no, for decades—until her back broke and she foundered and went down and all I could do was curse at her helplessly and beat her the more.

All this came to me in Kent and Hallby's. Luckily my mother squeaked as we sat down. There's a reason; if you sit at a corner table in Kent and Hallby's and see your face where the mirrored walls come together—well, it's complicated, but briefly, you can see yourself (for the only time in your life) as you look to other people. An ordinary mirror reverses the right and left sides of your face but this odd arrangement re-reflects them so they're back in place. People are shocked when they see themselves; I had planned to warn her.

She said, bewildered, "What's that?" But rather intrigued too, I think. Picture a small, thin, white-haired, extremely prim ex-librarian, worn to her fine bones but still ready to take alarm and run away at a moment's notice; that's my mother. I explained about the mirrors and then I said:

"People don't really know what they look like. It's only an idea people have that you'd recognize yourself if you saw yourself across the room. Any more than we can hear our own voices; you know, it's because longer frequencies travel so much better through the bones of your head than they can through the air; that's why a tape recording of your voice sounds higher than—"

I stopped. Something was going to happen. A hurricane was

going to smash Kent and Hallby's flat. I had spent almost a whole day with my mother, walking around my neighborhood, showing her the University, showing her my house, and nothing in particular had happened; why should anything happen now?

She said, looking me straight in the eye, "You've changed."

I waited.

She said, "I'm afraid that we—you and I were not—are not—a happy family."

I said nothing. I would have, a year ago. It occurred to me that I might, for years, have confused my mother's primness with my mother's self-control. She went on. She said:

"When you were five, I had cancer."

I said, *"What?* You had *what?"*

"Cancer," said my mother calmly, in a voice still as low and decorous as if she had been discussing her new beige handbag or Kent and Hallby's long, fancy menu (which lay open on the table between us). "I kept it from you. I didn't want to burden you."

Burden.

"I've often wondered—" she went on, a little flustered; "they say now—but of course no one thought that way then." She went on, more formally, "It takes years to know if it has spread or will come back, even now, and the doctors knew very little then. I was all right eventually, of course, but by that time you were almost grown up and had become a very capable and self-sufficient little girl. And then later on you were so successful."

She added, "You didn't seem to want me."

Want her! Of course not. What would you feel about a mother who disappeared like that? Would you trust her? Would you accept anything from her? All those years of terror and secrecy; maybe she'd thought she was being punished by having cancer. Maybe she'd thought she was going to die. Too scared to give anything and everyone being loudly secretive and then being faced with a daughter who wouldn't be questioned, wouldn't be kissed, wouldn't be touched, who kept her room immaculate, who didn't want her mother and made no bones about it, and who kept her fury and betrayal and her misery to herself, and her schoolwork excellent. I could say only the silliest thing, right out of the movies:

"Why are you telling me all this?"

She said simply, "Why not?"

I wish I could go on to describe a scene of intense and affectionate reconciliation between my mother and myself, but that did not happen—quite. She put her hand on the table and I took it, feeling I don't know what; for a moment she squeezed my hand and smiled. I got up then and she stood too, and we embraced, not at all as I had embraced the Little Dirty Girl, though with the same pain at heart, but awkwardly and only for a moment, as such things really happen. I said to myself: *Not yet. Not so fast. Not right now*, wondering if we looked—in Kent and Hallby's mirrors—the way we really were. We were both embarrassed, I think, but that too was all right. We sat down: *Soon. Sometime. Not quite yet.*

The dinner was nice. The next day I took her for breakfast to the restaurant that goes around and gives you a view of the whole city and then to the public market and then on a ferry. We had a pleasant, affectionate quiet two days and then she went back East.

We've been writing each other lately—for the fist time in years more than the obligatory birthday and holiday cards and a few remarks about the weather—and she sent me old family photographs, talked about being a widow, and being misdiagnosed for years (that's what it seems now) and about all sorts of old things: my father, my being in the school play in second grade, going to summer camp, getting moths to sit on her finger, all sorts of things.

And the Little Dirty Girl? Enclosed is her photograph. We were passing a photographer's studio near the University the other day and she was seized with a passionate fancy to have her picture taken (I suspect the Tarot cards and the live owl in the window had something to do with it), so in we went. She clamors for a lot lately and I try to provide it: flattens her nose against a bakery window and we argue about whether she'll settle for a currant bun instead of a do-nut, wants to stay up late and read and sing to herself so we do, screams for parties so we find them, and at parties impels me toward people I would probably not have noticed or (if I had) liked a year ago. She's a surprisingly generous and good little soul and I'd be lost without her, so it's turned out all right in the end. Besides, one ignores her at one's peril. I try not to.

Mind you, she has taken some odd, good things out of my life. Little boys seldom walk with me now. And I've perfected— though regretfully—a more emphatic method of kitty-booting which they seem to understand; at least one of them turned to me yesterday with a look of disgust that said clearer than words: "Good Heavens, how you've degenerated! Don't you know there's nothing in life more important than taking care of Me?"

About the picture: you may think it odd. You may even think it's not her. (You're wrong.) The pitch-ball eyes and thin face are there, all right, but what about the bags under her eyes, the deep, downward lines about her mouth, the strange color of her short-cut hair (it's grey)? What about her astonishing air of being so much older, so much more intellectual, so much more profes-sional, so much more—well, competent—than any Little Dirty Girl could possibly be?

Well, faces change when forty-odd years fall into the develop-ing fluid.

And you have always said that you wanted, that you must have, that you commanded, that you begged, and so on and so on in your interminable, circumlocutory style, that the one thing you desired most in the world was a photograph, a photograph, your kingdom for a photograph—of me.

SWORD BLADES AND POPPY SEED

For this was something new,
something distinctive of modernity
itself, that the written word in its
most memorable form . . . became
increasingly and steadily the work
of women.

—ELLEN MOERS,
Literary Women

Where do we writers get our crazy ideas?

Listen.

It was late in the autumn of 183—and I was still alive. I was leaving the theater. The play had been *Hernani*, the pit tumultuous, and my dress had passed unnoticed; thus I counted the evening a success. At the entrance to the street, lit on that rainy autumn evening only by the weak flicker of oil lamps—

But here I must refer you to the poem of my colleague, Madame Lowell, as the authority on how I and the old man met, talked, and walked—only bearing in mind that it was November and not April (as the American lady says the adventure happened to her), that there were certainly none of Madame Lowell's tramways in evidence, and that the comparative brilliance of gaslight lay decades in the future. (Nor did anybody even dream that some day cities would be lit by electricity.) Nor was the old man as much of an aristocrat as Madame Lowell (who is the sister of the President of Harvard) imagines, for to my eyes (and they were good ones then, for I was only twenty-seven) he had more the air of a robust old man of the people, shabby but keen-eyed and of fine bearing, blunt but with natural manners. Otherwise Madame Lowell has the matter perfectly; we met, he spoke to me as one man to another—no surprise!— and we talked. And although the old man's talk was equally fine in both cases (Madame Lowell is quite eloquent on this point), its flavor in my case was—of course—as Gallic as it was American in hers. In the main, however, events went much as the poet has described (you would do well to read Madame Lowell's account, which she called "Sword Blades and Poppy Seed" in her volume of the same title) and eventually we two came to the old man's shop, a large, low, rough building something like an inn, something like a tumble-down old mansion, something like a modern, bourgeois chateau, something like a peasant's hut, and more than all these, something very like—most unnaturally like—though I could not tell at the time exactly where the correspondence lay— the unfinished manuscript of my own novel, *Indiana*, which I had flung down on my writing table, in despair of ever finishing it, just before leaving for the theater.

"You are—?" said the old man.

"A first-year student," said I.

For the description of the shop you would do well to go to Madame Lowell, who does these things in verse, but as far as the prose of a mere novelist can follow, the interior presented to my eyes was rougher and more spacious than that seen by the American lady. I must admit that I found it hard to see in the uncertain firelight from the big hearth (like a country chateau's) which stood between the rough deal shelves that made up two sides of the room, but all the same it soon became evident to me in the twistings and turnings of carved and molded beasts and flowers, in the glint of edge and lip, that one-half the old man's shop was entirely given over to containers: pitchers, jars, jugs, pots, pipkins, mugs, canisters, chests, kegs, flasks, goblets, chalices, casks—as Madame Lowell says—though she does not mention the sewn African cloth and birch-bark bags, the glass phials, and the brown-paper parcels and other more modern sorts of wrapping. There were even copper kettles, contemporary hatboxes, and a few old barrels some where in the second rank of shelves—or was it the third?—at any rate in that puzzling and curious space beyond which one could not see clearly, a space which made the shop look so much (oddly) larger than it possibly could have been.

And the other wall! The prospect here was as flat, hard, and glittering as the first was capacious and rough, an expanse of steel that testified (or so I thought, for to tell the truth I was as fascinated and amused as Madame Lowell's poetic *persona* was frightened—or was to pretend to be—some ninety years later) to humanity's dual passion for cutting things to pieces and then putting them into containers afterwards. For here, displayed on one-half of the wall, were swords, daggers, spears, arrows, claymores, sabers, lances, dirks, stilettoes, scimitars, yataghans, foils, pikes (I am following Madame Lowell again), every sort of implement that could cut, slash, slice or rip (there are almost as many words for the acts as there are implements!), and on the other, although more civilian, the edges were of an even keener and more bloodthirsty nature, "every sort of cutlery" as Madame Lowell puts it in her mad war-dance of rhymes: knives, pruning hooks, razors, scalpels, lancets, shears, pen knives, kitchen knives, butchers' knives, scythes, sickles, more pairs of scissors (from blunt to fine) than humanity has arms *in toto* and "Every blade which man could mould" to separate one thing from the other or one thing into two, or twenty, or twenty thousand parts, and so get at death . . . or the truth.

I was, as you may imagine, somewhat taken aback—here was a fine adventure for a November night!—but my head most decidedly did not go round as Madame Lowell says hers did (though perhaps the American lady was merely in want of a rhyme). Instead I turned to the proprietor of this strange shop and asked, as you or anyone else might—it was surely a natural question—"Old man, what do you sell?"

"Sword blades and poppy seed," he said. "Dreams and visions there, over here, edged weapons. Both for your trade," and he handed me a card on which was printed, or perhaps embossed—

for the letters seemed to stand out and even glow a little in the gloom—*Marchand des Mots,* which means nothing else but "Dealer in Words."

Did my head go round? Did I weep? Well, it may be that I wept a little, thinking of my ambition, my unhappy marriage, *Indiana,* my poverty. It was unthinkable then for a woman to write. It was certainly unthinkable for a woman to leave her husband and live with whomever she pleased, as I had done. I was only twenty-seven. It may be that I intended to say, "Thank you but no; this preposterous game of words is not worth what I have gone through; for a woman to attempt fame or money or safety or all three by her pen is a ridiculous piece of nonsense; I'm for Nohant and my husband," but whatever I intended, I heard these words come out, "Which of these is for me?" But the French is stronger; it says *à moi,* which means Mine.

The effect of that *Mine* was extraordinary. At once the walls of the shop wavered and bent like paper in a fire. They were—or were not—no, they were *not* the boundaries of the room but only the first of rank upon rank of weapons here, and shelves of barrels and boxes and jars there, all stretching back to infinity as far as the eye could see; it was a vision, dizzying, unstable, palpable, of words in every language ever spoken (and some not yet), visions, analyses, arguments, flights of rhetoric—

"I see," said the old man, smiling in the firelight, "that you admire my Dutch blunderbusses, my horse-pistols, my sharp-shooters' rifles, my Martini guns, my weapons of persuasion and intellectual analysis! But never mind those farther shadows; they are not for you. One is a very interesting substance, that greenish glow, that poem of the future; he actually said *C'est du radium* (but I recall that only now; I did not hear it at the time). "I sold a few grains only recently to a young Englishwoman, a mere child of seventeen who does not know half its properties."

"No, Madame," he continued, "they are not for you. The suiting of the tool to the hand is a delicate business. I see your gaze wander to my gilt parcels and pharmacists' jars—that is laudanum, to be sure, but that? Not *Morphéus* for the god of sleep, but something very like it—only these are not for you either. I know my customers, Madame; you will want the rough poppy seed that gives true visions and not these smooth, modern substitutes which give nothing but anesthesia. I must carry the stuff; it's the law; but for you, Madame? Bah! Something different. Something entirely different."

There was much to say of this, you may be sure, and yet I said again only the main thing, "Which of these is mine?" So—and I had already vaulted the barrier to the shop, displaying (if I may say it myself) the daring and enterprise of the creator of Consuelo, and would have taken doubtless something quite inappropriate—the old man gave Madame Aurore Dudevant the tools of her trade. For that was my name then. But before he did, he took both my hands in his. He said, "Madame, this is a serious business that I do."

"I know it more than anyone," I said.

"Ah, these new customers!" exclaimed the old man, smiling affectionately and shaking his head. "One can explain nothing to them. And as for seriousness—so looked little Mary Godwin as she wrote *The Modern Prometheus*. Art is always a serious business but perhaps for these particular newcomers it is something even more—the Hampshire lady who was no more regarded in society than a poker or a firescreen, for whom her sister was the love of her life, and who painted on her "two inches square of ivory" more than anyone has yet been clearsighted enough to make out; the Yankee in her clean kitchen, writing a book condemning black slavery and thus, by a hidden meaning, her own; the young English girl who lost her baby and brought women's life-giving back into my trade with the myth of a monster that has made the world tremble. And you, Aurore Dudevant, what does it mean to you?"

"Give me what is mine," I said, "and I will show you." So there in the firelight the old man—or was it now an old woman?—handed to me the measure of poppy seed that was mine and the weapons and tools that were also mine, by right.

"Now pay me," said he.

Unlike the sister of the President of Harvard, who affects to be revolted at this point (but don't you believe it; it's all the exigencies of the meter), I am of good bourgeois stock, at least on one side, and know that what one gets one must pay for. But how? In what currency? And that was exactly the question I asked.

"With time," said the old man. "And work. The work of a lifetime, Madame." And then he called me by a name that was not my own.

I said, very quietly—for it had been in my mind to use just such a *nom de plume,* something English with the first part of Sandeau's name—"Why do you call me that? 'Madame George Sand,' that is not my name."

He said, "It will be."

And that is the end of my adventure.

But not of this story, for a question remains. Madame Lowell got sword blades and poppy seed from the old man (she has told us this in her poem) for no payment but a lifetime of work, which she gave, and Mary Godwin Shelley got radium, with which she wrote *Frankenstein*. But what tools, what visions, did this old man or old woman give me? What did he give Madame Stowe and the Mesdames Brontë and Madame Austen and Madame Dickinson and Madame George Eliot and Madame Stein and Madame Woolf and Madame Cather and Madame Hurston and Madame Colette and all the others? I have told you (with some help from Madame Lowell) where we got the tools of our trade, but do you now want to find out what those tools really were?

Are you truly curious?

Then read our books!

MAIN STREET: 1953

Who's Elaine Beach?

Just the one you'd expect. The shy one. The sandy-haired one with freckles. The unhappy one who isn't good-looking. The one who came back to town after a two weeks' absence, claiming she'd been to Chicago and had a baby. The one who's always listening to something else. The one who, on autumn nights, looks as though she can hear something else. The one who hates parties. The one who won't talk about it.

The one to whom supernatural adventures ought to happen.

In a car, coming slowly home from the Christmas dance in a blizzard, being driven by a boy she didn't like. The prairie stretching iron-grey and iron-hard for miles. In her lavender-organdie dress, sitting as far away from him as she can, in her fake-fur coat, in her dyed lavender pumps, her short hair fluffed up in the cold, her fingers drawing roses and daisies on the fog of the car window.

Didn't say anything.

At a crossroads, got out of the car and ran away. The snow so thick she could hardly see the Stop sign. A great, blowing white. She's in it, stumbling across the iron-hard furrows of the field.

Nature lies dead. Into a small fringe of trees standing alone on the prairie, she's dreamlike and hurting. Numb feet, snow blowing up the sleeves and down the neck of her coat, stinging pellets hitting her face and blowing in whirls and spirals past the dim dead branches.

The trees don't stop.

Somewhere, lost among the confusion of dead twigs and piled frozen rubbish is the place where the shape changes. Or something changes: the murmuring in one's head, the outline of things, there's an abstract difference, the dream as it wakes up. The sand picture.

And she does make it. Right into Broceliande. She's the same but being the same doesn't make the world the same; that's the difference. She's erased. Sobbing with relief in her heavy coat under the May-bloom, under the infinite milky light, delicate grey blossom against delicate grey sky and the round moon rising, colored like the inside of a peach. Broad, ivory-tinted rivers catch the first slash of pink light. To be able to walk farther and farther under the dropping trees, carelessly dragging her coat across daisies and fallen May petals, her skin dewing, all around her the loud sound of thawing water.

To be the same but to be perfect. Wandering in her stockings from one pale creamy heap of flowers to another in the beginnings of dawn. To know it goes on forever. To know that nothing changes.

To know there is no time passing.

There's cloth of gold and cloth of silver. Architecture like glass or ice. Living on snow-water that turns to wine as the sun hits it. Banners of all colors. The terrible, terrible temptation of spirit so intense and fiery that forms can scarcely contain it: bilberries and dewberries and cupcakes of music, living on music, metal-foil music, shapes of dazzling white, so sad and so gay. Music like cut glass. Daggers of music that enter the soul, sharp and unhuman in this forest of Broceliande that has barely five trees together but she made it; she got into it anyway.

Even faces.

She came back.

She said she'd been to Chicago and had a baby but shut up if anyone asked her about the details.

Got her old job back.

Stopped watching television except for the news, gets newspapers from all the big cities now: Chicago, San Francisco, New York, Los Angeles, Boston, Cincinnati.

Has taken down all the pictures in her furnished room and keeps instead old rocks she found out on the prairie or in town, pebbles ditto, old matchbooks, sticks and dried leaves, weeds, flowers, old tin cans.

She hints at important "theories" about current events but won't tell them.

Won't wear make-up, won't go out, won't buy new clothes, won't get married (that's too much like You Know Where, she says, at least the way they talk about it).

She says scornfully that she doesn't hear voices; that's just gossip.

She works well and quickly, filing things, and almost for nothing (in their back room) so they don't fire her.

She never goes to church now.

She says sometimes that she had a baby whose name was Elaine Beach.

If you get there—

If you come back—

Angrily kicking holes in the clay of the train depot in spring, in summer intently measuring how far grasshoppers jump, with an old tape measure she keeps always in the pocket of her shabby plaid skirt; she says she'll never go back. Moving farther out on the prairie (but she won't ever get in a car), eating snow greedily in winter and laughing, but never never ever going there again. That's final, she says.

She didn't come back to a long illness or to old age or some family tragedy, nothing bad.

But from Broceliande?

HOW DOROTHY
KEPT AWAY
THE SPRING

It had been a long season and a lonesome one, and Dorothy had often no employment but a sort of dreaming journeying. She wandered slowly upstairs and down, through the bare halls and the dusty, crannied places under stairs. She watched the snow whirl silently around the corners of the house and went into the kitchen to breathe on the windows' frost-jungles, but the housekeeper didn't want her there. Then Father would come into the hall and stamp to get the snow off his boots, and she would slide away and go sit under the stairs. There she would make up a long, elaborate daydream: that her dead mother had left something hidden somewhere around the house for Dorothy to find. It could take days and days of just looking and turning over clothes in her dead mother's closet, but of course she would recognize it instantly when she found it. Her cough kept her from going to school or seeing much of anyone. She would sit under the stairs and think a lot, and then, when it got dark and the five o'clock chimes rang from the bedroom clock, Dorothy would go down to supper.

He looked across the dinner table at his daughter, her round rimless glasses perched seriously on her nose. Her pigtails stuck out at an angle from her head. She had put red rubber bands around them as if she didn't care what she looked like.

"How was everything this afternoon, Dorothy?" he said. She stopped eating buttered carrots.

"Fine," she said. Her glasses slipped down and rested on her nose.

"Push up your glasses, hon," he said. She pushed them up with one buttery finger and watched him.

"Next week I'll be coming home a half hour early every day," he said. "Won't that be nice? We'll see each other a lot sooner."

She stared at him over the rims of her glasses. They magnified the lower half of her eyes and not the upper. She looked like a goldfish, somehow.

"Mm," she said. She took another mouthful of buttered carrots and chewed them slowly. After dinner he read to her and later, at her bedtime, asked the housekeeper how she'd been all day and what she'd been doing. He insisted on tucking her in himself when she went to bed.

Dorothy woke up in the middle of the night and listened to tell if anyone was awake. She knew it must be the middle of the night. It was dark and the house had become a great windy cavern that whispered and creaked and magnified the scurry of mice in the walls into thunder. Dim light leaked in under the window curtains. Dorothy sat up in bed, holding the blankets around her. She stuck her feet out of bed. Then she stood on the cold boards with her braids piercing the dark and her nightdress stirring faintly around her bare feet. She padded across the floor and pulled aside the curtains. It was almost light outside because of the snow; the sky was only a mass of falling, drifting flakes that passed inches in front of her eyes.

On tiptoe, barefoot, with her nightdress blowing as she climbed the windy stair, she crept up to the second floor. She passed her father's bedroom on the way, very quietly. There was the hall radiator—she ran her hand over it; it was so cold that the freezing iron burned like fire.

On the third floor there were full-length windows that opened out onto the courtyard. Dorothy leaned against them for a few minutes, staring out at the falling snow.

In her dream she put a hand to the mutely lit glass, and the window opened with a rush of air. The wind gathered around her; it whirled, lifted her, and dropped her slowly miles and miles through the falling snow. Snowflakes fell on her and lay unmelted. She liked that. She began to run. She skimmed swiftly over a long white country road, past windy hills, between the huge muted monoliths of the forest trees, past quiet avenues of hedges, through fields muffled in white, past tilted, half-buried cottages. There was a park she had once visited, with outdoor picnic tables spread in white, and circles of trees, each still branch ridged with snow. She smiled and let the pale folds of her nightgown drift around her feet, immensely pleased, her feet scarcely touching the blanched earth.

They were there.

One was thin, as hollow as a mask behind, of cold and cordial silver. A silver bow and long arrows lay over his arm.

You are a Hunter, she said, her voice deliciously quiet in the spreading quietness. Aren't you? He nodded. The two others were not as great. The taller one was a traveler with a clown's nose and peaked hat. His face was foolish and sad. The third was a gnome, chunky and thick, hardly anybody.

You seem to be a Clown, she said wisely to the one. And you—to the other—are very Little, although I don't know your name. Is there anything else?

The Clown spoke and his voice was absurdly high, thin, and sad. It was also silent.

We are adventurers, he said proudly. The Hunter smiled, although without a face and lips to smile.

Yes, yes added Little. We go to dethrone a tyrant who lives on a mountain. He holds a Princess captive in his castle.

The Hunter smiled and lightly touched his bow.

May I come? Dorothy asked. The Hunter extended one hand. It touched hers and its cold burned like fire.

We have been waiting for no one but you, he said, and his voice echoed light and hollow in the clearing. Dorothy unbraided her hair and let it fall loose. It grew long and hung to her waist. She turned and saw her father working his way laboriously toward them. He wore arctic furs and goggles and sank in snow up to his knees.

Don't vanish into silences, Dorothy! he cried. Come home, come home, come home.

She threw a handful of snow at him and he dissolved into snowflakes, gurgling:

You'll catch your death.

They rose and glided North under the heavy gray sky. Dorothy's breath made a frosty cloud around her. It was as warm as a coat. The snow was warmer, like cream, like white Persian kittens, like white fur, like love.

He looked across the dinner table at his daughter, who was seriously drinking her dinner milk.

"I guess your cough is better," he said. "Isn't it? I guess soon the doctor will let you go back to school. Won't that be nice?"

"Yes, daddy," she said.

"Well, winter doesn't last forever," he said. "Does it?"

"No, daddy," she said. She put down her milk, leaving a large white mustache over her upper lip. "Daddy," she said, "when I go back I won't know anything. I'll be behind."

"My daughter behind?" he said. "Don't you worry about that. You're smart, you'll make it up in a couple of weeks."

She nodded politely and finished the last drop of milk.

Once the Clown picked a flower. It was all white: petals, leaves, and stem, an odorless rose. He stuck it in his pointed hat, and all the travelers sang a song they had made up:

Our hearts fill
With good-will,
Four strong,
Marching along,
Singing this song.

The rose sang with them in a shrill voice, only singing "five" where they sang "four" because it seemed to think it was one of them. After a while the Clown dropped it out of his hat onto the snow, where it stopped singing and crumbled into a heap of snowflakes.

It died, said Dorothy. The Hunter shook his head.

It was never real, he said. But it didn't know that.

In the hushed white forest where the sky dropped slowly and perpetually, it was never day or night, only a muted gray, half like twilight and not at all like dawn.

Little asked Dorothy: Are you hungry? She thought and shook her head.

But she should be, the Clown protested, holding his own head anxiously to one side. The Hunter brushed a strand of hair away from Dorothy's face with one flat silver finger.

Not now.

After days the trees began to thin and dwindle, and soon they came upon an open plain where the sky arched like lead. This was a terrible place. Dorothy and the Hunter were not afraid, but the Clown and Little hung back and hugged one another—not, as they carefully pointed out, for fear—only for warmth to keep out the chill of fear.

The castle is up ahead! they whispered.

The Hunter strode lightly ahead, carrying his bow and arrows, and Dorothy walked in the downy brushings his feet left in the snow. She made angels and roses of them. The Clown and Little began to wait—not, as they quickly pointed out, for fear—only for noise to keep out the silence of fear.

At first the ground began to slope; then they were in hills; then the hills grew; there were palisades, cliffs, escarpments, rocks black as night, nights rocky as ravines, paths that could lose you forever, boulders that could come rattling down. On a monstrous rampart that humped itself nakedly in massive ribs and shoulders, at the highest point, over an immense abyss, was the Tyrant's castle. It hung half over a sheer drop. It gleamed blackly, turreted in midnight basalt. An obsidian-colored flag flew stiffly over it, stretched to tautness by the toothy winds of the mountaintop.

Here is the place, the Hunter said, his queer, chiming voice echoing even in the mountain pass. The Clown straightened his hat and smiled gently at Dorothy. I must look my best when going into danger, he said. A shrill wind hit them, lifting Dorothy's long hair over her head like a flag. They began to climb.

Her father found her leaning out of an upstairs window in a cotton dress, letting the cold wind blow around her. She was trying to keep a snowflake unmelted on her finger. He didn't scold her, but sent her to bed and sent the housekeeper up to take care of her. She lay in bed with her hands clasped across her chest, politely refusing to read anything. She said she was perfectly all right. She lay there all day. And thought and thought and thought and thought.

The door to the castle was brass; it swung open into a long hall when Dorothy pushed it with all her strength. They followed the hall until it opened up into a great, echoing room, hung with tapestries that depicted the four seasons, and haying, and mowing, and other mythological scenes. At the very end of the room, on a throne of flint, sat the Tyrant, his head sunk in sleep. He was huge and wavering and mist-gray; Dorothy could see through him to the wall behind. A circle of steel went round his head; it was his crown. Quickly Little ran to a trumpet hanging on the wall and blew three notes. The Tyrant started out of sleep, and as he rose, as he woke, his face became terrible with rage.

Push up your glasses, Dorothy! he roared. The Hunter drew back the invisible string of his bow and broke the steel circle with a frosty arrow. The Tyrant sank to the floor and spread in a puddle of tears.

Hurrah! cried the Clown. We have killed the Tyrant.

Hurrah! cried Little. I blew the horn that woke up the Tyrant.

Hurrah! cried Dorothy. I pushed open the door that let us into the castle of the Tyrant.

The Hunter leaned against a wall and said: Look. The Princess is coming.

The Princess blew down a corridor and into the room. She was all of fog.

Thank you for saving me, she said in a damp, rushing voice like water falling under stone arches. I am very grateful to you.

The Clown dropped to one knee. The pleasure is all ours, lovely lady, he said. She patted him on the head, and a little cloud from her hand caught on his hat and trailed from it like a breath.

They walked out of the castle. At once the fierce, grinning wind lifted the Princess and whirled her away in ragged, torn streamers.

What a shame, said Dorothy. Little nodded.

She was beautiful, declared the Clown sadly. I never saw anyone so beautiful before. Two tears rolled down his cheeks.

They walked easily down the shrunken mountain, and the castle, although not very far behind them, became a toy no bigger than Dorothy's hand. Then it disappeared. Snow began to fall; pearly covered trees and bushes rose silently around them. The light paled to a moonstone gray.

Look! cried Dorothy: Oh, look at that! and her voice seemed to seep away and lose itself in silences. There was a lake ahead, set like an opal between the fringed, drooping trees. Dorothy ran, she skated, she dipped and spun over the cloudy ice, whirling in tighter and tighter circles until she dropped on her knees and bowed and bowed while Little and the Clown applauded frantically. Then she saw through the trees a faint light, a touch of color, the very smallest kind of change.

There was a light in the East.

The dawn! cried the Clown. No, the spring! cried Little.

The spring, the spring! they sang, whirling about, holding hands and dancing in a ring. The spring, the spring, the spring's a thing when birds all sing and ice goes ching! and bushes fling and vase is Ming and flowers ping and hearts go zing and love's on the wing and life is king!

Dorothy, on her knees on the ice, said, No, no! It isn't going to come. I won't let it. But they danced on.

You can't stop it, they cried. The spring, the spring, the flowery spring! The glint, the chime, the sky, the blue, the joy, the jay, the jam, the rue!

And after that comes summer, you know, they added.

Dorothy began to cry, there on the pond. The Hunter knelt down and put one arm around her. Its touch burned like fire. He said, in his no-voice, his voice that was all the voices she had ever loved: You don't have to.

Then they were all gone and she was standing barefoot in her nightgown in the courtyard of her home.

The sun had risen in the East into a clear sky: the long spell of winter was broken. A face appeared at a second-story window. Come in here! it called crossly. You'll catch your death of cold. Quickly Dorothy ran upstairs to her room. She climbed into bed and pulled the covers up to her chin.

"Yes, daddy, yes, daddy!" she called. "I'm in bed now."

But she knew her mother's secret. She had found it.

The next day Dorothy was very ill, the day after that she did not wake up very much, and the day after that she died. At her funeral there were bunches of violets, banked azaleas, and lots of hothouse gladioli. It was like summer. Everyone said so. Dozens of people came to see Dorothy in her Sunday dress and many women wept.

In a pale forest, under still, white branches and a slowly dropping sky, Dorothy plucks a white rose for the faceless silver Huntsman. There's no place to put the flower but in his hands, for he's as hollow as a mask. Her long hair is knotted beautifully about one of his long arrows. Another pierces her heart. She smiles a little, rueful perhaps, happy perhaps.

I kept away the spring, she says to him. Didn't I? I really did it. I kept away the spring.

THIS AFTERNOON

A real mermaid in a real river, twenty knights on bay horses, Charles le Magne ceding to the Duke of Anjou, a bridge built on one side of the stage while on the other swarms of workmen methodically erect and demolish a miniature castle twenty-five feet high, the invasion of the north by the pagans, Eleanor the Fair brought with a train of horsemen, bridesmaids, nobles, counts, and servants to wed Louis the Pious "who never showed his white teeth in a smile" and through it all, here, there, everywhere, now cajoling, now laughing, now pointing, making faces, preternaturally active, skipping, calling on the music—the Satyr, the *genius loci* of the beech woods, whose gray, smooth, straight trunks surrounded the entire natural amphitheater, producing at the top a half-canopy of new leaves: limp, half-extended, like umbrellas with the skeleton showing through the early-spring substance and just the color of new lettuce.

It was very hot. Neon signs had been placed in the branches of the trees where they glowed in the daylight: pink, orange, lavender. The German tourists, in leather pants, traveling cheaply with knapsacks, sweated. The sparse crowd shifted on the benches under the particolored shadow of the sparse leaves. Behind the wooden benches set in the amphitheater a truck advertised a tour of the Auvergne.

With a roll on the drums, with multicolored lights and flares, with the mermaid flipping herself entirely up into the air and down into the water again, the stage went up in a bonfire of thin, colored flames. There was the sound of a loud explosion and a great deal of smoke. The crowd cheered. Down in the green floor of the amphitheater the Satyr bowed, strolled off to scattered applause, and vanished behind a tree, leaving the empty stage as smooth, as quiet, and as printless as it had been an hour before. The pageant was over.

An American on leave from the California Forest Service, who had sat through the performance with his collar opened, his jacket off, and his tie loosened because of the heat, took his jacket over one arm and walked down toward the stage. The audience was filing out, some of them into the truck. There under a beech tree the Satyr stood, still in costume, naked to the waist. He was scratching his sides vigorously and yawning; with a polite nod to the American he went over to the first row of benches, picked up a blanket left behind by one of the tourists, and put it around his shoulders.

"The signs are gone!" said the American, and so they were. The trees were bare. He blinked at the Satyr, and the Satyr blinked back at him, smiling in a friendly way, hunching his shoulders under the blanket. "I suppose they've taken them down," said the American. He slung his jacket over his back. "Your highway sign was not very large," he said. The young man was rubbing himself with the blanket precisely as if had been a towel and he an athlete; a young woman passing by with two small children remarked "It is all done vit' mirrors," and started up the green aisle toward the truck.

"Do you speak English?" said the American and the young man grinned; he ducked around the hedge that screened the back of the stage. The American followed, saying "Is this where you dress?" but the question didn't seem particularly important and it occurred to him that the heat was making him sleepy. A path led behind the hedge and into the woods; he walked along it with the Satyr, expecting any moment to come to a tent or a screen, but all they met on either side, on the forest floor, were broad green leaves a foot off the ground that shivered like hair or skin if one brushed against them, stretching off through ranks of trees like the undulations of hills and valleys, turning and tossing in the speckled sunshine, while above the new leaves made a translucent umbrella. The American yawned. He took out pipe and tobacco and was surprised to see his companion stop where he was, turning on him a look of such pleading, eager intensity that he laughed, a little startled, said, "All right, all right," and "There's certainly no danger of a forest fire now." The other suddenly looked acutely distressed, as if to say *Oh, but I've forgotten*—"I have another," said the American, "and I don't in the least mind lending it." So they both smoked under the trees, one sitting with his knees up and the other lying at full length on the leaves.

But what a strange fellow was this art student from Dijon or Brussels! (so the American thought), skinny as a man could be, with the muscles of his arms and chest like ropes, and yet leaning back in the leaves, staring dreamily up at the branches, and smoking as if sinking back serenely into time, or no time, quite unconcerned with anything, and thinking (to judge from the expression in his eyes) of nothing whatsoever. And here in the woods he was pale, extraordinarily pale, as if the shade of the trees had done something to him, so that the American found himself thinking, without quite knowing where he had heard them, of the words Hubert the Bold had addressed to an angel in the historical pageant: *Fair spirit,* (for so he had said, in Latin) *I do not know where you come from, but I take you to be from God the Almighty because of your bright and sweet looks; and do implore you to render to Him my faithful, loving, and complete service. For as no man here below is without a master, or if he is, is rightly thought to be villainous and untrustworthy, thus I wish no longer to be masterless, but to pledge myself to God and to enter willingly into His sweet service. Amen.* And there had been a devil. And colored fires. He yawned.

"If you like the woods," he said, "you ought to come to my country." The Satyr said nothing.

"Well, perhaps not," said the man from America, to his own

surprise. "Perhaps not; it is not quite so human as this, after all," and leaning back against the trunk of a beech tree, he looked up into the sky, the speckled foliage moving with the sun above him, the whole tree turning, as it seemed, round and round as if he were on a whirligig. Something very odd seemed to be happening up in the leafy roof, and it worried him; he turned to look into the face of his companion—so distinct, so bright—and something in that face worried him, too, for it seemed to him that he could not remember it for two seconds together, in spite of its distinctness. He said suddenly, "Where are the others?"

The Satyr smoked peacefully. The man from America knocked out his pipe and put it in his pocket; he got to his feet saying, "Well, goodbye," but his companion did not answer; he put out his hand, a little uneasily, to this young man who had been such an extraordinary source of quiet company; he nodded a little brusquely, saying again, "Goodbye to you," and left him half-sitting, half-lying, under the beech tree, the tourist's blanket spread over his shoulders. It was curious (thought the man from the California Forest Service) what a vivid presence the man had, although one could not remember his face; and how oddly the touch of his fingers remained, although he could not remember shaking hands; and how pathetic it was, and how strange (here he looked back) to see him, like a spot of sun, vanishing in successive, jerky displacements, farther and farther away.

Of course he must keep to the path. He had been told that. It was getting cloudy. Between the darkening roof of the beech leaves and the curious, subterranean, springing leaves that covered the forest floor, winding about the trees, disappearing here and there, was the path that led to the theater that led to the highway—no, the road that led to the highway, the bus tour of the Auvergne—perhaps it was getting late in the day. He mopped his forehead with his handkerchief. The man from California mouthed, "Actors!" in a tone far from complimentary. He stopped and shifted his jacket to the opposite shoulder. It seemed to him that he had walked at least twice as far as he should have to get back to the theater, so he stopped and tried to find the sun, but it was getting cloudy; then he imagined himself caught in a down-pour and said—aloud—that he wished he had never gotten mixed up with the whole damned business.

Then the path disappeared. For a moment he stood stock-still. Then it seemed to him that he saw the trail reappearing farther along among the trees, curving, slender and shadowy, and forgetting that he ought not to leave the path—for someone, he knew, had told him not to leave it—he stepped resolutely off into the leafy carpet, took three strides, and sank up to the knee in fire.

He had stepped into a metal trap. Shuddering, he raised himself on one arm, but there was nothing to see; the trees marched away in a straight file, gray and smooth; over the ground the deceitful, broad leaves undulated in a parody of hill and valley, hiding whatever was under them; and the far, shadowy reaches of the woods melted into darkness. There was nothing to see. He knew animals must have suffered like this. He could not see his own blood, for he could not move. But he thought, *Oh, nothing new!* and then fainted.

When he came to himself, it was all the same, quite the same; even the light had not changed. But through the trees—not in the direction he came from, but quite the opposite way, he saw as in the jerky enlargements of a picture in stages—the image growing bigger and bigger—the young man he had left. The Satyr squatted down beside him. With a coiling jerk of the arms he released the trap and delicately moved it to one side, putting his stolen blanket over the man. He sat and watched him. It occurred to the man from California that he was being watched without mercy, without kindness. "Why don't you get help!" he gasped, but the Satyr only stared, his knees drawn up in front of him, his face faintly luminous in the gloom as if he carried his own light with him.

The man from California thought with intense, hopeless longing of hospitals, of ambulances, bandages, surgical materials; he thought also of the animal blood shed on these leaves for thousands of years, watched perhaps by eyes just as cool; then he thought, *Man is an animal,* and then *Perhaps someone is coming.*

Something was being done to his injured leg. He let his gaze wander about, trying to penetrate the mysterious alleys made by the tree trunks, the darkness thickening between them; he saw a few white flowers peeping between the leaves of the ground cover, a few on the bare branches, and this pleased him absurdly until he discovered that he was shivering; he thought, *It's fever,* and then, as he saw the white specks sweeping across the gray trunks, thickening like a curtain, he realized that it had begun to snow. The Satyr, naked to the waist, sat beside him. The man from the California Forest Service raised himself on one elbow. "You must do something," he said obstinately. "You must, you must, you must do something—" He was shivering, cursing, and chattering all at once; he was much more frightened than he would have been if he had been alone, until without the slightest preamble, the young man caught him up in his arms as if he had been an armful of paper and strode off through the trees.

The American woke inside a forester's hut, lying on an empty bunk near the cold fireplace, with the blanket still over him and his own jacket under his head. He saw the Satyr's face in the dark. At first it seemed to him oddly old, or not so much old as tired, or not so much tired as worn away into a kind of shell, but before he could decide which of these was the most likely (he was a little delirious, he knew, and the whole question amused him) the Satyr turned to him, kindling, the life flaming up in him as it does in no living man, until his face and body burnt with that ageless presence known centuries ago to the fortunate ones who came in from the fields to find a *fair spirit* standing by the hearth.

"You've left the door open," said the American thickly. And so he had, wedging it with a stone. The Satyr smiled. The wind had increased tremendously outside, and gusts of snow came through the open door. Now and again the door itself blew open with the wind.

"I don't see," said the American, trying to sit up and glaring balefully, "how you expect me to stay alive with that—*that*—!" and as if to prove his words, an especially vicious gust of wind drove the snow across the little hut and over him in a fine sprinkle. The Satyr moved to the doorway and stood in it, blocking the wind.

"Blast you," said the American, "I believe you want to kill me," and carefully wadding his jacket in his hands, he threw it at the door. The young man stepped back a pace and caught it, laughing softly. He came up to the wooden bunk and bent over the sick man, replacing the jacket under his head and smiling at him—and not only in selfless charity. In the back of his delirium, at the bottom of his confusion, as if caught from the brilliant eyes looking into his, the man from the California Forest Service felt for an instant the loneliness of those who are not human but who need human company to live, the last of those who cling to a ground drenched with human history, the very woods where Charles le Magne rode with two thousand knights, where the Duke of Burgundy's men blazed the trees to mark their way, and where Queen Eleanor (but this is a fairy tale) was presented by Huon le Cor with three wishes and used them—as people do—very badly. He said heavily, "You wouldn't make it in my country," and the Satyr grinned with delight and touched the American's forehead—it was like being touched with fire. At the same moment a terrific clap of wind slammed the door of the hut, the stone rolled half on its side, and the door—after an instant's pause between life and death—shut. It shut very quietly.

It was like blowing out a candle. With a dim, terrible flicker, with his face a mask of sadness, the young man stepped back, spread his arms, and died. The man from America saw him die, saw him age and crumble in a few seconds, until like a pile of ashes that glows still in the dark, his bones lay half-sitting, half-lying against the floor of the hut. Four walls kill these creatures.

It was only then that the man from California saw the hooves and the horns.

THIS NIGHT,
AT MY FIRE

Someone has given me a pack of Tarot cards; they are very old and very heavy and the hanged man has turned up three times too often, but nothing else moves in this bungalow even though we are rushing toward Vega in the constellation of the Lyre at almost exactly one and one-fourteenth times the speed of sound. Very windy and black outside.

Half an hour ago L____ came in, fiddled with the stove, then took himself and his boots into the next room, from where I can see him sprawled ungracefully on the settle, his feet on the boards. Nobody else. I think L____ is listening. The clock on the stove points to ten o'clock. From above L____'s boots, from his leather jacket, comes half a groan and half a snore; I can see his blond head jerk awake and I turn over The Rising Sun, The Empress, Death. The Wendigo, that makes men dance in the black night until it kills them, rattles the electric lines but has missed L____ tonight; he would say "only the wind." I think he's asleep. But it's serious enough, I would think, to be traveling so fast with no idea at all where one is going.

Earlier tonight we were submarine but a great deal was going on, polishing the silver, with water outside the windows. Now we are bare; and as the clock ticks and I lay out my cards, the night passes in absolute silence. The wind is screaming too high to be heard although occasionally it thumps the side of the house. I listen. The Rising Sun and The Resurrection, followed by The Widow, Death, The Hanged Man, Greed, Resurrection. These cards are used only for fortune-telling now. Walking silently, so that the boards do not make noise, I go in to L____ and shake him awake, taking my hands away. He looks up stupidly, his hair falling over his face, this big, big handsome man.

"There's someone outside," I say. L____ stares. His woman has told him someone is outside. He gets to his feet. What a lot is going on tonight! So I tag along after him, and peep from behind his broad back and stand courteously to one side and motion the old man in. But L____ does not like it. I give him a look, a sidewise look, like that of creatures bright, much too bright, under leaves; let him in, be generous, let him in, why not let him in? and reluctantly, perfunctorily, tall as a tower, L____ swings aside. Why not let him in. Bow. Scrape. L____ is reluctant. The old man (where did he come from? it's a puzzle, L____ doesn't like puzzles) whom I don't, particularly, mind—O there is a great deal going on tonight!—has a turtle's neck and skin mottled like the underparts the sun doesn't reach, an old turtle, shuffles into the kitchen. This night, at my fire. My clock, my tables, my chairs.

"Make him something to eat," says my husband.

And I do. There is, in my stove, something dangerous; there is, hiding in the electric wires, something very bad; but not half so bad as outside. I watch him eat, quite interested, I am interested in everything, and I watch L____ too: his long, sloping arms, his hands, the muscles in his thighs. There are reasons, I suppose, for everything. L____ goes into the next room and leaves me alone with the old man; I start to put out my cards. He picks one up.

"What's this?"

"Ah! that's Death."

"What's this?"

"The Resurrection."

I start to deal them but he wants them all, the peevish creature; and I complain, and L____ tells me to let them alone. From inside. Long distance. But I never mind. I let him have the whole future right in his hands. We continue at that same mad pace; the whole house hums; now the old man has thrown down all my cards, he pushes them crazily off the table. "I want!" he shouts, "I want! I want! I want!" rocking crazily.

Slowly, slyly, I pick them up; I explain to him that the cards symbolize the world, that the world is made up of opposite forces, that the earth turns round the sun, that the universe is flying apart. Circumambulating the table like a diver, I pass them in front of him: Death, Death, Death—which deliciously I know how to do.

"Do you know," say I, "what this means? This means Death."

"Do you know," say I, "what this means? This means Death."

"And this means," say I, "the forgetting, and this means The Glorious Resurrection, and this means The Power and The Virtue." Late at night things often become fields of power: my wicked big white box, rattling, clicking, my tablecover dipping down into nothing, the shadows behind the doors, my radiant red-green-yellow-blue pasteboards, compelling and beautiful. He watches me and he knows. Oh, how he watches! And how he knows! I have always and ever called people my darling; thus witches are domestic women, and so I tell his fortune with my man in the next room, with the earth turning round the sun and the sun round a star; all flies with frightening impetuosity through the heavens, and L____ stirs and turns dizzily in his vacant sleep, tall as a tree, and ploughs the floor with the heel of his boot. And wakes.

"Get him out of here," says my man.

The old man starts; his mouth falls open, stuttering.

"Get him out," says my man, standing in the doorway as broad as the doorway, he always forgets what the world is made of, and the old fellow with the mottled skin beats on the table with one hand, uttering noises like a deaf-mute.

"I can't," say I, my eyes down. L____ stands in the doorway, cold as sin. He strides forward and picks the little fellow up by the neck, pushes him out the kitchen door and locks it; and says: "You'd let every beast in here."

I avert my eyes modestly. Soon it will be time. But I am only very bright and very little: what harm in poor me? and at this moment the wind—in which a quantity of things are riding tonight—crashes against the kitchen door to deliver me a present, that wind which is O! full of murders tonight.

L___ stands up. He looks out the door; and starts. And utters a hasty exclamation of dismay. And skews his face to one side, and climbs his eyebrows and drops his lips unhealthily over his teeth. My darling, my sweet, my love, now he sees what I see and hears what I hear, and he sweats and clings to the doorpost with a groan.

The old man has hanged himself on our doorstep.

Now the dizzying ride of this world has made him sick, my man, endlessly sick at last, never to be well again, his head turned completely.

Not like me. For I am all right.

"I HAD VACANTLY CRUMPLED IT INTO MY POCKET . . . BUT BY GOD, ELIOT, *IT WAS A PHOTOGRAPH FROM LIFE!*"

In an ancient rooming house in New York, where the dirt covered the molded plaster ceilings, where the creak of the stairs at night echoed like pistol shots in the dark, amid the rickety splendors of peeling red velvet wallpaper and indescribably varnished furniture, Irvin Rubin lived. He was a bookkeeper in a cheap publishing house: *Fantasy Press*; he worked there for the discounts. He told this story to a woman in the office, and she told it to me, one winter morning in a cafeteria with steam that covered the plate glass windows running down in clear patches that displayed nothing at all, so distorted were they, but drops and streaks of the scene outside. Irvin Rubin, who never ate without a book propped up in front of his plate, his pale eyes fixed on it, his cheeks rhythmically bulging, and his fork blindly hunting in front of him, took all his meals in cafeterias. Then he read in his room. He had nothing in particular to do. He knew nobody. The woman who worked with him had tried to engage him in conversation, but fruitlessly, for Irv had nothing to say except shrill denunciations of the latest writers put out by *Fantasy Press* ("he called them a bunch of hacks," she said) or complaints about his desk, or his office-mates, or his salary, for on other topics he had no opinion at all, but one morning he came over to her desk and stood with his hands behind his back, red, sweating, and trying visibly to keep calm.

"Miss Kramer," he said to her, "where would you take a girl?"

"Goodness! do you have a girl?" she said lightly. He looked a little dazed.

"Where would you take a girl?" he repeated plaintively, apparently twisting his hands behind his back; then he said, "Where would you take *a real lady,* Miss Kramer?"

"I don't know," said she, "I don't know any," and Irvin—vastly relieved—dropped into the seat next to her desk. "Neither do I," he said simply. At this point (she told me) he smiled and June Kramer saw with something like dismay that for an instant his face became distinctly human, rather young (he was twenty-eight), and even genuinely sweet. He frowned and the effect vanished.

"I certainly wouldn't ask *anybody else,"* he said significantly. "I wouldn't ask anybody else in this joint." He got up; shifted from foot to foot. He frowned again. "Do you think she'd like to read something?"

"Well—" said Miss Kramer, "I don't know—"

"Do you think she'd like to come to my place?" he burst out.

"Not right away," she said, alarmed. He looked at the floor.

"Perhaps you should go for a walk," said Miss Karmer cautiously, "or—or maybe she would like to go to the movies. Maybe you could see," (here Irv, looking at his feet, muttered "it's all trash anyway") "well, maybe you could see—" but before she could finish her sentence, Irv started violently and then walked jerkily away—scuttled, rather. He had seen the supervisor coming.

"How's the nut?" said the supervisor in a whisper to June Kramer, who looked at him over her glasses, set her lips severely, and said nothing.

It turned out that Irv had met his girl near Central Park, walking two dachshunds on a leash, though neither June Kramer nor I could see what such a girl would want with him. Perhaps she was not a girl exactly, and perhaps not exactly a lady either, for although he always described her as a compound of a "real lady" and a "glamor girl" with "that husky sort of whisper, Miss Kramer" like you-know-who in the movies, Irv Rubin's girl friend always seemed to me like the women drowned passively in mink or sable in the advertisement sketches—lost, lifeless, betrayed, undoubtedly kept by some rich sadist—at least that's how they strike me. He had caught glimpses of her many days before he actually met her, for Irv's furnished room was located in the decaying blocks near the rich section of Central Park West, and he had followed her pure profile down many side-streets and even into the Park, catching glimpses of her black coat and bobbing, straining, double dogs in unlikely places—once, I believe, the supermarket.

Irv loved his girl. He dwelt on her obsessively with Miss Kramer, in a way that seemed new to him, as if he were awed, almost (said June Kramer) as if he were frightened by her superiority, by her elegance, by her fashion-model paleness, and most of all by the silence with which she tolerated him, by the way she listened to him as if he had a right to talk to her, to take her on walks, and to tell her (with spiritualized earnestness) that Howard Phillips Lovecraft was the greatest writer in the world.

He had met her, he told June Kramer, on Central Park West, on a cold, blue, brilliantly sunny Sunday afternoon, when every tree in the Park was coated with ice and icicles hung from the eaves of the buildings along the street. Sundays were bad days for Irv; the bookstores were shut. (He gave Miss Kramer a recital of all the places he had been to on the last nine or ten Sundays; I forget most of them, but he went three times to the zoo and once rode up and down Fifth Avenue in a bus, though he said looking at expensive things in windows "was as nothing compared with the Imagination;" his own clothes were so old and in such bad repair that people noticed him in the street—at any rate, it was a pitiable catalog.) He had seen the girl sitting on a park bench, reading a book, with her twin dachshunds nosing about in the snow in front of her, and he had crossed the street with his heart beating violently, knowing that he must speak to her. Luckily the book she was reading was by his favorite author. His voice cracking horribly, he had managed to excuse himself and inform her that the edition she was reading was not as complete as the one of 193—, and "pardon me, but it has everything; I got that book; it's much better; do you mind if I sit down next to you?"

No, she didn't mind. She listened to him, her thin, handsome face pale and composed, giving every now and then a little jerk to the leashes of the dachshunds who—thus caught up rather drily in their explorations—whimpered a little. ("She's got real leather gloves," he told Miss Kramer, "black ones.") What she told him I do not know, for he couldn't remember it, but whatever it was (in her hoarse, husky whisper) it sounded to him like the assurance that he was the most intelligent man she had ever met, that she too thought the books of H. P. Lovecraft of the utmost importance. ("He's a real writer," Irv used to say) and she thought she would like *very much* to take a walk with him. He told all this to Miss Kramer. He told of their walk through the park, amidst icicles falling to the ground with a *plink!* and everything shiveringly, blindingly bright under the sun—the mica in the rocks, the blue sky, the shriveled leaves hanging infrequently from the trees, the discolorations of the snow where mud, or dogs—or her dogs—stained the white. All the time his radiant companion (she was a little taller than he) walked beside him, with her black coat blossoming into a huge, enveloping collar that half hid her face, with her black elegance, her black stockings, and crowning all a hat—but not a blue hat, a hat almost violet, a hat the color of twilight winter skies where the yellows and the greens and the hot, smoky pinks riot so gorgeously in the west while all the time you are freezing to death. He really made it come across. The hat she wore was made of that silky, iridescent, fashionable stuff, "and get this!" (he said) "get this, Miss Kramer, that hat is the *exact same color as her eyes!''*

Alas, poor Irvin Rubin! Miss Kramer thought, but his lady did not get tired of Irvin Rubin. They went to the movies. They went on walks. They went to bookstores. I saw them myself, once, from a distance. And every evening Irv's girl waved goodbye (though it is impossible to think of her doing anything even that vigorous) and walked into the Park, into the blue with her blue eyes shining like stars. She lived on the fashionable East Side. Late one Saturday afternoon Irvin knocked on Miss Kramer's apartment door in the Stuyvesant Town project, and then stood there miserably with his hands balled in his jacket pockets while she fumbled with the latch. She had women friends in for bridge, who were playing cards in the living room.

"Miss Kramer!" said Irv breathlessly, "You just got to help me!"

"Well—well, come in," said she, sensing uneasily that her guests had stopped talking and were looking at Irvin in surprise. "Come into the kitchen. Just for a moment." He followed her like some ungainly creature in a fairy tale, only stopping to remark in surprise, "Gee, you're all dressed up," (her hair was newly set and she wore a suit), but otherwise taking no notice of his surroundings, not even the extreme tininess of the little kitchenette when the two of them had crowded into it.

"Now what is it, Irvin?" said Miss Kramer somewhat sharply, for she was thinking of her guests. She even made a mental note of the number of clean coffee cups left on top of the refrigerator. He looked vacantly round, his mouth open, his hands still in his pockets, one side of the ancient plush collar of his jacket turned up by mistake.

"Miss Kramer—" he faltered, "Miss Kramer—please—you got to help me!"

"Yes, what about, Irvin?" said she.

"Miss Kramer, she's coming up to my place tonight. She's coming up to see me." ("Really!" thought June Kramer, "what's so awful about that?") He dropped his gaze. "What I mean, Miss Kramer—I mean—" (he breathed heavily) "I don't want her to think—" and here he lifted his head suddenly and cried out, *"Please, Miss Kramer, you come too!"*

"I?" said June, thinking of her guests.

"Yes, please!" cried Irv, "Please! I want—I mean—" and with a sort of shuddering sob, he burst out, "I told her there would be people there!" He turned his back on her and doggedly faced the refrigerator, rubbing his sleeve back and forth across his nose.

"Irvin, don't you think that was wrong?" said she. No answer. "Irvin," she said gently, "I think that if this girl likes you, you don't have to invent things that aren't true and if she doesn't really like you, well, she's going to find out what you're really like sooner or later. Now don't you think it would have been better to have told the truth? Don't you?"

"I don't know," muttered Irvin. He turned around. He looked at June Kramer silently, doggedly, the tears standing in his eyes, those pale-blue, protuberant eyes that should have been nearsighted but were not, alas, too nearsighted to see silent, passive charmers sitting on park benches across Central Park West.

"Oh all right," said June Kramer; "All right, Irvin," and she abandoned her friends, her cards, her little party, to make Irvin's girl think Irvin had friends.

"That'll look respectable, Miss Kramer, thank you," said he, and then he added—with a cunning so foreign to him that it was shocking—"She'll be impressed by you, Miss Kramer; you look so nice."

So Miss Kramer put on her coat with the rabbit's fur collar (to look nice) and they went to Irvin's boarding house, first on a bus that churned the slush in the roads, grinding and grinding; and then in a subway where the platform was puddled with melted snow—but no weather, bad or good, ever drew a comment from Irvin Rubin.

It was cold in the hallway of his boarding house, so deadly cold that you might fancy you saw the walls sweating, a kind of still, damp, petrified cold as of twenty winters back. The naked radiator in Irvin's room was cold. He took off his jacket and sat down on the ancient four-poster—the room held only that, an armchair, a dresser, and a green curtain across a sort of closet-alcove at the back—in nothing but his shirtsleeves. June Kramer shivered.

"Aren't you cold, Irvin?" she said. He said nothing. He was staring at the opposite wall. He roused himself, gave a sort of little shake, said "She'll come soon, thank you Miss Kramer," and relapsed into a stupor. It had begun to snow outside, as June saw by pushing aside the plastic curtains. She let them fall. She walked past Irvin's bed—the bedspread was faded pink—past the dresser whose top held a brush, a comb, and a toothbrush, and whose mirror (set in romantic curlicues) was spotted and peeling, so that the room itself seemed to disappear behind clouds of ghostly shapes.

"This could be quite a nice room if you fixed it up, Irvin," she said brightly. He said nothing. She saw that he had gotten a book from somewhere and was reading; so she walked about the room again, glancing at the armchair, the bookshelf under the single window, and the bridge lamp under which Irvin sat. Shoes protruded from under the green curtain. Miss Kramer sat down in the armchair, beginning to feel the cold, and noticed that Irvin had pinned a snapshot on the wall next to it, in the least accessible part of the room, a photograph apparently taken many years ago, of a boy standing with a dog under a tree. It was the only picture in the room.

"Is that you, Irvin?" said Miss Kramer and Irvin (after a pause in which his eyes stopped moving over the pages of his book) nodded without looking up. Miss Kramer sat for a moment, then got up and walked over to the bookcase (it was full of *Fantasy Press* books), again parted the plastic curtains, again looked out into the snow (it was beginning to stick to the cleared sidewalk and the streetlight), again contemplated the photograph, whose faded sepia seemed to have reduced the tree to a piece of painted canvas, and finally said:

"Irvin Rubin, are you *sure* this girl is coming tonight?" This question had a surprising effect on him; hastily slamming down his book, he jumped to his feet with both mouth and eyes open, his face working.

"Oh, please—" he stammered, "oh, please—"

"Oh, I'm sure she's coming," said June, "but is she coming *to-night?* Are you sure you didn't get mixed up about the time? I don't mean to suggest—" but here he ran over to the alarm clock that stood on the floor by the other side of the bed and shook it; he listened to it; he tried to explain something to her, stuttering so that he frightened her.

"That's all right!" she cried; "That's all right!" and Irvin Rubin, his chest heaving, stood still, subsided, wiped his eyes with his hand, shuffled back to the near side of the bed where—oh, wonderful Rubin!—he recommenced reading his book. She thought of asking him to put it away, but she was afraid of him, and afraid too of the silence of the room, which seemed to warn against being broken. I think she was afraid to move. It was not only the human desolation of that room, but the somehow terrifying vision it gave her of a soul that could live in such a room and not know it was desolate, the suggestion that this bleak prose might pass—by a kind of reaction—into an even more dreadful poetry. June Kramer began to wonder about Irv's girl. It occurred to her with agonizing vividness the number of evenings Irvin had come home to that awful room, had come home and pulled out a book and peopled that room with heaven knows what; and then gone to bed, and got up, and gone to work, and eaten and come home and pulled out a book again until it was time to lie in bed for eight long hours (Irvin was a punctual sleeper), dreaming dreams that however weird—and this was less disturbing—were at least more like the lives led by others in their dreams. But now he read. She almost fancied she saw a kind of cold mist rise from the page. At last (she was stiff with sitting tightly on the horsehair seat of the arm-chair) Miss Kramer struggled to her feet and said in a voice that sounded weak and feeble in her own ears:

"I'm afraid I have to go, Irvin, I really can't stay any longer." She saw that he had closed his book and was staring at her with his brow wrinkled. The light from the overhead fixture gave him an odd look.

"Don't go, Miss Kramer," he said in a low voice.

"I'm sure your young lady meant next week," said June desperately. "Or tomorrow. Yes, she'll come tomorrow—"

"Please! Please!" cried Irv, "Please!"

"I'm sorry, but I have to go," said June. "I have to," and quite unreasonably terrified, she turned and rattled open the latch of the door, letting in at once a draught of that cold, dead, still air from the hall. All at once she knew perfectly well what she had been comparing it to all this time, and as she dove downstairs, followed by a distraught Irvin Rubin, crying breathlessly about his girl and this the first social event of his life, she saw before her only the open grave into which she had stared some forty years before, when as a small child she had been forced to attend the funeral of her youngest sister. In the street she ran away from him, clutching her purse to her side, but as she reached the corner and slowed down, something—she never knew exactly what—made her stop and turn around.

Irv's girl had come. She was standing next to him on the steps. June Kramer saw clearly the coat and hat Irvin had described. She could even make out the black leather gloves and the black stockings. Although she could hardly see Irvin himself in the light from the street lamp, she saw every feature of the girl's pale, powdered face as if it had been drawn: the thin eyebrows, the expressionless profile like a sketch on paper, and most clearly of all, those wonderful, wonderful violet eyes—"she's got such *pretty eyes,*" Irvin used to say. "She's here, Miss Kramer, she's here!" Irvin was shouting cheerfully, beaming down, coatless, at his pale, real lady, when a gust of wind momently froze the street. Irvin's shirt flapped, Miss Kramer's coat performed a violent dance about her calves, but the strange lady's black envelope did not stir, nor did her black scarf, but hung down in carved folds as if it had been made of stone, as still as her hands, as cold as her face and as dead as her expression, which seemed in its pale luminosity to be saying to June Kramer (with a spark of hatred) *I dare you. . . .*

But here Miss Kramer, although she knew she was imagining too much, gave way to cowardice and ran, ran, ran, gasping, until she had reached the subway station and could—burying her face in her handkerchief—give way to tears.

After that Irv was not well. He missed days. He came late to work. When she spoke to him he answered her shrilly, denouncing the office, the people, the books, the world, everyone. It was impossible to talk to him. Three days before he finally disappeared, he cornered June in the stockroom and cried out to her, with an air of pride mixed with defiance: "Miss Kramer, I'm going to get married! My girl is going to marry me!"

She said congratulations.

"We're going away, to stay at her folks' place," he said, "but don't you tell anybody, Miss Kramer; I wouldn't want any of those—those *shrimps* who work in this office to know about it! They're just cowards, they're stupid, they don't know anything. They don't know anything about literature! They don't know *anything!*"

"Irvin, please—" said Miss Kramer, alarmed and embarrassed.

"Go on!" he shouted; "Go on, all of you!" and then he turned his back on her, rubbing his eyes, mumbling, looking at one title after another on the stockroom shelves—though all of them were the same, as June Kramer told me afterwards. She thought of touching him on the shoulder, then she thought better of it, she thought of saying "congratulations," again but was afraid it would set him off, so she backed off as quietly as she could. She paused unwillingly at the door (she said) and then Irvin Rubin turned round to look at her—the last time she ever saw him. His defiance and his pride were both gone, she said, and his face looked frightened. It was as if human knowledge had settled down on him at last; he was ill and terrified and his life was empty. It was like seeing a human face on an animal. June Kramer said, "I'm sure you'll be very happy, Irvin, congratulations," and hurried blindly back to her desk.

This is Irvin Rubin's story as Miss June Kramer told it to me one winter morning in the cafeteria with the windows weeping and the secretaries clattering their coffee and buns around us, but it is not his whole story. I know his whole story. I saw him enter the Park early one winter evening with a young lady—it was probably the day he left work—and although I don't know for certain what happened, I can very well imagine their walk across the Park, the young woman silent, Irvin slipping a little on the icy path, turning about perhaps to look at the apricot sky in the west—though, as June Kramer said, natural phenomenon never got much notice from him. I can guess—although I did not actually know—how Irvin's true love opened her automatic arms to him in some secluded, snowy part of the park, perhaps between a stone wall and the leafless trees. I can see her fade away against the darkening air, that black coat that holds nothing, that black scarf that adorns nothing, her iridescent hat become an indistinguishable part of the evening sky, her legs confused with the tree-trunks, and her eyes—those wild, lovely, violet eyes!—kindling brighter and brighter, radiant as twin planets, brilliant as twin pole-stars, out of a face now grown to the hue of paper. I can see them melting, flattening, and diffusing into a luminous, freezing mist, a mist pouring out from sockets that are now sockets in nothing, doing God only knows what to poor Irv Rubin, who was found the next morning (as the janitor of my apartment building tells me) flat on his back in the snow and frozen to death.

A few days afterwards I saw Irv's lady-love across Central Park West, on a bright February afternoon, with the traffic plowing the snow into slushy furrows within ten feet of her and the dogs of twenty blocks around being walked up and down to leave their bright pats in the snow. She was reading a book, turning the pages effortlessly with her gloved fingertips. I was even able to make out the title of the book, though I rather wish I hadn't; it was Ovid's *Art of Love*, which seemed to degrade the whole affair into a very bad joke.

But of course by the time I managed to get across the street, she was gone.

COME CLOSER

Well, I'll tell you, it began the day I was out on the Jewett Ridge looking for Sarah Howe's little boy that had got lost. All the school mothers were out that day. I took my husband's pickup truck because he was in Orne, talking to the contractors, and I loaded the back seat with blankets. That was for the boy; you know, it gets pretty cold up here in November. I don't know my way around too well and it was the afternoon before I got to the Cox house. I thought—well, you mustn't be too sensitive, so I parked the truck in the driveway. I thought maybe someone new had moved in, even though people from around here don't like the place because it's set back so far from the road and that makes it hard in winter because of the snow. But it's a good, big place and a pretty place, and I don't care what anybody says, that's important; I think it's important to have a nice-looking house. The people who lived there before the Coxes planted some kind of trees along the driveway that stayed green all year; I don't mean pine trees, I mean real, green leaves. I think it must be a comfort for a woman to look out of the kitchen window and see a green tree in the middle of the snow. And they had squares of leaded glass set on each side of the front door, too, which is very pretty.

When I got there the trees had fruit—just imagine, fruit in November!—something like black plums, though the leaves were like *japonica*. Why, I was even going to pick some of it but then I saw that the trees had more and more as they went up nearer the house and the last one was bowed down just like a picture book. Somebody was living there, all right. The paint was no good—you have to be careful up here because the weather gets at it—but there were clean curtains in the window and flowers, too. I think they were zinnias. I don't know where they could get zinnias in November. I thought I would leave the truck and pick some fruit from the second tree, and then I thought, no, I would wait until I got to the next one because that had so much more, and then—well, I went up to the last one of all. I thought nobody would miss a plum from the last one. Only they weren't plums; I couldn't tell what they were. But it doesn't matter. I had only just put my hand up when a woman opened the kitchen door, near the window with the flowers, so I pulled my hand back right away. You never know how people are going to take things. She was a tall, thin, gray-haired woman and to tell you the truth she didn't look any too nice. Most of us don't dress up exactly, but we don't go around in a faded dress that's down to the ground almost and lisle stockings.

"Goodness! you scared me," I said. She didn't say anything. I thought that there was somebody behind her, so I backed off a little and I said, "I'm sorry; I didn't mean to make any trouble." Then I got up my courage and I said, "I'm looking for a little boy. He's lost. He's wearing a blue raincoat."

Here she opened the door a little wider and she said, as if she'd just remembered it or maybe was ashamed of not being more neighborly, "Come in. Come in, Mrs. Mill."

"I don't know," I said, "I have to keep looking," but she shuffled her feet so in those awful, dirty slippers and I thought maybe she hardly saw anyone from one week to the next, poor soul, and had forgotten how to talk to people, so I said, "Yes, I will," and then I said, "Thank you kindly."

Well, I have never seen such a place! That's all I can say. I don't mean it wasn't neat, because it was; it was neat enough to make you wonder if anybody lived in it. But the dust! It was full of it.

That woman took me into the kitchen, that was just as bad as the rest of the place, and padded around in those awful slippers opening cupboards and drawers and there was hardly a stick of food in the whole place, just a few old jars and things and a package of tea up on the shelf. She was humping her shoulders in the queerest way and she looked as if she were going to cry; she just stood in front of me with her head hanging down. I thought she must be some kind of loony so I said, "Don't you fret; you don't have to make me tea."

"Mrs. Mill," she said, "Mrs. Mill, Mrs. Mill, Mrs. Mill," over and over and I thought to myself *Oh, no, she's crazy!* I turned to get out of there, but in two steps I had walked right into somebody and did I jump! I ran back into that kitchen as if I'd seen a ghost. But it was only a man—I guess it must have been her husband because he was just as old, only real dark like the Portuguese they have working on the roads. I don't mean he was one, I mean he was a dark-looking man.

"Don't you mind Millie," he said. "You just tell me your business." Then I saw he had a gun that he put down against the wall; I guess he must have been hunting. I told him I had come to ask about the little Howe boy and he nodded. He said, "Millie can't tell you anything. She don't know anything," and then he gave her a push out of the kitchen. "Millie!" he shouted, "you show this lady upstairs."

"I have to be getting on . . ." I said. He nodded.

"She don't know anything," he said, "but you ask my boy. He knows," and he picked up that gun of his. I tell you, I felt better when I saw him go out the front door! His wife went up the stairs and I followed her, but I didn't dare say a word; I didn't know what she'd do. She would go into one room and look around it, and then into another, and it was one of those big farm houses, you know, that have ten or twelve rooms, and each time she went in she would stand still in the middle. But there was not a thing in one of them, not even a stick of furniture. When we went into the last one she stood there without saying a word, even though I asked her twice where her boy was. I went in to get her, but the moment I walked in that room somebody jumped out from behind the door and knocked into me.

"Oh, watch what you're doing, can't you!" I said, for it was a big boy of fourteen or so, very tall but still full of baby fat. I supposed he thought it was a joke. "Mind yourself!" I said, real sharp, and then I turned to her and said, "Is this your boy?" But she only said, "We haven't got it."

"What do you mean?" I said. "What haven't you got? What are you talking about?" The boy bumped against her, foolishly, the way you'd kick somebody under the table to remind them of something. "What are you doing?" I said. He ran to a closet and searched around inside it—though from where I was standing it looked just as bare as bare—and he pulled out. . . .

"That's Sarah's little boy's raincoat!" I said. "You give it to me!" but the big silly thing ran around behind his mother. I thought to myself that I had had just about enough and in a minute I was going to cry and I said, "You make that boy behave!"

"We haven't got it," she said.

"You give it to me!" I said. Then she lifted her head and looked me right in the face, and I tell you, my heart nearly stopped. I never saw such a face. She looked like a witch. She looked as if she'd killed somebody and was glad of it. I thought maybe they had killed the boy. I backed toward the door. Just when I reached it, I heard the pickup truck motor starting up outside. I guess that did it! I mean, I know how my husband would feel if anybody took that truck. Why, our living is from that truck.

I didn't even stop for a moment; I ran right down the stairs and out the front door. I didn't even think of the poor little boy. I just ran to that truck and drove down the road. It wasn't till I came to the next house that I remembered that nobody had been in the truck, even though I heard it start up. And how did she know my name? I just drove away; I had the funny feeling that if I went back the house would be just the same, with the front door shut even though I'd opened it and nobody around anywhere, just the house and the line of trees with the last tree loaded with fruit.

* * *

When I got to the village I went to Mrs. Post and told her the whole story. She'll tell you what I said. I had just got to when I came to the house when she broke in and said, "Honey, nobody lives there."

"Oh, yes they do!" I said.

"No they don't," she said. "Not in that place." She was sitting at the kitchen table with me. She pooh-poohed to herself the way she always does and pushed away a whole pile of papers to make room for the tea.

"Nonsense, love," she said, "I know the people who used to live there and they're dead. The Coxes. They died fifteen years ago when you were a girl. Everybody knew about it. Millie Cox turned the gas on herself and the other two. And I don't want to be mean, but it was a lucky thing for all, I'd say." Mrs. Post is the Notary Public for the whole ridge so she knows just about everything. "Millie was a distant cousin of my mother's," she said. "Everybody's related around here. She was a jealous, grabby woman."

"But I saw *somebody.*"

"What did her in was that thing that happened to her boy," said Mrs. Post. "Not that he wasn't miserable enough before. He cried in school and tried to run away time and again. She couldn't leave him alone, I suppose. Well, when he was nine or so he ran away for good and when they found him a couple of days later—well, dear, we know it must have been strangers; it couldn't have anything to do with any of us—well, the truth of it is that the child said something about 'some men' and then he never said another word. It was clear to everyone that the boy would never grow up. Not in the mind, I mean.

"Well, we were sorry, of course, but Millie wouldn't hear a kind word. She kept to herself and brooded over it and brooded over it for nearly six years before she did it. Why, she would stop people in the street and ask them was it fair *her* boy had been chosen? She would come into school and make scenes; she would blame everybody; she would say she couldn't bear to see everyone else's lovely children—why, what's the matter with you, love, you're shaking like a leaf!"

"Oh Mrs. Post," I said, "Oh Mrs. Post," and I spilled my tea because my hand was shaking so. "They'll have to burn it down and take up the cellar!" for I had just remembered something that bothered me when I first walked inside and didn't know what to make of it.

Those flowers in the window were as dusty as everything else, and withered too—but only on one side. They looked so fresh from the outside, and the windows were so clean, and the window-curtains so white! But flowers can't be withered on just one side. I thought about the house again, the way it had looked, so homey and pleasant, with the line of trees winding up to it and bearing fruit even in November, with the best fruit always on the next tree, each tree saying: Come a little closer, come a little closer. . . .

It was a child-trap.

IT'S IMPORTANT TO BELIEVE

That they plucked her from the muddy pond where she lay, breathing life back into her. That they emptied the stones from her jacket pockets. That they took off her clothing and dried her, wrapping her in something invisible and warm. That the one with the fur and tail and six fingers opened the walls and showed her the shining dance floor of the Heavens. That they fed her and she didn't refuse, no longer believing the body to be horrible. That there were vines and little creatures like chickens. That there was soft laughter. That King George did not talk in the shrubbery. That she was not shut up. That she wanted her books and they got them. That she asked for her manuscripts and they had them. That she loved one who loved her.

That they went there.

That it was a good place.

(For Allie Sheldon, who wrote "Beam Us Home," and for Jessica Amanda Salmonson, who had the idea that it would be marvelous if time travelers or aliens went back to England in 1941 and rescued from suicide by drowning You Know Who . . .)

MR. WILDE'S SECOND CHANCE

This is a tale told to me by a friend after the Cointreau and the music, as we sat in the dusk waiting for the night to come:

When Oscar Wilde (he said) died, his soul was found too sad for heaven and too happy for hell. A tattered spirit with the look of a debased street imp led him through miles of limbo into a large, foggy room, very like (for what he could see of it) a certain club in London. His small, grimy scud of a guide went up to a stand something like that used by ladies for embroidery or old men for chess, and there it stopped, spinning like a top.

"Yours!" it squeaked.

"Mine?"

But it was gone. On the stand was a board like the kind used for children's games, and nearby a dark lady in wine-colored silk moved pieces over a board of her own. The celebrated writer bent to watch her—she chanced to look up—it was Ada R——, the victim of the most celebrated scandal of the last decade. She had died of pneumonia or a broken heart in Paris; no one knew which. She gave him, out of her black eyes, a look so tragic, so shrinking, so haunted, that the poet (the most courteous of men, even when dead) bowed and turned away. The board before him was a maze of colored squares and meandering lines, and on top was written "O. O'F. Wilde" in coronet script, for this was his life's pattern and each man or woman in

71

the room labored over a board on which was figured the events of his life. Each was trying to rearrange his life into a beautiful and ordered picture, and when he had done that he would be free to live again. As you can imagine, it was both exciting and horribly anxious, this reliving, this being down on the board and at the same time a dead—if not damned—soul in a room the size of all Aetna, but queerly like a London club when it has just got dark and they have lit the lamps. The lady next to Wilde was pale as glass. She was almost finished. She raised one arm—her dark sleeve swept across the board—and in an instant her design was in ruins. Mr. Wilde picked up several of the pieces that had fallen and handed them to the lady.

"If you please," she said. "You are still holding my birthday and my visits to my children."

The poet returned them.

"You are generous," said she. "But then everyone here is generous. They provide everything. They provide all of one's life."

The poet bowed.

"Of course, it is not easy," said the lady. "I try very hard. But I cannot seem to finish anything. I am not sure if it is the necessary organizing ability that I lack or perhaps the aesthetic sense; something ugly always seems to intrude. . . ." She raised her colored counters in both hands, with the grace that had once made her a favorite of society.

"I have tried several times before," she said.

It was at this point that the poet turned and attempted to walk away from his second chance, but wherever he went the board preceded him. It interposed itself between him and old gentlemen in velvet vests; it hovered in front of ladies; it even blossomed briefly at the elbow of a child. Then the poet seemed to regain his composure; he began to work at the game; he sorted and matched and disposed, although with what public in view it was not possible to tell. The board—which had been heavily overlaid in black and purple (like a drawing by one of Mr. Wilde's contemporaries)—began to take on the most delicate stipple of color. It breathed wind and shadow like the closes of a park in June. It spread itself like a fan.

O. O'F. Wilde, the successful man of letters, was strolling with his wife in Hyde Park in the year nineteen-twenty-five. He was sixty-nine years old. He had written twenty books where Oscar Wilde had written one, fifteen plays where the degenerate and debauché had written five, innumerable essays, seven historical romances, three volumes of collected verse, had given many public addresses (though not in the last few years), and had received a citation (this was long in the past) from Queen Victoria herself. The tulips of Hyde Park shone upon the Wildes with a mild and equable light. O. O'F. Wilde, who had written twenty books, and—needless to say—left his two sons an unimpeachable reputation, started, clutched at his heart, and died.

"That is beautiful, sir, beautiful," said a voice in the poet's ear. A gentleman—who was not *a gentleman*—stood at his elbow. "Seldom," said the voice, "have we had one of our visitors, as you might say, complete a work in such a short time, and such a beautiful work, too. And such industry, sir!" The gentleman was beside himself. "Such enthusiasm! Such agreeable docility! You know, of course, that few of our guests display such an excellent attitude. Most of our guests—"

"Do you think so?" said Mr. Wilde curiously.

"Lovely, sir! Such agreeable color. Such delicacy."

"I see," said Mr. Wilde.

"I'm so glad you do, sir. Most of our guests don't. Most of our guests, if you'll permit me the liberty of saying so, are not genteel. Not genteel at all. But you, sir—"

Oscar Wilde, poet, dead at forty-four, took his second chance from the table before him and broke the board across his knee. He was a tall, strong man for all his weight, nearly six feet tall.

"And then?" I said.

"And then," said my friend, "I do not know what happened."

"Perhaps," said I, "they gave him his second chance, after all. Perhaps they had to."

"Perhaps," said my friend, "they did nothing of the kind. . . .

"I wish I knew," he added. "I only wish I knew!"

And there we left it.

WINDOW DRESSING

Mannequins—as everyone knows or should know—have only one aim in life: to make some pervert fall in love with them. It is because no one loves them that they have no souls, and because they have no souls that their lives, perfect and beautiful as they are, are so queerly disconnected, for every mannequin dreads that time of night when the lights are turned off in the windows. Then, not being seen, she ceases to see herself, and the memories dictated to her by the dress she is wearing (mannequins change their memories every time they change their souls) completely disappear. Then she falls into an uneasy, troubled sleep and dreams vague, unpleasant dreams of the factory in which she was made, of plaster, paint, and lumber, of spinning down conveyor belts, of horrid whirrings and grindings—but then she wakes up. The sun is out, oh bliss! and she wears a hostess gown and remembers, as clearly as clearly can be, dinner at the St. Regis and a drive in Central Park. It is a great comfort to exist again. They know, of course, that they will eventually die, having first been chopped up or melted away or crushed for industrial fill or land reclamation, but even though they know it, they are brave and there is always the chance that someone—someone—

Marcia was wearing a bathing suit when William first saw her. She had the stiffish, uncomfortable look mannequins adopt at such times. She knew that the bathing suit (it was a revealing one) showed the lines where her hips joined her waist, and in a helpless, frustrated rage she arched her arms, spread her fingers, and threw back her whole body as if to say, "Do with me what you please; I'm still more beautiful than *you!*" But William did not know this. Had Marcia only been aware of it, it was all the same to William whether she had a crack at her waistline or not, for he had never seen a real woman in a bathing suit, being far too terrified to look at one. He was not afraid of the mannequins, however. With deep respect he investigated her perfect feet, her aristocratic legs, her gay arms flung back; he even returned his glance to her suit (she had no navel) and tried to pierce the obscurity of her dark glasses to see what painted, fretted, moth-lashed eyes could match that tip-tilted nose and that enchanting, pouting, fashionable mouth. He stared at her, moving his tongue slowly over his front teeth. Marcia could not move, of course, but she could see him plainly, a fat young man in a zip-front cloth jacket and glasses, and she was in ecstasy. A radiant flame seemed to bathe her from head to foot. To her he was in every way the handsomest and best of mankind, for mannequins know nothing of men; the male figures they sometimes have to associate with in window displays are, without exception, sheep-faced juveniles with nothing at all on their minds and hardly more on their faces. Moreover, as the mannequins say, "*They* can't do anything for a girl." Thus Marcia kindled, thus she bloomed, thus she threw back her arms more gaily than ever, and pouted and posed and tried (even though she was wearing a bathing suit) to show him how she appreciated, no, how she loved him, and how happy she would be if only he could transport her to Southampton or the West Indies to wear her Bergdorf bathing suit on the real beach under the real sun, and to be a real woman forever. William, on his part, gulped, swallowed, stirred a little, and then went away. And that was the beginning.

Now the year wore on, and William went away and came back; the leaves fell in the park and Marcia wore a raccoon coat and carried a little flag; William pressed his nose, morning and evening, against the glass; it snowed and Marcia was clothed in a black evening gown; William came on his lunch hours and Marcia noticed that he carried books; William waved and Marcia radiated. She began to look respectfully (as well as she could without moving her eyes) at the objects placed in the window with her, especially the books, for she thought, "I shall have to read things and go places when I am a woman." One day the designer (toward whom the mannequins feel as toward God) came into the window and clothed Marcia in a pink cocktail dress reminiscent of the twenties. He put shoes on her feet and a headache band on her head. He adjusted the pole that held her up and arranged her arms and legs so that she seemed to be dancing. He left a copy of a novel by F. Scott Fitzgerald open at her feet and Marcia tried to read the back jacket, for she thought, "I shall have to know about such things when I am a woman." William came at six o'clock when the street lights were lit and the snow gleamed in the park. He stared at her for a long time. One of Marcia's arms was up and one was down; her body bent forward and one pointed foot barely touched the ground, its knee glowing rosily through the pink silk fringes of her dress. Her blue-gray eyes beamed softly, her mouth laughed, her enchanting nose enchanted twice as much as it ever had before. Slowly, glancing first to each side of the street to make sure that nobody saw him, William printed a kiss on the glass; then suddenly, with a leap as if an electric shock had run up the sidewalk into the soles of his shoes, he shouted one unintelligible word and raced away. Marcia was desolate. She tried to move. She could not, of course, but the headache band unaccountably slipped down over her face (an indignity that frightens and disgusts every mannequin). Her mind was in complete turmoil; why had he run away? Why had he come at all then? Had he changed his mind? She was not used to such perplexities. She laughed and danced in her window, although she would have wept if she had been a woman, and when the lights went out late at night she had very unpleasant dreams, dreams of bumps and shocks, of strange sounds, of swinging up and down, of stopping and starting, of something flapping, smothering, and crushing her in folds. It was the worst nightmare she had ever had. She tried to cry out but mannequins cannot speak; she tried to wake up wishing urgently, bitterly for daylight, and as the last series of shocks stopped—something bumping rhythmically on her head—there was light, she was someone, she was somewhere, and she woke up.

William was kneeling before her. She was in a room unlike any window she had ever lived in. "Is this where Daisy lives?" she thought wonderingly (for she had read about Daisy on the book jacket the day before) but just at that moment an excruciating pain, a sort of dissolving sting, shot up her arm; William had kissed her hand.

"Oh you moved, you moved, I knew you would!" cried he, burying his face in her skirt, and throwing his arms around her knees, he proceeded to tell her all about himself. The same unbearable pain flashed through all of Marcia's plaster limbs but she kept quite still for mannequins have great pride of *métier*, and even when the pain was at its worst she did not move, only rocking back and forth a little as William hugged her. He was kissing her all over her face. Then he stood back and beamed. He scurried to the other end of the room and washed his hands and face, drying them on an old towel. He squirmed out of his jacket. "You can trust me," he said. "I used a glass-cutter. They'll never find you." He smiled slyly. "I knew you were looking at me," he said.

"I love you," said Marcia. William dropped his towel.

"You spoke to me!" he cried. "You spoke to me!" She smiled.

"Yes," she said. It was difficult to speak. It was difficult to smile, or to move, but she smiled again (a little stiffly) and moved (a little stiffly) until William prevented her walking toward him by rushing up to her, grabbing her hand, and dropping to his knees. "Speak to me," he said.

"Hello," said Marcia. She felt light as air. "You're charming," she said. "Do you think I'm charming? Do you read F. Scott Fitzgerald? Is this that Colony? Can we dance here?"

"No," said William, a little crestfallen, "I don't dance."

"I do," said Marcia, "I dance the Charleston," and she went dancing around the room, her skirt swinging, filled with delight, crying "Charleston! Charleston! Charleston! Charleston!"

"Sssh!" cried William, "Sssssh! somebody'll hear you!"

"Charleston, Charleston, Charleston!" screamed Marcia, "Oh—how—I—love—the—Charleston—"

"Stop it, stop it!" shouted William, and chasing after her, he tripped and fell on top of her to the floor where she still sang out "Charleston! Charleston!" her legs moving as if she were dancing. Mannequins never take much notice of what position they are in, since the pole holds them up when they are vertical and they are often stored horizontally in warehouses. But after an instant Marcia realized the position she was in, whereupon she said very reproachfully, "Oh William, you're taking advantage of my position," and smiled very sweetly as he let her get up. It was easy to smile now.

"My name is Marcia," she said. "Is this the Colony?"

"Uh . . . no," said William.

"Then I can't stay here," said Marcia, looking in William's shaving mirror (which hung over the bureau) and fixing her hair. "Because it's not the Colony, you see." She turned to look at him. "Are you F. Scott Fitzgerald?" she said.

"No," said William.

"Are you a Princeton man?" she asked.

"Uh . . . no," said William, his head sinking.

"Not a Princeton man!" cried Marcia, shocked. "Don't tell me you're a Yale man!"

"Uh . . . no," said William.

"Where *did* you go to college!"

"Uh . . . nowhere," said William.

"Nowhere!" she cried.

William bowed his head. Marcia was silent. After a moment she stealthily pulled her skirt away from contact with him and slid one foot toward the door, but William—anticipating her—rushed between them. Marcia pouted. William wrung his hands. Marcia tapped her foot. She shrugged angrily and, practicing little dance steps, began to move toward the door, but William, in terror at her leaving him, ran after her and clutched at her dress.

"You're not a gentleman, you're not a gentleman, stop it!"

shouted the mannequin. William grabbed her arm and Marcia struggled; William tried to kiss her and Marcia began to cry; William begged and pleaded and Marcia maintained stubbornly that this was not the Colony, she knew it was not the Colony, and why was he keeping her from the dance? She could not get rid of the idea that there was a dance going on somewhere nearby. William glared and panted, terrified that she might run away from him into the street; Marcia beat at him with her hands and tried intermittently to dance; William pulled at her and Marcia screamed: William grabbed her by the dress—and the dress ripped from top to bottom. Both stood stock-still. Marcia did not breathe. At this sacrilege, this desecration, she could scarcely keep on her feet; she felt her personality, her whole world, her very consciousness totter. Hardly knowing what she did, she ran to the window; windows had always been her friends; she had lived all her life in windows; and it was with a confused idea of getting back to Bergdorf's and the designer, back to the beautiful backgrounds and the still, shining lights, that she climbed up on to the sill and jumped out.

William restrained her. Unfortunately her head fell out of the window in the process. He stood stupefied for several seconds. Then as the sound of Marcia's head shattering on the sidewalk below penetrated his mind, he dropped what was left of her, her headless body, her dress, her shoes, and all the rest in one convulsive movement, leaped violently into the hall, and ran out of the house. He never came back.

And Marcia? She lay in William's room for almost a week. Then, as the room was to be rented, she was put out into the street along with the china figurine of a dog, a load of William's books, and some garbage for the Sanitation Department. A painter from Hoboken found her first. He took her to his studio where he propped her against a wall among the mice, the dropped paint rags, and the used-up tubes. He gave her shoes to one friend and her dress to another; now he uses the sheet he had draped about her to wipe his brushes. Even without a head a mannequin is sentient in a blind, slow, slug-like way, and the various giggles, shrieks, and titters Marcia perceives from time to time distress her very much. They do not seem quite proper. Very slowly she is turning into a thing, forgetting her window at Bergdorf's, forgetting William, forgetting everything—no personality can come to her from the sheet and the paint for these are too real, and in a few months she will be nothing but a piece of plaster. Every once in a while the painter takes his latest girl to see the headless body, and the girl—a plump, coarse-skinned travesty of a Bergdorf mannequin—laughs at her.

"*That's* Pop Art, if you please!" says the artist.

He despises it.

EXISTENCE

Imitatio Quasi Imago in Honorem
Jacobi Blish Multa Cum
Admiratione Felicitatis Sui In
Artibus Reconditioribus *

It is impossible to call up the Devil when women are present, I mean real women, that is to say hermaphrodites, for men (real men, who exist) are the people who look at the women, and the women are therefore the people who are looked at by the men. So that women (when they are alone) must be either men or nothing. There are a great many women who were supposed to have called up the Devil, all those witches and so on, but the question remains: what did they really call up? Or better still: did they exist? Maybe they called up something else. Or if it was true, and women really can *call up* the Devil, what does that make the Devil? Or are women really male? I have no answers to these questions.

With men, there's no problem. See the men? There are four of them. They have good, straight, legal, logical, one-track, masculine minds. Wicklow, the fat one, wants to blow up the world; Ludlow, the *magister magici*, is going to do it for him; Albano, the third one, will try to stop it (they have to have him there for legal reasons); and the fourth man—oops, it's a woman—is Mr. Wicklow's private secretary. One could be forgiven the mistake. He employs this woman because she has an

---

* "Representation in the form of a picture in honor of James Blish, with much admiration for his felicity in the more recondite arts."

eidetic memory and no mind of her own; she's been in love with him for years. Her name is Estrellita Baines. Estrellita means "little star."

The men have no first names. Why should men need first names?

Wicklow, the bully, fat and merry, who bullies his secretary.

Ludlow, indescribably commonplace, lean, smells bad somehow (through no fault of his own, you can't place it), and takes no pleasure in the mauling that interests Mr. Wicklow. Has awful eyes.

Albano, the monk, who's been taking a lot of spiritual mauling lately, the solid, stolid peasant with big feet. Nurses impossible dreams of personal glory and is violently ashamed of them. He's not speaking to anyone.

Wicklow: thick cream, *lots* of money.

I

All around the marble chamber (which resembles a Greek columbarium at Forest Lawn) in various positions on the tessellated floor, posing against the walls like figurines, like lamiae, like snakes, are the bad doctor's demon assistants, girls with big eyes, girls with silky thighs, lovely girls with undulant bodies, golden hair, arms like waves, moist pits, impossible bones. They smile or scowl.

> Beat me.
> Tease me.
> Love me.
> Rape me.

II

All around poor Estrellita Baines in her gray suit and her rimless spectacles. She wears a skirt and carries a pocketbook so you can tell who she is. Her hair is pulled back in a tiny bun. It just won't grow, no matter what she does.

It matters what women look like.

III

Then they got tired of waiting. After discussing what the catastrophe is to be—Plague or the Bomb—they disperse to their separate circles. Demons are not allergic to electric light, and so the lights go on. Circles, pentacles, alb, stole, cope (you can read all this in books). Insofar as she thinks at all, Estrellita Bains thinks that whatever Mr. Wicklow wants must be right. The world is lucky to be done in by him when it's going in any case. Mr. Wicklow is feeding the fire on the lamia's magical body. Ludlow's fat cat is very regardant and strange by the altar at Ludlow's feet, from time to time turning his huge eyes on his own ginger fur and giving himself a self-regarding lick. He weeps like a human.

". . . *mulier hominis est confusio*. . . ."

Estrellita Baines wonders why she feels so sleepy. The room is filling with smoke.

". . . *felix conjunctio*. . . ."

Frater Albano wonders at the words. Ludlow sounds like a bandsaw; it's impossible to make anything out.

". . . *quicquid, te, cara, delectat. Quid iuvat deferre, electa?*"

Wicklow feeds the fire.

". . . *ave, formosissima . . . iam, dulcis amica, venito. . . . Vestiunt silve tenera merorem virgulta, suis onerato pomis. . . .*"

What *is* the man saying? The cat lies on its back and bats at the air. Something cold seems to glide in across the floor under the smoke. Wicklow, shaking himself awake, drops more resin into the fire: resin and honey; sparks snap from the dead body of the lamia. Ludlow has explained everything very carefully; magic is an art, like science. *I mean* (thinks Wicklow) *like mathematics.* Or *perhaps an exact art, that's better.* Anyway, there are rules. Inflexible rules. It's all to do with the nature of the Personages that lie behind the appearance of things—or in connection with the appearance of things? Wicklow shakes his had to clear it, earning a sharp look from the magician. *And Albano is here because of some pact the Devil has made with God, or God with the Devil, who can tell? But he must only observe, not interfere. That's clear. Why? The limits on Good. Evil breaks the rules, Good must obey the rules. Very simple. And to our advantage.*

". . . *imperatrix mundi.* . . ."

". . . *Dione.* . . ."

". . . *mundi luminar.* . . ."

And the cold, rising, somehow does not clear the smoke, but makes it blacker. Frater Albano is almost entirely lost in the dark. The empty pentacle in front of the altar begins to glow, not light but rather darkness visible, and into this column whirl the magician's girl-demons, sucked around and around, distorted souls flattened and glowing, somehow dimmed as if caught in a waterspout. A mutter comes from Frater Albano's direction, absolutely contrary to the rules.

"*Aliquid mihi faciendum est!*" cries Ludlow. The altar flames. Stifled words come from Albano, and much coughing.

". . . *veni, vidi.* . . ."

"*Quid nunc, O vir doctissime, tibi adest?*" exclaims Ludlow.

". . . *vici.* . . ." finishes Albano in his corner, barely able to speak.

"*Veni, audivi, exii!*" Ludlow shouts, and as these last words sink into the cold (sink into it but do not penetrate it, do not neutralize it, refuse to mingle with it, but only trail wisps of human heat after them), the light in the pentacle condenses to a tiny star, a mote of light that seems to drift farther and farther away. It does not become less, but somehow draws back as if in obedience to the laws of some other perspective, until it is very far away (but still within the room); and then—at the point of becoming too small to see—it expands soundlessly until it fills everyone's sight, a magnesium flare, intense and colorless, in which one looks at one's neighbor and sees bleakly and without emotion that he has not even greed or wrath, but that he is hollow.

"I don't like this," says Estrellita Baines. Ludlow raises his wand, black eyes blazing like balls of pitch. A head seems to be forming in the room (they are all inside it). The head grins, mottled, quicksilver-mouthed, simultaneously behind the doctor and before him, at the ceiling and around their ankles; Estrellita Baines says more positively, "I don't like this *at all.*"

"And why," she continues crossly, "do you always have to grin like a wolf? It's so dull. Why can't you grin like a chihuahua?" At the sound of her voice, the ceiling and floor exchange places, causing an almost unbearable nausea. They settle, and Ludlow raises his wand. *If she moves . . .* ! And simultaneously, Frater Albano disabled by coughing, manages to croak *"reprobare, reprobos!"* which is the end of a verse that can be used only once; and somehow in the world, now shaking and gliding like a crack-the-whip, up and down, back and forth, racked with alternate light and darkness, the *magister magici* sees dependable Estrellita Baines preparing to step out of her circle. The lenses of her spectacles reflect the fragmented images of a dissolving world. He raises his wand to blast her.

Broad daylight. Silence. Sunlight streams over the raised gallery at the end of the room. The Sabbath Goat sits on the edge of the gallery, swinging His animal's hooves. He is as solid a horror as anything can be, emblematic from the crown of lit candles on His human head to His erection to the Star of David on His forehead to His oozing breasts to His slit-pupiled eyes. Goats and cats belong to Him. Estrellita steps out of her circle, foolish and confused. She says, "You look silly." He lifts His head and opens His mouth; the magician's cat backs carefully onto Ludlow's feet and settles there with a groan. Estrellita has taken off her glasses, as if trying an experiment (can she see without them?), but this is one of those ladies who looks even worse that way; nobody says, "You're beautiful without your glasses." So she puts them back on. She wanders out between the chalked figures on the floor, studying them with interest. Her voice, one knows, will be strong but not sweet:

I don't fancy giving you my world to play with.

Give up, magician. I don't exist apart from the particulars, so you can't touch me.

"I thought," says Frater Albano, finding the words, or the words finding him, "that you would be more beautiful."

Why? I'm not a picture. And I'm not the Virgin, either. She hikes up her stockings and begins to climb the stair at the side of the gallery. Albano covers his face with his hands. Holding her drab skirt above her knees with one hand, she trudges up the steps—dogged, plain, and slow. She kicks off her shoes.

I could be beautiful if I wanted to. I could be anything if I wanted to. But there's nothing emblematic about me; I must use what's to hand. So if your aesthetic sense isn't too violently offended, gentlemen, I'll stay as I am.

The Sabbath Animal yawns. Little Star climbs the steps. Either the steps are higher than they look or she isn't really walking, for it seems to take her forever to get there. And as she toils away from the three on the floor, she grows larger—though still climbing one step at a time—until, miles away, large as a monument at the head of a stair, huge as a pyramid, she can pick up the Goat in one hand, which she does. Her spectacles flash like the Lunar Apennines. He wriggles furiously in her fingers, and she brings him close to her face, to look at him. Sitting on the gallery, feet reaching the floor and head bent to avoid the ceiling, she presses her knees carefully together, ladylike. The gallery sags and creaks. She puts her free hand behind her back, and when she brings it out again, there is in it another furiously wriggling little man. A golden squiggle to match the red-and-black squiggle. She holds them almost at her nose.

Neither of these is the genuine article. Of course, there is no genuine article.

Ludlow breaks his wand in two and points the raw ends at Little Star. She does not look up.

No use, magician. What a funny little man you are, with your hot temper and your subtlety and all your logic! You have played for years with your pacts and laws and compulsions without the slightest suspicion that anyone was trying to cheat you. And you spoke for years with what you believed to be Infernal Personages without ever once thinking that the real mark of a Personage—as distinct from a Thing—was Its ability to change Its mind. Someone has been making fun of you.

Ludlow continues his incantation.

If the characteristic of a Thing, says Little Star, *is its invariability, then surely the characteristic of a Person is passion, volition, and reason. And where is that to come from if not from you? Ah, We had grand times in the early days when there were only vegetable and animal souls to draw our being from, grand times but bland times, I must admit; then you came along and We have developed amazingly since. We have developed into beauts, doctor, if I may so express myself, into real lolla-paloozers, the human coloration of which never ceases to amaze me.*

"Who are you?" says Albano in a croak.

I (says Estrellita Baines), *am The One Who Puts Things Back Where They Belong. I am She Who Confines Fancies to the Space Between the Ears, The Lady Who Makes Things Concrete, The Woman Who Insists on Facts, I am The I-Am, I am The What-Is. Something of a paradox, you will admit, for a supernatural being. But I am one of the two real Personages.*

"Why are you here?" cries Wicklow. "Why are you interfering? And why are you my secretary?"

Because (says the woman-mountain) *I am The Decider Who Decides That To Make A Real Bang You Must Use A Real Bomb. Anything else offends Me.*

"That is not logical," says Ludlow, the master magician, in a hard, tight, furious voice.

It is not, says Little Star, *but it is both reasonable and real,* and thrusting both arms under her skirt, she appears to release Good and Evil into the space between her legs, then doing the same with the magician and the monk, whose arms and legs twinkle a violent protest as they are shoved back into the womb. She seems to get no pleasure from it. Her lips are thin and priggish. The huge hand lowers above Wicklow, who throws himself flat on his face.

"I don't believe it!" Boss Wicklow shouts. "It's not possible!"

Why not? I am the effluvium of billions of souls, a billion and a half women who turn uneasily in their sleep, a billion and a half men who resent the uneasiness of the women. My brother is What-Is-Not and he is also my father, my lover, and my son: The One Who Broadcasts Dreams. The Man Who Believes, The Inside Turned Outside, The Yes-It-Is, The All-Is-All, The Great Somebody Else. And to complicate matters still further, we are really each other, but since that's impossible, we take turns. It's the women's turn today; it'll be the men's tomorrow, when the men become women, when the women become men, when they both become zebras. I'll still be here.

"Go away!" He shuts his eyes.

The trouble with men is that they have limited minds. That's the trouble with women, too. But I know everything.

"GO AWAY!"

All right.

He opens his eyes, to find Estrellita Baines—his own size now—kneeling over him. There is a very disapproving look on her face.

"Mis-ter Wick-low!" she says.

"I'm all right," says merry Wicklow.

"I think," says Miss Baines, "that we had better go home, Mr. Wicklow, and that after this, Mr. Wicklow, you had better consult me about anything you plan to undertake. You have wasted both your money and our time."

"All right," says rich Wicklow.

"And I think," continues Miss Baines, "that, while I'm at it, I might as well tell you the plans I have for this palazzo, which is to be turned into a karate school for high-school girls. Your life will not be worth living, Mr. Wicklow."

"I know it," Wicklow groans.

"You will not like it, Mr. Wicklow."

"Yes, yes," he says.

"Considering what I know about the firm, you may even have to make me a partner, Mr. Wicklow."

His head snaps up. "Miss Baines!" She is standing just inside the door to the great marble room. She's sizing him up. She's wondering mildly where that idiot Albano and that idiot Ludlow and the cat and all those silly girls have got to. She seems remarkably graceful. She pirouettes on one heel; it's wonderful how good a woman can look when she knows there's no competition around. He hates her.

"Mis-ter Wick-low!"

He follows her.

Appendix: The Latin

It's no wonder they call up the Great Mother, considering the invocations they use. If you are interested:

mulier hominis est confusio—Chaunteclere to Pertelote, woman is man's damnation

felix conjunctio—happy conjunction (of a boy and girl)

quicquid, te, cara, delectat, etc.—everything, dear, to delight you.

ave, formosissima, etc.—oops, can't find it; more medieval love poetry

imperatrix mundi—empress of the world

Dione—another name for Aphrodite

mundi luminar—light of the world

Aliquid mihi, etc.—There exists something which must be done by me. (bad Latin)

Quid nunc, etc.—a facetious cry for which I am indebted to T. H. White's *Mistress Masham's Repose:* "What is biting you, O learned man?"

veni, vidi—I came, I saw
vici—I conquered
Veni, audivi, exii!—I came, I heard, I left!
magister magici—nasty neologism
reprobare, reprobos—to reprobate reprobates (written by one)

FOUL FOWL

Grim-jawed they were, seven feet tall. Heroes. Immunized against every known disease. Wow!

They shouldnta come down on Fifth Avenue, I had a married daughter she was going to this exclusive dentist on Park, now no more Mother-and-Son dance at the high school.

Utter, Utter Contempt. (We shall make you all slaves, et cetera.) Myron Goldfarb, M. D. extraordinaire, amateur Cordon Bleu, better than Brillat-Savarin (it is whispered "meilleur que Brillat-Savarin! N'est-ce pas?") prepares the meal for the conquerors: who have—poor things!
(hey, they're cute!)
been fed on a totally balanced diet of synthetic proteins, and so forth. We'll cure them of *that*.

> *VIZ:*
> *Red carpet*
> *Gold pillars*
> *Plush curtains*
> *Pretty girls (shame!)*
> *Royal Doulton Dinner Service*
> *Gold silverware*
> *Tablecloth from India (we help you in your need,*
> *   please pay by next mail, 10% off)*

And:

>Entrechat aux mushrooms
>Seafoods variés (in cream sauce)
>Nutmeats (allsorts)
>Cheese bleu
>Cheese red
>Cheese yellow
>Fish
>Meat
>Fowl
>French bread (best in the world)
>Café au lait
>Lait (milk)
>Mousse au Chocolat (defies translation)
>Fraises (Strawberries, you fool, kiss me)

Oh, how people got killed! It was awful! (With a look.) And they spared *nobody*. Not even the entire senior class of the Maryland Women's Academy, which really should've known better than to hurl panties and paper bags full of water at them. One week later after subduing the entire globe (gah!) they again ate:

>Entrechat aux mushrooms
>Seafoods variés (in cream sauce)
>Nutmeats (allsorts)
>Cheese, bleu, red and yellow
>Fish
>Meat
>Fowl
>French bread (a little stale)
>Café au lait
>Lait
>Mousse aux Chocolat
>Fraises

Their table manners defied description. Who could have thought a mere M. D. could have been so diabolically clever, eh, Shirley?

> First they began to cough.
> Then they began to sneeze.
> Then they broke out in red spots.
> Then they itched all over.
> Then they began to wheeze.
> Then their faces swelled up.
> Then they got AFRAID.

"We are immunized against every known disease!" they cried piteously.

"We have tested this food for poison and found none!" they cried even more piteously.

Then Myron Goldfarb led them off, sneezing, coughing, itching, wheezing and swelling, to get a shot full of Antidote.

"How did you do it?" everyone cried, overturning the Royal Doulton Dinner Service, the French bread, the chocolate pudding, the mushrooms, the seafood—shellfish, caviar, etc.—the milk, the strawberries, the fowl, the meat, etc. while the pretty girls all crowded around Myron Goldfarb, who had returned and was rather enjoying himself as they kissed him every which way where.

"Oh, shucks!" said Dr. Myron Goldfarb.

"Well, I haven't been an allergist for twenty-seven years for nothing," added Dr. Goldfarb modestly. "I imagine any of you folks here, like this pretty child on my lap, for example—no, don't get off my lap, pretty child—well, I imagine any of you folks here if you were presented with supreme examples of the culinary art and had lived all your life on gloop and such, why you would devour it right up. And if you ate any of the common substances to which we frail humans are so vulnerable, alas, like unto milk, wheat, eggs, chocolate, fish, shellfish, strawberries, mushrooms and nuts, and then ingested these delightful confections say a week later, you too might induce an allergic reaction and produce this, say, histamine and swell up and get red spots and all the rest of it."

"Dr. Myron Goldfarb," (said they all solemnly and vowfully) "if whenever and again I find myself susceptible to the pollens shed by the common ragweed in September, O loveliest of months, or the grasses of June, O most delightful of blooming seasons, or the rose, the emblem of True Love, or the trees that blossom in spring tra-la or any other histaminic ills of this mortal flesh, it is to you and you alone that I shall turn, for you are a pearl among allergists and a Cordon Bleu of great price, which you should be written up in the Guide Michelin as the savior of the human race. *Vive* Myron Goldfarb!"

"Jolly-O," said Dr. Goldfarb.

"By the way," said the Secretary of State, "what infallible Antidote are you administering to those weak-hived tyrants in the next chamber?"

"Potassium cyanide," said Dr. Goldfarb.

Vive Terra!

A SHORT AND
HAPPY LIFE

Skinner-Waxman was hiring.

To this end, they sent out several students to measure the
    height of a public building with the aid of an extremely
    handsome
    sensitive
    solid
    and more or less vertical

Barometer.

One said:

I was at first determined to measure the height of the Civic
    Depositors' Bank and Guaranty Income Trust by measuring
    the air pressure at the bottom and comparing it with the
    air pressure at the top.

But then I thought: *That has no style.*

I then decided to measure the shadow of the barometer—
    stuck upright in the ground—and the shadow of the
    Bank, Bank being to Barometer as Shadow to Shadow.

But shadows change and pass and clouds may come alas and
    the sun moves as the grass withers and all is mutability.

And I thought: *Death comes.*

So I went to the top of the Civic Bank and Guaranty Income
    Depositors' Trust with the intention of dropping the
    barometer off the roof and timing its splat, but it

occurred to me that it might fall on someone's head,
on the head of a worthy father of a family, on the
head of a girl, on the head of a girl in a summer dress
who walks with her dress clinging and her hair swinging,
with beads of sweat on the nape of her neck, looking for
the right building and the right typewriter below the
horrible chances of sixteen feet per second per second
off the top of the Depositors' Trust.

And I thought: *There must be trust.*

So I went to the janitor of the building and said "What information will you give me in exchange for this handsome,
vertical, solid, and extremely sensitive barometer?"

But although we had several drinks together and he was
extremely
handsome
vertical
solid and
sensitive,

He knew nothing.

So I took a train to the plane and the plane to the city
and the city to the bus and the bus to the library and
my feet to the archives and got the whole thing out of
a book.

(We told you, said the interviewer, to use the barometer.)

I did, said the student, I used it to hold down the left-
hand pages whilst I looked at the right-hand pages and
I may say, Sir, that your barometer is sadly wanting
in construction.

For although it is extremely sensitive, handsome, sturdy
and comes in an attractive leather case, it has one
fatal tendency, to wit: to roll.

Although (he added) that may be considered natural enough
in a more or less roughly cylindrical object;

For as Lao-tse says: *That is the joy of barometers.*

* * *

They rejected him.

(They even gave his barometer to someone else.)

He joined—never mind what, it was a great secret and
    is a great secret to this very day, and died several
    years later off Alpha Procyon while in the performance
    of his duties, which may not be spoken of, mentioned,
    described or referred to, here, there, or anywhere else—

Flash-frozen like a can of soup, died laughing, was frozen
    laughing, remains laughing to this very day.

He thinks (while circling around the green star in a sit-
    ting position):

How pleasant to laugh!

Skinner-Waxman still uses the barometer, WHICH IS NOT PER-
MITTED UNDER ANY CIRCUMSTANCES TO ROLL.

NOTE: Skinner-Waxman is the name of a multiple-choice test used
to measure creativity.

    What?

THE THROAWAYS

They met in a cafeteria (kah-*fet*-er-*ee*-yuh, n. origin unknown. An establishment where fet may be obtained) and the Traditionalist took one slot while the Fashionable took the other. Both were young, barely ninety. Clothes were a bit drab that week and the Fashionable was wearing the "natural look," somebody else's body, of which she had several spares at home. She had also thought of bringing along an extra head, but did not wish to appear gaudy. The Traditionalist, on the other hand, was genuinely in her own skin. Nothing but. The Fashionable said, after the proper polite pause:

"Your clothes are really custom-made, aren't they?"

"No," said the Traditionalist. "They're me."

"Ooh, you're a Traditionalist!" cried the Fashionable, and then she added in a rush, "Would you tell me, really, if you don't mind, about you people, do you—"

"No," said the Traditionalist rudely. There was a moment's silence.

"I was only going to ask," said the Fashionable timidly, clearing her throat, "whether you come here often."

"Well," said the Traditionalist, relenting, "not as a general rule. I am not especially fond of fet."

"Aren't you?" said the Fashionable. "Oh, *I* am! It wiggles about so. It's so loovy. And one doesn't need to scoop it up with one of those little shovel things you're using—be careful, you'll get it into the disassembler—you just open your mouth and the fet jumps right in. Fet is *in* this year."

"Not in me," said the Traditionalist, eyeing her tangle of fet with new distaste. Steaming, writhing fet hung in the air before both ladies, little pieces detaching themselves from the main mass now and again and drifting gently from side to side.

"It practically *begs* to be eaten!" remarked the Fashionable. There was another silence.

"I suppose," said the Fashionable finally, "that you Traditionalists must lead very exciting lives. I don't. Of course I often had thoughts about turning Traditional when I was a girl, you know, just giving up everything and stripping myself bare, just going out into the bush, as it were, but—" (and she finished with a sigh) "here I am living in a plain old Disposable."

"Mmmm," said the Traditionalist.

"It's a nice Disposable," said the Fashionable. "You know how they work. Ours is automatic. You set the machines in the walls to extrude the proper furnishings and accessories for each particular time of day and then you set the pattern control: French Provincial, Haiti Regression, Moon Maroon, or even Random. Well, you know."

"A plethora of things," said the Traditionalist, "and a remarkable paucity of ideas."

"You can even," continued the Fashionable, unheeding, "set it to repeat the same pattern all the time if you want. For a whole day, say. I had a friend who lived with Severe Plutonian for ten days—a whole ten days, mind you—but she said her family nearly died of boredom. She'll never do it again."

"I dare say," said the Traditionalist grimly.

"Of course," said the Fashionable, "they say there's—uh—a certain something about living with a design for a day or two. They say you become attached to it, in a way. Still, it must be awfully eerie to wake up, you know, and see exactly the same things you saw the night before. I don't think I'd care for it."

"No, not you," said the Traditionalist.

"Of course," said the Fashionable airily, "I *certainly* wouldn't live in a woom! Not even a furnished woom. That's a little too far out." She lowered her voice carefully. "I know for a fact," she said, "that besides the instability of having the thing *flowing* around you all the time and turning transparent and heaving and all sorts of impossible colors, that there are absolutely authenticated cases of a woom going berserk; it's something about their glandular system; they get this overwhelming longing for their own planet and the first thing you know you're barreling past Pluto in a fetal position until some Pleezeman picks you up." She nodded her head vigorously. "No, no," she said, "no woom for me, thank you! I'll stick with my Disposable.

"Of course *you* don't live in a Disposable," she added, narrowing her eyes at the Traditionalist, "and I'll bet anything that you wouldn't even touch an Instantaneous."

"Don't even mention—!" shouted the Traditionalist, starting to her feet.

"No, no, no," said the Fashionable quickly, "of course not; I wouldn't live in one myself. Of course, a friend of mine has one; they do seem to be coming in. I visited her and I must say there's something about those Instantaneouses. Of course they make you feel awfully passive. But sometimes it's nice to be babied a little, have your needs and desires anticipated all the time. Why, when it felt me coming in, it turned from Lunar Black Crust White to Saturn Stipple (that's a sort of conservative purple-pink, you know) and all the walls went concave. I must say I was impressed."

"I can anticipate my own needs and desires!" snapped the Traditionalist.

"Well, I suppose you can," said the Fashionable with a sigh. "You Traditionalists are so decisive. Tell me," (and she giggled slyly) "what *do* you live in?"

"I," said the Traditionalist, anticipating her reaction with grim relish, "live with solid walls and Throaways."

"Throaways!" gasped the Fashionable.

"There's a little shop where you can get them," said the Traditionalist, lowering her voice. "Illegal, of course. A factory in the Rockies. I go there every week and pick out everything. Guaranteed for a week. They're delivered through a secret underground organization. At the end of the week my husbands and I smash the hard things with our feet and put the whole mess down the disposal chute. Then I go back again."

"Oh!" gasped the Fashionable. "Oh, my!"

"It's the only way to live," said the Traditionalist. "You people will never know." She rose to go, but the Fashionable held her back, grasping her by the arm. There was a strange light in the Fashionable's eyes; she was licking her lips. She even glanced furtively about and motioned the Traditionalist closer.

"Did you ever hear," she hissed, "of Things?"

"Of what?" said the Traditionalist.

"Things," said the Fashionable breathlessly. "Just Things. You make them with your own hands. Everything. To sit in. To sleep on. To eat from. You just make them. First you make them and then you put them around and then—" (she almost choked) "then—you just leave them there."

"You leave them there?" said the Traditionalist slowly.

"Yes," said the Fashionable faintly. "You just leave them there. They're permanent."

The Traditionalist jerked away. She tottered. She turned ashen. She almost fell. "Permanent!" she cried in horror. "How can you say such a thing to me? I may be a Traditionalist but I'm not a—savage! A pervert! A—*nonconsumer!* Permanent? I'd rather die!" And putting both naked heels into the ejection cups at footlevel, she was instantly reassembled at the exit to the cafeteria. There a robot dorman (*dor*-man, n. origin Old French dormir, to sleep. Originally an ornamental construction extruded by residential buildings while all the inhabitants were in a state of unconsciousness) approached her. He was so handsome, so perfect, so shimmering, so golden and so multi-fingered that all human beings naturally loathed him on sight. He said:

"Pardon, sirormadm, but you are in state of high distress. Must fix or not proceed."

"I *will* proceed!" cried the Traditionalist heroically, striking a pose.

"Pardon, sirormadm, but as you know, this my function. Am

psychotherapeutic device to mediate psychic conflicts arising from too-sudden change of environment, i.e., between sheltered, semi-specialized milieu of commercial nature and public freeforall. Allow disturbance mediation or further egress impossible."

"If you detain me," said the Traditionalist, "you will be the cause of my becoming emotionally distressed in an even more serious manner. I will become extremely disturbed. I will have a fit."

"Fit?" said the robot dorman.

"I will become unconscious," articulated the Traditionalist with great care. "I will fall to the ground. I will foam at the mouth. My emotional stasis will be irreversibly impaired. You will have interfered with my business."

"Where go?" said the dorman.

"To blow up a public monument," said the Traditionalist.

"Pardon," said the dorman. "You are Traditionalist. Please pass. Nearest monument available to Traditionalist for blowing up yet unblown that way. I summon beam transport, yes?"

"I will proceed by helicab," said the Traditionalist, "if there are any left, which I doubt. It is the Traditional way."

And so she did.

And the Fashionable, tears in her eyes of somebody else's body, rather wished she had brought along that extra head after all. It might have made her cleverer. The fet wreathed itself into the most enchanting, heaving, iridescent shapes, but it did not charm her. She dug her nails into her palms and whispered desperately to herself:

"I don't care if it's bad. I want it. I want it so much. I must have it. Permanents. Oh, *somebody* must know where to get them! *Somebody. . . . Somewhere. . . .*"

THE CLICHÉS FROM OUTER SPACE

I have a friend who has put together an anthology of feminist science fiction stories. Actually I have several friends who have done so, but the friend I am referring to here is an imaginary one, so I shall call her Ermintrude.

Ermintrude is keen of eye, brilliant of brain, intolerant of nonsense, and has surprisingly powerful forearms. (Editors develop these by screaming and tearing their hair a lot.) So powerful are her forearms, in fact, that it is possible for Ermintrude—even when overworked, underpaid, and suffering from schlockfever (this is a disease editors get from reading too many stories submitted by the general public) to carry up to ten-and-a-half pounds of vividly purple prose in her arms at any one time. However, a pile of manuscripts does tend to be unstable, and upon visiting Ermintrude recently I found her supine on her living-room rug and up to her frontal sinuses in vast quantities of rejected fiction. The stuff had slipped and fallen, as usual, and out of sheer discouragement (I think) she had followed. Anyway, she lay sullenly upon the (really rather aesthetically interesting) pattern of rejected manuscripts and pronounced, in a voice I shall never forget:

"If I get *one more story* about weird ways of becoming pregnant—"

"Oh, come on," I said. "It can't be as bad as all that. I know there are men who can't imagine women having any other adventures than biological ones, which is why they write such guff, but—"

"Read one," said Ermintrude.

Well, after I had, and had helped Ermintrude up, and we had kicked the manuscripts about a bit to relieve our feelings, I went home, Ermintrude got out her anthology, and I thought I'd heard the last of the business. But that pile of rejected mss must have been the vehicle for a curse, or *geas*, or malevolent principle, or at any rate some kind of filterable virus which had clung to me, saturated my clothing, or otherwise affected my person. The whole business was *not* over. How do I know?

I began to write trash.

No, not the kind I usually write, a different kind. Actually I was not the active agent in the writing of the stuff at all. To this day I don't know who—or what—is. I began to have strange and horrible dreams in which the boundaries of history and logic disappeared, fulgous luminescence streamed from old copies of *Conquer Absolutely Everything* and *The Sexist from Canopus,* and teenaged male science-fiction readers vanished screaming into geometrically impossible bull-sessions located in the fourth dimension. A certain obscure invocation ('male bonding ritual' is the closest I can get to actually pronouncing the phrase) recurred constantly and throughout my dreams there grew a frightful din, an alien, rugose drumming, horrible, mind-blasting, and obscene, which finally roused me one night from the worst (and last) dream to discover that—

My typewriter was typing all by itself!

Mind you, I don't say "writing," for after I left a sheet of paper in the machine the next night (if not to satisfy the alien intelligence which had obviously traveled from Ermintrude's rejected mss to the sort of tacky metabolism—a Sears Electric—which suited it best, at least to mute the noise) the creature stopped, as if panicked by the actual sight of its own words. Then slowly it attempted a few scattered phrases like "mighty-thewed" or "her swelling globes." Lately it has got more enthusiastic and its efforts have begun to bear a definite resemblance to conventional prose narratives of the science-fictional kind. In the forlorn hope of satisfying the damned thing (otherwise there will be nothing left but exorcism, and I don't *want* to type all five hundred and twelve pages of *Sexual Politics* on the machine—think of the time involved, let alone the increasing cost of typing paper!) I am attempting to have the following—well, fragments—published. Maybe this will content the Thing in the Typewriter. I have had to read all sorts of fiction in my career as a teacher and so has Ermintrude (as an editor) but nothing—nothing!—could be as abominable, as mind-destroying, as abyssal, and as dull, really, as the following collection of:

CLICHÉS FROM OUTER SPACE

The Weird-Ways-of-Getting-Pregnant Story

Eegh! Argh! Argh! Eegh! cried Sheila Sue Hateman in uncontrollable ecstasy as the giant alien male orchid arched over her, pollinating her every orifice. She—yes, she—she, Sheila Sue Hateman, who had always been frigid, nasty, and unresponsive! She remembered how at parties she had avoided men who were attracted by her bee-stung, pouting, red mouth, long, honey-colored hair, luscious behind, and proud, upthrusting breasts (they were a nuisance, those breasts, they sometimes got so proud and thrust up so far that they knocked her in the chin. She always pushed them down again). How she hated and avoided men! Sometimes she had hidden under sofas. She had stood behind open doors for hours on end. Often she had wrapped herself in the window curtains, hoping to be mistaken for a swatch of fabric.

But this was . . . different.

Ecstasy pounded through her every nerve. How she had wanted this! Now she could have children. Would they have tendrils? Roots? Would they emerge as a bushel of seeds? A tangle of leaves? Would one of her toes fall and root itself in the ground? It didn't matter. Whatever her son would be like (and she knew, somewhere deep inside her, that she would have a son) she would love it because it would be His.

Realization poured through her: *She really loved men!*

She had loved them all along. But she had been afraid. Afraid of their strength, their attractiveness, their gentleness, their cute way of coming up to her in the street and saying, "Hey, honey, that's a great pair of boobs you got there," which had set her heart racing.

She remembered Boris's direct, strong gaze, and the crushing power of his beautiful arms as he had attempted to rip off her clothes.

She remembered Ngaio's twinkly, humorous politeness as he said, "The reason that you keep disagreeing with my intellectual conclusions, Sheila, is that you're a bitch."

She remembered José's tender, masculine protectiveness as he had said, "We can't hire you, Sheila, because this is a man's job. It's too difficult for a woman."

She really loved men.

Eegh! Argh! Oh! Oh! Argh! Eegh! cried Sheila Sue, convulsing all over the place.

The giant orchid tenderly wrapped its fronds. . . .

(to be continued—unfortunately)

The Talking-About-It Story

"Oh my, how I do love to live in an equal society," said Irving the physicist, looking about with pride at the living room of their con-apt, which Adrienne, his wife, had decorated the interior of with her brilliantly intuitive flair for interior decoration. Adrienne had been a plant geneticist, but had decided that what she really wanted was to stay at home, have eight children, interior-deco-rate, garden, cook organically, grow herbs in the windowsill (it did seem to be rotting the wood a little), and go barefoot. She was very close to the earth. There was nothing feminine about that;

it just happened to be that way. It was her decision so Irving respected it.

"Yes, wouldn't it have been awful to have lived in the old unequal society?" said Adrienne. She went into the kitchen to see how the alfalfa soufflé was getting on.

"Yes, living in a sexuality egalitarian society is absolutely the best thing there is," said Joyce, the laser technologist who was taking twenty years off from her career to raise four children because that was what she really and truly wanted to do. "Just imagine how horrible things must have been in the old days!"

Her husband, George, an IBM executive who made six billion new dollars a year, smiled fondly at Joyce. "Yes," he said, "now that men and women are equal, things are so much better. I hate to think of what they used to be like!" He loved and respected Joyce and had built her a little workshop in the basement where she could practice laser technology in her spare time.

Their Black maid, Glorietta, came in and announced. . . .

(to be dealt with—severely)

The Noble Separatist Story

"Tell me, Mommy," said Jeanie Joan, snuggling up to her beautiful, strong, powerful, gentle, wise, loving, eight-foot-tall Mommy who was President of the United States, "why aren't there Daddies any more?"

"Well, Jeanie Joan," said her Mommy, "once there were lots and lots of Daddies. Daddies were nasty, vicious men who went away to something important called "jobs" while Mommies and babies lived in little prisons called "homes" and pined away for lack of healthy exercise, intellectual freedom, and the ability to earn their own livings. Daddies weren't brutal (usually) and didn't (always) beat up Mommies and babies with baseball bats. Mostly they just passed a lot of laws saying that Mommies weren't equal and had silly thoughts and raging hormones and couldn't work or think properly except for taking care of "homes" and babies. So the Daddies had all the nice things to themselves."

"What nasty Daddies!" said pretty little Jeanie Joan.

"Yes, weren't they all?" said her Mommy, carefully pushing off her left knee *Moll Flanders, Das Kapital,* Engels on the family, John Stuart Mill's *On the Subjection of Women,* and the complete works of George Bernard Shaw. Jeanie Joan might misinterpret them. She could study them when she was older.

"And then what happened?" said Jeanie Joan, well on her way to becoming a beautiful, strong, powerful, gentle, all-wise, loving, eight-foot-tall, completely perfect Mommy herself who would never swat anything in anger, not even a mosquito.

"Well, dear, after a while all the Mommies got together and they saw how silly everything was. And they passed a lot of new laws saying that people were equal no matter whether they were Mommies or Daddies or whatever color they were, and after that everybody loved everybody and there was no more war or poverty or racial discrimination or greed or selfishness."

"But the *Daddies*—!" said Jeanie Joan, kicking her Mommy gently in the ankle.

"Well, Jeanie Joan," said her Mommy, "the reason everything got so wonderful was that the Daddies just couldn't stand a world without war, poverty, racial discrimination, greed, selfishness, or hate. They weren't really human at all, you see. So they committed suicide, every one of them, within three weeks. And so did the little boy babies. We call that 'raging testosterone' or 'constitutional inferiority' or sometimes just 'discouragement.'"

"What big words!" said little Jeanie Joan thoughtfully.

"Yes," said her Mommy, carefully removing from her right knee Marabel Morgan's *The Total Woman,* a biography of Phyllis Schlafly, Queen Victoria's denunciation of women's rights, and six thousand copies of *Vogue.*

They might accidentally fall on little Jeanie Joan's head and bruise it. She could read them later, too.

"Tell me, Mommy," said Jeanie Joan (she was a talky little thing), "why—"

(to be avoided—at all costs)

THE TURNABOUT STORY
or

I Always Knew What They Wanted to Do to Me Because I've Been Doing It to Them for Years, Especially in the Movies

Four ravaging, man-hating, vicious, hulking, Lesbian, sadistic, fetishistic Women's Libbers motorcycled down the highway to where George was hiding behind a bush. Each was dressed in black leather, spike-heeled boots and carried both a tommygun and a whip, as well as knives between their teeth. Some had cut off their breasts. Their names were Dirty Sandra, Hairy Harriet, Vicious Vivian, and Positively Ruthless Ruth. They dragged George (a little sandy-haired fellow with spectacles but with a keen mind and an iron will) from behind the bush he was hiding in. Then they beat him. Then they reduced him to flinders. Then they squashed the flinders to slime. Then they jumped up and down on the slime.

"Women are better than men!" cried Dirty Sandra.

"Lick my boots!" cried Hairy Harriet.

"Drop your pants; I'm going to rape you!" cried Vicious Vivian in her gravelly bass voice.

Ruthless Ruth said nothing (she never did; it was rumored among the gang that she had never learned to talk) but only chewed her cigar and flicked open an eight-inch-long, honed-steel, poisoned, barbed, glittering knife! Growling, she moved toward George.

And these women are financially supported by their husbands!

thought George. *Those poor, terrified males fastened to the bedroom door by diabolically constructed chain-link thongs, which only let them loose to make money!*

Our hero thought his end had come. But suddenly Ruthless Ruth turned green, smoke came pouring out of her ears, her facial expression changed, and she fell to the ground, writhing.

It was that time of the month!

Dirty Sandra and Hairy Harriet likewise turned green, lost their judgment, dithered, turned six or seven colors, and groaned, wallowing on the ground and clutching their stomachs. They were in no condition to do anything to anybody now.

That left Vicious Vivian. In mid-snarl she changed, too, but differently; she slank toward George, her mouth pouting, her body inviting, her large, moist eyes pleading with him to give her what she needed.

It was the other time of the month for her.

"Tell me, Vicious Vivian," said small, sandy-haired, iron-willed, spectacled, heroic George, "where is your center of command, who is your leader, and what are your battle plans?"

"I will tell you everything," sobbed Vicious Vivian in a gentle soprano, melting to her knees and embracing George's calves in the extremity of her biological need. "I adore you. I want you. I need you. I can't help it." And she told him everything, nibbling at his knees and sighing between-whiles. "Oh, take me with you!" she cried; "I love you and I have betrayed The Cause!"

"You couldn't help it," said George compassionately, and stealing her motorcycle, he rode off into the sunset. He must get his secret to the Humane Instruments of Monumentality in Sausalito. Now he knew why female factory productivity only reached the norm four days out of every month. Now he knew why female scientific brains only worked in the rare few days between that time of the month and the other time of the month. Once the H.I.M.S. had this information (and a calendar) they could use it to take the world back from Women's Liberation and build a truly free and equalitarian society for everyone, not just men but women, too (taking into account their special physical needs, of course).

George's bad back, stuffed sinuses, flat feet, trick knee, migraine headache, hayfever, bladder infection, and angina pectoris began to. . . .

(to be burned—with tongs)

ELF HILL

Thank you, I'm *quite* all right now, really. It wasn't anything only. . . .

Well, that book with the pictures.

Fairy tales? Oh, yes! I'm sure they're harmless; I certainly didn't mean there was anything wrong with them. They're quite pretty, even the ones—what is it called, "Elf Hill"? All those people who are hollow behind, you know, like a mask. I don't suppose they'd strike most people as horrible, but. . . .

It's just that they remind me of something.

May I? Oh, thank you! I haven't seen a real window—except one—in ever so long; and yes, that's the bridge over there—it's quite clear today, only a faint sort of fog and all that marvelous yellow-brown color—and one can see the tops of the buildings as nicely as on television.

Would you? It's nothing; only I've just been to see my mother at Sunset Estates. I don't want to be a bore; everyone knows the feelings you have about your mother can be—

The pictures?

Well, that's just it. It isn't my feelings; it's something else. At least I think it is. It's about the place, you see, and I don't know enough to decide what to do, and yet I have to do something. I mean—that's why I came here. I suppose you have the fairy-tale books for when you see children, don't you, although I do think they'd be frightened at pictures like that. But then maybe I'm the only one to be frightened. Which is why I'm here, you see.

I've just visited Mother at Sunset Estates. Oh, I told you. Well, there's only me now, ever since Michael got that wonderful job— but so far away, out past the Rings, you know!—and Father has been dead for ever so long. Before retirement, too, although back then retirement wasn't so important because people weren't so old—so many people didn't get so old, I mean. You know the statistics; I'm not expressing it well, but you know what I mean. Anyway, I'm the only child and the only daughter too, and I used to spend all my weekends with her when she was at home. I liked to do it. It wasn't hard for me, as it is for some people; we've always gotten along. But then Mother moved to Sunset Estates and you can't visit there more than once; it's simply too expensive. After that you have to be content with video calls and not even live ones, either, because the reception is so bad. They don't tell you why but it is. Mother said she knew why but couldn't say on a tape, so of course I had to go and see her in person.

Well, I couldn't leave my job during the week because they take that out of your pension—which is such a struggle nowadays!—so I took the BosWash loop Friday evening and stood on line to cross the Atlantic and then again to get the Shuttle over the Arctic. I can't say that I wasn't annoyed at her for being so far away—they say it's normal to have bad feelings about your parents as well as good ones, so I suppose I shouldn't complain—but Mother's awfully lucky to have gotten into Sunset Estates at all. She might've had nothing but a bunk in Happihomes or some awful place like that if she hadn't put all her saving into her retirement—and I help just as much as I can, and Michael sends us both a great deal. He says, "Thank time dilation and Einstein for the favorable rate of exchange." I'm not sure what that means, but it *is* some sort of miracle; that I know. Anyway, I didn't get into the terminal until the next morning and even then there was a delay and an awful scare—about scrambling people as they went through the transformer—so it all took much longer than I expected. Then there's the difference in the time zones. I never quite understood how that works, but I know it's on account of mother's being so far away. It was very early there and I tried to rent a chair in a transient hotel but the automatic entrance had set the rates too high, even at that hour. Then I tried to phone Sunset Estates, but the local reception wasn't just bad (as Mother had warned me it would be); it was terrible. So in the end I had to take a subway without calling ahead. I didn't know if she had stayed up to see me or even if she thought I was lost—capsules get fed into the wrong branch lines all the time, you know—or even if she thought I might be dead in a transformer accident. But when I got out of my capsule before the elevator bank and managed to find the one with the right number—and *then* made sure I punched the right location—but why do you think they say "punched" all the time?—really, it's more like tapping with your fingers—anyway, they do, especially on television—so I got to the anteroom of Sunset Estates and there she was.

Oh no, she was fine. There wasn't anything wrong. At least I didn't think so then. The anteroom was awfully small and dirty, but most of them are; it's just that I thought Sunset Estates, being so expensive, would have a better one. Only it didn't. And the corridor beyond was perfectly awful too—chipped plastic panels covered with grime, as if nobody ever washed them—and in one place two old women and an old man sitting on the floor in the strangest sort of way—one old lady was actually *poking* the old man!—and he was pulling at the old lady's hair, only not hard, of course, since all of them were quite old, but in an odd sort of stupid way, like an old baby.

I said, "Good heavens! Who's that?" and they stopped and stared at me in the oddest fashion, as if they were going to cry. Mother said, "It's only the Hallers; don't mind them." Then one of the old people tried to get up, but they looked awfully thin and feeble, you know, and really very sick and I said, "Shouldn't we tell someone?" but Mother jerked me by the sleeve to make me go faster and said, "If they want help, they shouldn't be out in the hall." This wasn't like her, for she used to be very kind, but she looked as if the Hallers—if that was their name—were too disgusting to bother about. Then I thought they mightn't belong to Sunset Estates at all, since if they did they would surely choose to visit each other's apartments instead of sitting in a dreadful, dirty, bare corridor four feet across—which is all it was, really. Certainly that seemed to explain it.

I supposed we hadn't come to the apartments yet, since the doors were so close together—just like closet doors, actually—but Mother said we had. They were "branch doors," she said. So she turned a combination in one and there was another door and then another and then another, each just a few steps from the last and each with another panel of buttons. And there were other old people by each of them, looking terribly ill, so much so that I was concerned. But finally it was the last door and we were in Mother's apartment.

It was *lovely!*

I don't think I've seen anything so wonderful since I was a little girl, back when there was room for everybody. I'm so used to living with everything folded up into everything that the sheer space of it made me dizzy. At any rate something did as I went through the doorway; why, Mother had to hold my arm for the first few minutes, I was so stunned.

We had come in on a sort of balcony a few steps above a living room that must've been thirty feet either way, and all of it carpeted in pale blue just as thick as thick, and creamy-white walls with fruit and flowers modeled in them near the ceiling—like plastic, you know, only heavier and thicker somehow—and chairs and couches in pale stuff that shone and shone, not like plastic, either—and pictures on the walls with real paint on them (I don't think they were the sort of pictures Mother liked, though she said she'd gotten to like them) and little tables like the "wood look" only different, so wonderfully different, like everything else! And here were flowers woven into the carpet in all sorts of rich, pale colors, and here and there doors leading to other rooms as wonderful as that one—only think, *ten rooms*—with a television set and a modern kitchen five times as big as mine, and here and there flowers in vases on the tables, and such bright colors that I thought they couldn't be real!

But they were. They really were: roses and lilies and gladioli and I don't know what. There was a television room, too, and a sewing room and closets everywhere just full of clothes—oh, I can't tell you! So soft, so bright, so—so very shining and *good*. And then Mother took me through all of it for the biggest surprise of all. This was at the back. I had thought Sunset Estates, being so far up, might have a common room or dining room where the old people could look outside, but Mother said no. There was no common dining room; you cooked in your own kitchen or you dialed meals to be sent to you, just as you could dial clothes from the catalog. (We could do that, she said, and eat in the dining-room—imagine, a room just for eating!) I was saying how sad it was not to be able to look out, if only a little, when Mother touched something on the wall of a small room with curtains about it on three sides and a sort of lounge chair and table in the middle. I thought it was a sun-room, and when the curtains moved back there would be silvered plastic plates with lamps behind them, the way they have in the sun-bathing clubs.

It was nothing like that at all.

The walls were glass and outside there was sunlight and a breeze, and huge, creamy, piled-up clouds on the horizon—which was oh, so far away, miles and miles!—and nearby what must have been at least a whole square mile of lawn with flowering tropical shrubs on it and palm trees, just like the ones you see on television, and in one place a lake with birds swimming in it. Everything was rich and winding and lovely. I can't do it justice, I really can't.

I think I began to cry then; I was so happy for her and so relieved she hadn't gone to Happihomes or Endfun Acres, which she would have had to do without that little extra bit from my salary. In fact, it was all too much for me and I wouldn't let her open the sliding glass doors, though I made her promise we would go out later.

The first thing I said in the kitchen (which was wonderful and had all sorts of machinery for cooking, most of it automatic) was "But how? How do they do it?" For surely everyone at Sunset Estates couldn't have such a marvelous apartment, let alone that huge park out there, all to themselves.

Mother was choosing food for us, watching the steel arm of the freezer choose a piece of corn-on-the-cob and move it into the microwave oven. She didn't even look at me. I said, "But Mother, how?"

She said, "What would you like to eat, dear?" in the same voice she had used when I was little and was doing something I shouldn't—a sort of bright voice but not really—so I knew she didn't want to tell me.

Instead she showed me all the machinery in the kitchen, which would do everything without her lifting a finger except to press a button, and then the hothouse room (only she called it a conservatory), and then all the glass and silver and crystal, and bone china in the dining room, and then length upon length of fabric if she wanted to sew or embroider. Then we were back in the kitchen and this time I wouldn't take no for an answer. I said, "I want to know *how.*"

Mother said, her head tilted to one side, "Why dear, we share. Isn't that the secret of everything?"

I said, "But how can you share this? It isn't possible!" and she looked kind but impersonal, the way she used to do when she was explaining to Michael and me why we had to be good in school or how people didn't feel anything after they died or what an atom was. Mother used to be a teacher, you know. This time she said, "It is all, Mary Ellen," (that's my name) "on account of Space and Time," and then she told me how Sunset Estates could have twenty million retirees in its home and yet each one of them could have an apartment just as lovely as hers. And how each one of them—except for the Hallers, who didn't like such things—could even have a park, like the one I had seen, all to himself or herself.

"Imagine, Mary Ellen," (she said) "that this apartment is like a cube, solid matter like a piece of wood or a lump of clay. Now if twenty million people all want that one piece of wood or lump of clay, there's no way you can give it to each of them, is there? You can shave the piece of wood very thin and give each one a thin sheet, but anyone can tell the difference between a solid cube of wood and a little piece of veneer, can't they?"

I said, "Mother, why—" but she put up her hand for silence, the way she used to do in the classroom.

"You can't give everyone the same solid piece of wood," she said, "if you divide it this way" (she moved her hand up and down) "or this" (she moved her hand from side to side) "or even this way" (and she moved it forward and back) "so what can you do with those twenty million people, who all want the same cube of wood? Well, you might divide it up along the dimension of time, mightn't you? That way you can have it for a second, and I can have it for a second, and somebody else for a second—which means sixty people in a minute and three hundred and sixty in an hour and so on."

I burst out, "But we already do that!" for it was only taking shifts, you see, which everybody does at work or at the museums or the movies, things like that. Mother knew what I was going to say, I think, because she smiled the way she had in the old days in the classroom and raised her hand again.

"Right, Mary Ellen!" she said. "What good is a wonderful apartment like this if you can only have it for a second every hour or every day? That's no good at all. It might work if the people could be made to live only that second in the day and the next one in the next day—and one could do that, you know, dear, or at least have them live one day out of the year—one could give them drugs or put them into electrical stasis or freeze them or something along that line. But then we old people would live a very, very long time, wouldn't we?—and there would be more and more old people retiring every year and all of them living practically forever—three hundred and sixty-five times slower than normal—which wouldn't help matters any.

"No, Sunset Estates does nothing like that. It couldn't possibly. All the same there are twenty million people and only one apartment and yet everybody has his or her own apartment all to himself or herself."

Mother paused for a moment. I didn't say anything, for I was just as much under her spell as when I had been a child and she ran around Michael to show how the earth and sun moved in relation to each other and how you could see it as either one moving—though I didn't understand that then and don't now, to tell the truth.

"Mary Ellen," said Mother then, her voice sinking in the old, thrilling way, "Time and Space are not separate things, they are really one and the same. I know that's difficult to understand and you always had trouble with it at school, but it's quite true. Here at Sunset Estates it isn't merely Time that's shaved into slices (so to speak) or even the wood cube itself—when I say the wooden cube I'm really talking about this lovely apartment and grounds, of course—but the two together that are divided up. Each minute here lasts exactly one minute. Each piece of my lovely furniture and beautiful crystal and marvelous clothing is as real and solid as it can be. Yet I share all of them with twenty million other people. At Sunset Estates it isn't just Space and Time that are shaved thin, but the combination: Spacetime. And Spacetime is Reality itself. It is Reality itself that is shaved into twenty million slices at Sunset Estates."

I said, "But, Mother, how can we exist there, then? How can real people fit into something so . . . so thin?"

She said, "The people too are shaved thin at Sunset Estates."

I didn't understand at first, but she went on explaining, that most of the cost of Sunset Estates was the machinery that took you and made you thinner at each of the doors you went through; that each door was a different setting, to make sure nobody went into the wrong slice of reality, which the machinery couldn't handle; that two people could never be in the same slice together unless each of them came from outside (they were different slices of the original apartment and so could never be brought together without ruining the separation of all the slices); and that for the same reason no mechanical signals, like television, could pass directly between one slice and another. That was why phone and TV reception were so bad. Mother said that the remaining mass of each person—the nineteen million, nine hundred ninety-nine thousand, nine hundred and ninety-nine parts that were not in use—was stored somewhere else in a huge barrel of metal and were—I mean was—inactive. I don't really understand how they managed people doing different things in the apartments—I mean in the one apartment—but she said they "synchronized" everyone at the end of every month so that anything you changed in that time (like sewing or things you moved or the food you used up) just changed back in the middle of the night. Until then it was a strain on the machinery to keep all the slices so different (Mother said, I think, "accommodate to different interstitial stresses"), which is why a relative's visit was so terribly expensive for anyone at Sunset Estates. The retirees could occasionally make tapes and have them "solidified" by the machinery (to send outside, you see) or even "solidified" and then "attenuated" for another retiree, but that was rare. It was all very, very expensive. Everything was far too expensive except the apartment itself and the lovely grounds.

I said, "Then nobody sees anybody, ever!"

Mother said, "Except the Hallers. But *they* don't like to share. *They* are using up their funds and will have to leave very soon." She said this in a scornful voice, with her face all mean and pinched, not at all in the gracious and noble way she had been explaining things before. She said, "They're disgusting."

I kept thinking *The people are shaved thin, too.* But I couldn't feel it. The huge, heavy kitchen machinery was visible all around us behind its transparent plastic wall—one whole wall was for food and showed rank upon rank of frozen things and looked just like a factory—and it seemed to me that this was the machinery for slicing everything thin and that in a moment my presence would be too much for it and it would blow up or run down and twenty million other people would explode into the kitchen. It was as if we were inside one of those toys where you open a little figure only to find another, and so on, because they're all hollow. I imagined other apartments packed all around us like a nest of larger and larger boxes. It wouldn't have been so bad to think of the things being stretched thin, but the people, too—!

I said to my mother, "But I don't like it. There's something wrong with it. There must be!"

She said, "Then, Mary Ellen, you had better go home."

I said, shocked, "Something's happened to you!" and Mother said, "Nonsense! What a silly idea," but it was in that oh-so-bright voice she used years ago to say things were all right when they weren't. She told Michael and me that Father was dead in that voice. I wanted to stay but it was just then that a chime rang in the antique French porcelain clock on the dining room wall—I could see it from where I was in the kitchen—and Mother jumped to her feet, saying in the same too-bright voice. "Oh, how kind! They're warning you not to overstay your time," and then somehow she was rushing me through all those lovely rooms—though without touching me—crying brightly, "Don't phone; it can't get through, you know," and "Don't write, dear; they'll let you know if anything happens," and "Tell Michael how terribly happy I am!"

That's all. I never got to walk outside in the park among the hibiscus and the palmetto trees, though I'm sure that if I had nothing would have had a proper smell, not even a green smell, even though they were real flowers, and all those lovely things felt—I don't know how to put it—funny, somehow. Dim. After all, something has to disappear when nineteen million nine hundred ninety-nine thousand nine hundred and ninety-nine parts of you are somewhere else, doesn't it?

And mother never even touched me.

Oh, I don't know what to think! I want her out of there, I do. But where is she to go when the only other place is a bunk in Happihomes or a nasty hallway with dirt all over the floor? That's what the "Hallers" are, you see, people who come out into the halls of Sunset Estates to die because they can't stand to be alone; they think it will drive them mad, I suppose, being alone with most of themselves put away somewhere else. Or perhaps they've already been driven mad and can't find their way back to the right slice of reality. That's why Mother hates them, because they're real and dying with each other. And now I can't get messages through to that place where Mother is, where everything looks so splendid but when you touch it or smell it, it's a little dim or flat somehow. I can't keep her with me—there's hardly room in my apartment even for one—and I couldn't pay anything at all into my pension fund if I had to take care of her—Sunset Estates is cheaper than living on the outside, after all.

No, that's not my problem. She wouldn't come if I asked her. She was insulted by my so much as saying I didn't like Sunset Estates; I could never persuade her to come. Anyway, it's not really *my* problem, is it? Unless I sign up for Sunset Estates, too? Oh, you don't know how lovely it was!—ten rooms, the smallest at least twice the size of this one, and the huge library of television tapes; and music and books, and anything at all you wanted to eat, and that beautiful, beautiful park all for one's own, and somebody else to clean while you sleep—they do, you know, they store that last little slice of everyone for an hour in the middle of the night and a team of skilled people comes in to set everything to rights—and all of it so big and clean, so fresh and lovely. Maybe I'm wrong about the way things felt; maybe it was my imagination. It could have been, couldn't it? Or maybe the machinery is just a little bit overloaded with twenty million people. But they're going to have two apartments soon; they said so.

Maybe then it will be all right.

It's bad to be alone, of course, but is it worse when there's twenty million to a room and you don't see anyone else or like Endfun Acres where there are twenty old people jammed into one room and do you see them? And can't help smelling them too?

I don't know. I'm worried about my retirement. Last night I dreamed I was back in the kitchen of Sunset Estates and I asked my mother where my father was. She pointed at the floor, which became transparent, you know, and there he was, buried under the floor but looking as if he were alive. I recognized his white moustache at once. Then all the walls became like glass and there were corpses buried all around us. We were surrounded by twenty million dead people who looked as if they were buried alive. *I woke up thinking, At least I'll be near her.* I thought, *Every time I do anything I'll be able to think: Mother is doing this, too. We'll be so close together, in the same place, eating the same food, looking at the same television tapes, sitting on the same chairs, even though we can't touch.* Then this morning—I mean in reality, after I'd waked up—a brochure came in the mail.

It was from Sunset Estates. . . .

NOR CUSTOM STALE

They had discovered immortality. Oh not for people, not at all;
it was Houses that were immortal. Harry and Freda's House had
been in their family for fifteen generations. Of course fifteen
generations then meant much more than fifteen generations
did ten or twelve centuries back, for the Houses, with their atmosphere of protection and their soothing monotony, pro-
longed people's lives for a good many years. They were proud of
their House, for, as the Company always said (after proving to
Harry and Freda that their House was in perfect working order),
"Our Houses last, not a lifetime, but forever."

The House was attractive and semi-spherical and stood on a
little hill some three or four miles from the highway. On fine
days, Freda could walk out on to the hill and watch the cars
shooting past, but she usually preferred to watch the artificial
scene (of the same thing) as the House showed it to her in the
artificial window. One artificial scene she liked especially—that
of a little girl in a red dress who ran out on to the highway to
pick up her toy sand-pail. Freda often wished that the little girl
would raise her head and look into the living room, a small
adjustment for the House to perform on its artificial scene, but
of course no one would think of altering any part of a House.
The House was perfect. It gave them Air (for all the windows
were sealed), it gave them power, and it would let you choose

any delicious dish you wanted and then send its electric voice call-ing and calling to the nearest city to bring it to you. Or if you wanted Food to cook yourself, it would make that for you too, from the rock under its own foundation. For there, sunk miles into the earth, was the source of power for the House, a fierce hot dan-gerous heart that no one must ever come near. It ran everything and chewed up rock to make Air and Food, and powered Harry's Car, which was attached to the House down below the level of the ground in a little extension built out from the side of the House. Harry and Freda were not rich people and they had not gotten a Car, a Real Car, until their children had grown up and moved away; you were not wholly comfortable and protected until you had a real Car. With a Self-Powered Car, one actually had to walk in the open air from the Car to the house and then of course one didn't put on one's muffler or one's gloves (for such a *little* walk) and so one got a very bad cold. For Harry and Freda lived in what had been Canada and the winters were very severe. But now they had a Car; Harry could go right from it to the House through the tunnel the House had for that very purpose.

It was the night after Harry's retirement party that something first went wrong. They had all been talking about something scien-tific that Freda did not understand, with Wilberforce from Harry's job insisting that life meant risk and Harry insisting no, and then Harry saying that the life-lengthening properties of Houses were due to the fact that they never changed.

"Why," he was saying, "change a person's life and right away *they* have to change. They have to make decisions. They have to age. Thing to do is *not* change, not a particle, not a molecule." And Wilberforce (whom Freda had always thought far too rugged) had gotten angry and shouted that Monotony is Death and Harry had shouted Monotony is Life, so the end of it was they got very angry and Wilberforce said he hoped Harry would have a real dose of Monotony soon to make him see how fast *he'd* age. The guests had been getting into their cars at the extra Car Port in the basement, when Freda noticed what was wrong and came over to her hus-band, down the basement stairs.

"Harold," she said, "there's something wrong with the House." But Harold was busy telling Wilberforce that Change was Death and the highest human wisdom was to find the perfect moment and live it over and over.

"Harold," said she, but then the guests were gone. They went into the living room and there as Freda pointed out—there on the Panel set into the wall, there on the Panel that controlled everything in the House, there was a red light shining steadily like a ruby eye.

"Something is really wrong," said Freda. Harry fetched the House Manual and held it up near the eye, but the eye did not go out. He opened the manual and riffled through it.

"Transport III," he said. "Not serious." (Freda said "oh!" with relief.) "Not serious. As any red light on your Panel indicates, there is a small leak in your Fuel line. *Do not start or use your Car.* This is very important. A small leak can be magnified by use of that section of your House until it becomes a large leak, indicated by a green light. Large leaks are highly serious."

Freda and Harry looked at each other. Everyone knew what that meant. Once—and once only—had a family's large leak become serious, but everyone would remember that for the rest of their days. Harry looked grave.

"Freda," he said, "I'm going to disconnect the Car. And you must call the Company."

But when, in an overcoat and muffler, he had shut the car door and pushed the proper buttons. Freda was more upset than before.

"They won't come," she said. "No. Harry, they won't come; they said they have too much business—and not enough help—and besides it's the middle of winter and repairs like that can't be made until springtime. There was a perfectly impertinent young girl on the phone and she said didn't we think we could live without our Car for a while and besides it was after hours, call back tomorrow."

"Now dear," said Harry, "it's not serious."

"But Harry—"

"Look on it as a vacation, dear. It's not at all serious so long as we don't use the Car. These things take time, and now that I've retired, we can treat it as part of our vacation. Anyway" (and he looked smug) "I'm almost glad this happened; I'd love to show old Wilberforce how young you can stay if you don't go ragging your mind to pieces and changing things all over the place! We'll treat every day just like every other day and you'll see how fast time will fly."

So Harry and Freda had a vacation. They watched television, they had the House bring them all the new publications through its mail tubes, and for the first time Freda made the House give her Real Food, Food she could cook herself, instead of ordering meals from a faraway place. The House made the Real Food itself, chewing up the rocks on which it stood and changing them into whatever you asked it to. It was a very happy day. Freda called up a few friends and said that Harry and she were having a vacation and not to call them for that winter because . . . well . . . well, it was a kind of experiment.

The next morning another red eye had appeared on the Panel.

"Oh, look!" said Freda, annoyed, for she had gotten used to the idea of a small leak and it no longer worried her. "Look, what is it this time?" and while Harry went through the Manual she thought of the scathing things she would say to that young woman at the Company and the stern way she would look into the screen when she called her up.

"It's the phone," Harry said. For a moment he looked troubled. But then he closed the Manual with a snap.

"So much the better for Wilberforce," he said.

"But don't you think I ought to write somebody?" she said. After all, their situation was somewhat isolated and she had just told her friends not to call and—

"No, don't be silly," he said. "We're in a civilized community."

"But don't you think I'd better write them now?" she said.

"Of course not."

"But Harry, suppose the Air goes, or the Heat—"

"Then I'll put on my coat and walk a mile down the road to Wilberforce."

"But Harry, I think I'd better—"

"Oh, write then!" peevishly.

She turned into the kitchen, to dictate to the Mailing Extension, but as she did so, another red light appeared on the Panel. Harry looked through the Manual.

"It's the Mailing Extension," he said. "Now Freda—" but she just stared at him.

"Oh yes," she said, after a moment, "another of those little lights and it's nothing; but Harry, Harry, I'm worried. Put on your coat and go down the road."

"But it's a mile away," he said (reluctantly, for it was very cold out).

"But darling, suppose the Air is what goes next."

"Darling, if the Air goes, then we'll do what it says in the Manual."

"It says call them up and we don't dare."

"No, it says to open the front door and let some Natural Air in."

"I hate Natural Air."

"But Freda—"

"And besides, it's cold out and we'll get cold."

He got up wearily, ready to go ("Where's my muffler?" he said) but then he suddenly looked determined and sat down again.

"Now dear," he said, "look at it this way. It's not serious."

"Well—"

"It's not serious until there's a green light, which means a Large Leak. And you know them . . . the family who . . . well, *they* lived with a green light for six whole months until— And they simply didn't bother to look it up in their Manual. If anything goes wrong, I'll run down the road to Wilberforce's." He looked gravely at his wife. "Freda, don't you trust our House?"

"I think so," she said.

Nothing changed the next day, but there were no more lights on, either. Newspapers arrived. Movies were on call. Freda began to do a book of crossword puzzles. She cooked Real Food in the kitchen, happily glad of the leisure given to her by the House. In the evening she moved from the warm, sunny noon of the kitchen (perfectly imitating real sunlight) to the mellow afternoon of the living room and finally to the soft early evening of the bedroom. The days fell into a pattern—newspapers, books, magazines, movies. Breakfast, then lunch, then dinner in the twilight of the dining room: always twilight, with the artificial windows just darkening into the first clear blue of evening. As Harry wisely pointed out, the House was obviously a good House, since the first trouble (in fifteen generations, too) had occurred in inessentials, in the communications, which had really been added on after the house was built, the extra limb of the House, so to speak. And, he said, if there were any real trouble like Air or Heat, then of course he would put on his coat and go immediately to the neighbors down the road. Then the Company would rush over, but if the trouble were only incidental, naturally they had a good deal to handle. And fixing Fuel lines was a tricky job; they would naturally want to wait until spring. But of course what Freda had told the young lady at the Company was undoubtedly on file there. Houses, said he fervently, Houses were the greatest thing the genius of man had ever perfected.

It was only a few weeks later (or was it months?) that a fourth eye joined the third—magazines and newspapers stopped coming and they could not use the movies. But as Harry pointed out, the House seemed to be wisely spending its restorative powers (for Houses do repair themselves, to a degree) in keeping its main function well and fit. Freda could not call for ready-fixed meals, but then did she want to? No. No, no, he would say (shaking his head) they could watch filmed movies instead of broadcast ones, they could eat Real Food for a while; it would not hurt them.

In the morning Freda would get up at exactly 8:30 by the electric clock and make a breakfast consisting of scrambled eggs and real bacon. At 9:30 she would wake up Harry and the two of them would eat breakfast. While the House cleaned the dishes and made the beds, they would do the morning's crossword puzzle (one apiece) and then read a book until lunch time. At lunch they always had the same menu and at dinner, too (after finishing their books). And then after dinner they would watch a filmed motion picture program. And then, at twelve o'clock precisely, they would go to bed. Then the next morning, Freda would get up at exactly 8:30 and the morning after that she would get up at exactly 8:30 and then the next morning . . . .

Of course, after a while they had seen all the films and read all the books and it got a little boring. There was nothing to be done but read them and see them over, forgetting when she had read a book before. Every morning after she finished the crossword puzzle, she would erase it; luckily the puzzle was made of synthetic paper and never wore away.

"I really wish," she would say, "that it would be spring soon." (Unfortunately one day Harry had been trying to do something to the electric calendar, and now when you looked at it it always said "March 17.") "I wish," she said, "that it would get warm," though it was warm enough inside the House, very comfortable and warm. Every morning after she finished the crossword puzzle she erased it and then the next morning she got up to 8:30 precisely and, after breakfast, did it again and erased it again. The days went on; surely it had not been so long since the first ruby appeared on the Panel; and only two strange things interrupted the pleasure of the vacation.

They had made all the windows opaque and projected artificial moving scenes upon them, so they did not notice the young man until he shouted through the speaking tube by the front door to let him in and with him came a great gust of snow and the coldest, bitterest air Freda had ever felt. When they asked him if his Car had broken down, he laughed in an idiotic, slack-jawed, foolish way and then when he tried to speak to them, they found they could not understand him.

"Did your Car break down?" said Harry, very slowly and carefully, but the stranger only looked bewildered. Finally (whispering to Freda, "I think he must be deaf and dumb"—or maybe he had a cleft palate—) Harry wrote out on a piece of paper, "Did your Car break down?" and to their surprise the stranger wrote "Yes, yes" underneath. "He has a cleft palate," whispered Harry.

The stranger drank their Real Food milk, smacking his lips and then ate their doughnuts. When Harry wrote, "Do you have to get to the city?" he wrote below it a great scribble of words, of which every second one seemed to be some kind of slang.

Freda was getting to be afraid of him. Harry wrote on the paper. "I'm afraid it's time to go," and the stranger howled with laughter, hysterically gasping and choking over his milk. But he got up and wrote "Thanx" and then below it something that didn't make sense—"blank blank old-fashioned"—only his spelling all along had been much stranger than that, and Harry had to puzzle out every word.

"Old-fashioned?" said Freda, coldly.

"Old-fashioned?" said Harry. "Look here, young man, if we don't know about the newest things, that's only because our House hasn't been working for a couple of months. Believe me, young man, when the Company gets here in the spring—"

This time the young man wrote down "archaeological survival"—or at least that's what it seemed—and when Harry angrily tore up the whole paper, the young man gathered his blanket around him and got up. He was wearing something very like a blanket; they supposed he had put it over his clothes to keep warm in the Car. He began to bow, one time after another, till Harry was sorry for tearing up the paper and wrote:

"Won't you come and see us in the spring?" at which the young man turned quite white and dashed out the door. Freda sighed in relief when he had gone.

"I really think he was mad, Harry, don't you?" she said. Her husband nodded.

"I don't think he had a thing on except that blanket," he exclaimed. "And did you see his spelling? They don't teach children the way they used to when I was young." He thought for a moment. "Freda, let's make the windows opaque all the time and let's lock the door at night."

Which they did. And for a while, nothing out of the ordinary happened. But then one night—

One night Freda had a bad dream. They had gotten up at the usual time, made breakfast, done the crossword puzzles, read books, and in short gone through the day as usual and were lying in bed asleep, when Freda began to dream. She dreamed she saw a tall man striding through the great, snowy forest near the House. He was not like any man she had ever seen, for he was dressed entirely in furs from head to foot, a great tall man with his face almost covered with furs. At his waist he was carrying an electric light that swung back and forth as he walked and lit up first the snow and then the bare trees, the rocks, the snow-laden pine trees among which he walked. The snow was very deep, she dreamed, and packed; he was not walking through it but on it because it was so packed, and he was holding some kind of little instrument in his hand. The instrument chattered; first he turned it one way and when it chattered louder, he went that way. If it chattered less, he want back and turned it another way. Then Freda dreamed that the little instrument led him to their front door and he began knocking on the door with his heavy, fur-gloved fist, pounding on the front door and shouting. He tried to batter open the front door but it was sealed for the night, and he could not shout through the Communications tube because the House was too efficient to open the Communications tube to the cold night air. His heavy fists pounded on the door, great bruising blows, trying to wake up the people inside, and Freda dreamed that he was shouting to her, something terrible about time, too much time, not enough time. She woke up.

"Harry," she gasped, "Harry, there's a man outside." He turned over in bed.

"There's a man," she said. "A man pounding on the door. And he's saying something terrible about how we must go away."

"Wha'?" said Harry sleepily.

"There's a man," she repeated, "outside, all in fur, a huge big man who wants us to open the door."

"You're dreaming," her husband said, and certainly it seemed like it when she looked around the bedroom. The pink-shaded lamp cast its light up to the ceiling, the cozy, familiar furniture stood in its usual places. The room was warm and quiet (absolutely soundproof, in fact) and covered with a thick, luxurious rug (which renewed its own nap). Certainly there could be no man outside, and yet Freda almost thought she still heard the faraway vibration of blows. . . .

"Harry," she said, her voice shaking, "he was saying something terrible, something about it was too late and we must all go away."

"Where?"

"I don't know, somewhere, but it was too late. He was looking for people that had to go away with the rest of them."

"Who?"

"I don't know. But he was. Harry, what day is it?"

"Lord, Freda, the end of March sometime. I don't know. But—"

"But it was all snow out."

Silently Harry got up and stood on the deep rug. His slippers slid obediently across the floor and squeezed under his feet. Wearily he plodded out toward the living room and the front door with his wife behind him. Everything was absolutely quiet.

"If it's March, there shouldn't be so much snow," said Freda. Carefully Harry turned on the front lights, flooding the area in front of the door. The snow was only a few inches deep.

"See," said Harry.

"But," said his wife, "we're on a hill and the wind would blow it all away. Down there it was much deeper."

"How do you know?"

"In my *dream.*" Her husband looked amused.

"Freda," he said, "you're getting upset. These few weeks have been too much for you." He switched the light off. "Now suppose there are footprints out there; I think I saw some, as a matter of fact, being covered by drifting snow, but what would that prove? That another young man's Car had broken down, that's all. Like the one last week."

"Oh no, it was a month, dear."

"Not that long."

"Oh yes, a month."

But of course there was no way to prove which it was, since the calendar had broken down, but it must (thought Harry) have been only a week ago, since it was so obviously winter out. A very odd winter, he thought (they were going back to the bedroom now) for it seemed to be colder than any he remembered. A vague thought moved in his mind; in the moment he had the front-door lights on, he had happened to glance at the thermometer near the door and it seemed to have burst at the bottom.

Very strange; it was supposed to go down to eighty below, though of course they had never had weather like that. He climbed into bed beside his wife, dismissing the thought. The stuff they made nowadays was shoddy. Not like his House.

"Good night, dear," he said. "We must be missing the newspapers on the biggest cold spell in history."

"Yes, Harry," she said.

"You need a good night's sleep."

"Yes, Harry."

And they settled down once again to wait for spring.

Freda finished the crossword puzzle and put it down on the kitchen table, as she did with a new crossword puzzle every morning, now that their Communications were out of order. The thought occurred to her that there would be no new one the next day and she had better erase this one, so she did. But of course—wait—this was yesterday's. Or was it from the day before? No, yesterday's; she was quite sure of it. Behind her the Real Food chute was humming preparatory to delivering her Real Food after-breakfast coffee, as it did every morning. *That* was still working, at least; it would be a shame to send Harry out in the cold to a neighbor's because their House had broken down. But of course a few days' deprivation of Communication wouldn't hurt anyone.

Yawning, Freda went into the living room and sat down with her crossword puzzle by her favorite window, the one that overlooked the highway. She began to do the puzzle and then suddenly realized she had already done it. But had she? It was perfectly blank. No, no, she thought, don't be silly; of course you did it. You always do it in the kitchen and here you are in the living room. Harry was still asleep, of course, but then he had been working only a few days before, so naturally he enjoyed the vacation more than she did.

She watched the Cars shooting past on the highway. Some day she really must put on an artificial scene. But was this an artificial scene or not? She couldn't decide. Suddenly she noticed that the trees outside the window were in leaf, full green leaf, oh how lovely! She jumped up to tell Harry (the puzzle falling from her lap), but then a fancy took her that this was only an artificial scene after all.

I must, she thought, go outside, but there was some reason she could not go out. It was too cold. But how could it be too cold if the leaves were out? And there, by the side of the highway, a little girl in a red dress ran out to retrieve her sand-pail and then turned and ran back among the trees. They must be having a picnic, the first of the summer. No, no, wait—something moved uneasily in Freda's mind. She had seen the little girl before. The morning before, the little girl had run out in just that way. And the morning before that? Yes, the morning before and the morning before.

"Harry," called Freda uncertainly, "how long—" but that was ridiculous, she thought. It could only be a few weeks. No one had come to see them.

(Ah yes, said her thoughts, but you told them not to call, and then you disconnected your mail and your phone.)

No one had come from the Company.

(You never called them back.)

There was no dust, no scratches, no wear of any kind.

(The House cleans and renews itself every day.)

How long had it been? she thought: a month, several months, a year? Could it have been a whole year? Or ten? Or twenty?

"We haven't gotten a day older!" she exclaimed in fright.

(But, said her thoughts, every day was like every other day. Maybe if you do the same things every day, and say the same things and eat the same things, always at the same time—)

"Harry!" called Freda, but not loud enough for him to hear in the bedroom. Oh, it's silly! she thought; so to make herself feel better she went back to looking out the window. The Cars were still streaming past. A little girl in a red dress ran out to retrieve her sand-pail and—

"Oh really, it's stuck!" said Freda, for the scene had suddenly stopped, frozen in place like a photograph. Oh dear, oh dear, she thought, frightened, so it is an artificial scene after all.

The novelty of something actually changing in the House oppressed her so that she could hardly breathe. She would have to put on another scene, just when she had gotten used to that one, and then Harry would be angry and say that every change in their routine would make them grow older. Freda pulled the switch that cleared the window and made it transparent. As she did so the leaves on the trees, the trees, the Cars, the road, all wavered, blurred, began to melt and slide like water. Freda sat in her chair inside the warmth and comfort of the House, impatiently, somewhat nervously waiting for the window to clear and the outside view to show through. The window cleared. Freda began to tremble.

She found herself looking at a wall of snow. Perpendicular, straight as steel, it towered above the house and way above it, way past the very top of the window, were stars in a nighttime sky. The sky was so very black and the stars so very bright that they lanced through Freda's eyes and made her lower her gaze to the wall of snow again.

Even without the light from the House she could have seen the snow, for the light of the stars seemed as intense as moonlight, and it spilled down the sides of the wall of snow. The wall was some twenty feet from the side of the House; it stood impenetrable, terrifyingly solid, but there at the edge of the wall where the heat from the House had cleared a space around it, a very strange thing was happening. The snow melted but it did not melt; it exhaled, it breathed white vapor, it boiled, it whirled and writhed upward in a hundred fantastic shapes, hurrying swiftly into the black night sky above. On the top of the wall (barely seen from the House) were shining, sparkling pools of liquid, pools that moved sluggishly this way and that.

Behind Freda the House spread its usual rosy warmth, noon in the kitchen, afternoon in the living room, twilight in the dining room, but here spring, summer, fall and even winter had died. For this immortal cold was a sun away from winter.

It *was* deeper in the valleys, thought Freda idiotically, and when all the air on earth froze, most of it must have drifted down there and my dream was right. But no, no, it could not have been air in my dream, for there was a man walking on it; that must have been a long long time ago. How long, a hundred years? A thousand? A million? No, no, she thought, longer than that, much more than that but . . . but could it be? The House had begun to break down only yesterday. I'm sure, she thought, that it was only yesterday.

Harry came out of the bedroom, yawning as he always did at the time he always came out every morning, and as he looked and saw, Freda turned. The Panel near the window glowed with its five ruby eyes. Five? No, six. Twelve. Twenty. Then more and more until the whole panel glowed red as a cluster of cherries. In case of failure of Air, she thought, throw open the front door and admit Natural Air into the House. "Oh Harry, what shall we do?" she said, but there was no particular need to answer; the cherries dimmed, darkened, and then became green, green as beech leaves, green as the young green on hedges.

Freda had time only to say, "Oh, Harry!" and he, "Freda, what—" when the House gave a little tentative shake and then another and then shivered into a hundred—no a million—no many, many more atoms, atoms that threw the airy snow up in a great billowing rise. The crisp noon kitchen, the mellow, living room, the Real Food chute, the self-renewable rug, the sealed windows—all in a tremendous whoosh into the air. But not into the air, rather into the space above the air, and then it settled down on the frozen air, on to the sluggishly living pools of liquid hydrogen, bounced a little, billowed a little, and finally lay quietly, invisibly, over a radius of some hundred miles.

The House almost *had* lasted forever . . . as such things go.

THE EXPERIMENTER

Well, Gentlemen! Another two seconds and I would have been dead, lying with a knife in my throat on the deck of one of the ugliest yachts ever built—killed by my own friends, gentlemen!

What? Put this thing on my head so I can understand as well as be understood? (For I take it that's what your gestures mean.) What a pity. So instantaneous. We could have taken six months; you draw little diagrams, you teach me the words for past, future, present, I fall to my knees calling you gods—Sorry.

I'll stop joking.

Three months ago—no, of course I can't tell you what year it was unless I can put our two calendars together; what does a number like twenty-two something-something mean to me?—anyway, the whole thing started three months ago when the barbarian and the boy and I were riding off the Southern coast of—never mind; names change so, even locally. It was night-time. Our barbarian, with his uncivilized addiction to cleanliness, was taking a bath in the sea, and the boy was scraping the dinner pots. I was leaning over the rail, watching our wake, that true Southern phosphorescence you never see anywhere else, that luminosity that seems at any moment about to condense into the bodies of the drowned, the souls of the dead, floating up and drifting just under the surface of the water, whispering perhaps, smiling, gliding. . . .

Then the boy gave a yell and I nearly pitched over the side. The three of us stared. Then the clouds must have parted or some low mist blown aside. There it was.

"A town," said our barbarian, Sam.

What's funny? The machine does the translating, not me, doesn't it? I told you we saw a town and I told you Sam said so; and after months at sea you are supposed to go wild; you think of *restaurants*, you think of *women*, you think of *money*, though not necessarily in that order.

All except me.

Now I want to explain this right now; in what I did I was never for a moment actuated by personal malice. I'm a sociable man; I like people and I like to see them enjoy themselves. But once in a while . . . never mind, perhaps I've sold my soul to the devil or he sold his to me! Anyway, Sam was the first to speak, all *pronunciamento* and seven feet tall.

"Everyone," he said, "must take a bath except me, because I have already had one."

"Oh gods, I have to shave," said the boy.

"Not with my knife," I said. I've never met anyone so mad for growing up. I had stowed our good clothes somewhere months before and was looking for them behind some of our coiled rope and other gear when I collided with my tall friend. I have always called them my friends, gentlemen, but the truth is I have never understood them. Never at all. I put my hand on his shoulder to stop him and said, "Look here, what do you want? What do you really want?" He looked back at me in the half-dark, above the lantern we keep in the bow, and his face looked like a statue carved out of stone but that was only a trick of the light because these Northerners' eyes are blue and you can look right through blue eyes into the sky behind, like looking through the eye-holes of a skull.

"To be rich," he said. I've never understood that. The boy will end up going home, of course, because this is only a vacation for him—but I—

"Look," I called after Sam, "I'll get it for you. A fortune. For both of you."

We landed at night. A nice clean little harbor with native craft, mostly; you couldn't have told, give or take fifty miles, where you were. You've never landed on the commercial waterfront of a small city at night, have you?—indeed, with a room full of such extremely interesting equipment, why should you?—no, of course not. Well, you can have no conception of such a place unless you've been there. It is exactly the same wherever you are. It is sinister and it is homely. The shadows are deep, the streets narrow, here and there a light above an inn or coming out of an open doorway, and higher up you get the poor quarter, and higher up still the commercial quarter, and if you know towns the way I do (they all fit the land they're on as animals fit the lives they lead) you can work your way to the center in little over an hour. Likewise the politics. I stopped a native.

"Where is Main Street?"

"What?" he said.

"Great Street," I said, "Large Street, Wide Street, Market Street, Big Street, Important Street—" Thus you run down the list. We found it (Long-and-Large Street), then found we had to register at a government shed, which contained some truly horrendous warnings against coining. When I told them my plan Sam and the boy didn't oppose me—nobody ever does, somehow, when the fit is on me—so we stripped the ship and sold everything, including the compass, to buy clothes. We had to put on a good show as gentlemen. I told the other two I was going to get arrested and to stick with me; so the next morning, brilliantly dressed, I went up to a flower-seller's booth on Second-Biggest Street, took out our last gold piece, and bought a bouquet. Something called Tyrrhenian Violet Mix, as I remember.

"My dear elevatedness," crooned the florist, "allow me the nearly unbearable pleasure of giving you your change." The gold was making him tremble with greed.

"No, no," said I, assuming an unidentifiable foreign accent.

"But yes," he said. "But please. Allow me. Make me happy!" He doubled up over the counter like a snail.

"Oh well," said I; "if you insist, give me one small coin for this darling child who assists you in tying up the flowers and I will place it in his hand myself."

He gave me my change. I looked at it casually; I stared at it hard; I turned pale; I bit it; I cried:

"Counterfeit!"

One doesn't wish to be arrested for criminal misbehavior, you see; that doesn't get you anywhere. This was a very strictly governed little town. I will mention only in passing the heads stuck on pikes along the battlements of the Governor's palace on High-and-Handsome Street, the lists of taxes, and the license hanging in the inn where we had spent the night. As a common brawler, I would have been in a mess; but here I was the complainant. We were flanked by the local gendarmerie in what must have been record time (thirty seconds), in ten minutes we were in front of a judge, and in fifteen minutes the coin was pronounced genuine. I had rather hoped it wouldn't be.

"Fraud!" I cried.

"Arrest him!" said the judge, waking up for the first time during the entire proceedings.

"For what?" said I. "I have said nothing."

"Quiet!" shouted the judge, really angry this time.

"Only," I continued imperturbably, "fraud, which in my beautiful, rich, and very far away country signifies distress and extreme pain of mind. I have an imperfect understanding of your magnificent language. Would a wealthy man like myself"—here the courtroom grew very quiet all of a sudden—"would wealthy men like the three of us, I repeat, millionaires with commercial connections all over the known world and in some other places too, be concerned with anything but the principle of law involved in the forging of a small coin? Of course not."

"Alas," I continued, "that I cannot now import into your oh-so-desirable country the gold with which I had hoped to start three or four of my world-wide, extremely money-making enterprises. But principle must prevail. Honesty—"

"You're under arrest," said the judge. "And I'll examine you in private. Keep those other two in custody."

"Ah," I said. "Good."

Look here, gentlemen, don't you talk to me about luck. I always know what I'm doing. Once I'd read the notices in that damned registry office!—there were such heavy penalties for bribery, you see. Do laws punish what nobody ever does? His Wisdom got us into an ornate little stone room at the back of the court, fitted up with carpets (and gilding), locked us in, took out a bottle of something—

"Thanks, no," I said, dropping my accent. "I prefer to talk business." He dropped the bottle. Luckily there was a carpet on the floor, too. He stared at me, but I said nothing. I had my back to the window, which is always nice. He was a silly man; the first thing he did was get up and make for the door.

"Please, please," I said, "I am defenseless. Besides, your admirable door locks with a key, not a bolt or latch, and I managed to abstract the key whilst you were busy with the bottle; I would advise—"

"Murderer!" he said. He had turned pale and was attempting to ring a bell set under the table without my seeing him do it.

"Don't," I said. "Besides, you are quite safe. I'm a reasonable man. I really do like to make money." I smiled. "And I like to see other people make money."

"But you have money already."

"Not a penny," I replied. He went for the door again.

"Please," I said. "Please, my dear fellow, do be calm. Do you think I want to hurt or rob you? If I do either, I shall undoubtedly be sawed in half, or whatever nasty method of execution it is you use in this part of the world."

"Then—" he began unhappily.

"Why go through such an elaborate farce? That's of course what you were about to say, since you are such an intelligent man.

The answer is that for political purposes—which I shall go into presently—I needed to get in touch immediately with someone of great importance. Someone of great intelligence." I spread my hands. "Yourself."

"Polit—" he said.

I leaned forward, speaking in a very low voice.

"I must know," I said. "Are you for the Governor or—"

"Guards!" he screamed. He had backed away from me as far as he could go, bending himself uncomfortably into the doorknob. He turned and rattled it piteously. "Guards!"

"Do," I said, springing to my feet and altering my whole manner. "Do. Protest your loyalty. Swear. Will they believe you?"

He sweated, poised on one foot like a top.

"How do you know who sent me?" I went on grimly. "Eh? How do you know what *they* want, what *they'd* like? How do you know what they've *found out?*"

"Guards," he squeaked. I shrugged elaborately. I threw myself back into my chair. I began to play with the pair of gentleman's gloves I had bought that morning, magnificent things, really, openwork of leather and gold; they seem to make them very well in that region.

"You don't have to make the decision yourself," I said.

"No?" he said.

"No," I said, looking very grave and compassionate. "No indeed. Mind you, I'm only telling you this because of my regard for you. I hate to see people be—but never mind. Don't you think the best thing to do would be send me to—ah—someone higher up? I won't say a word if you do."

He had been standing on one foot all this time, I swear it; now he descended to two, so relieved to be bipedal again. He sighed and wiped his head. He smiled pitifully. He held out one hand—heartfelt—then snatched it back again in evident fear that I would garotte him.

"Never mind," I said. "Not all of us are cut out for the—ah—real complexities of—well, you know what I mean."

"Yes," he said, collapsing into his chair. "Oh yes. I do. Yes, yes, I do."

So that's done.

Was I at my ease? To tell you the truth, no. But I could deal with him. He was a lean, dry, cleanshaven old man in a voluminous crimson tent. He leaned on two sticks. He made me sit down and then he staggered up to me so that his parchment face leaned over mine, trembling as he said:

"How old are you?"

"Twenty-two," said I.

"Ha—hmmmmm." He cleared his throat, and then spat, and then looked absently out of the window of his reception room. You saw the marble arches and the whitewashed walls, and trees and hedges outside, very pretty if you didn't notice the soldiers. He gathered the stuff of his robe between two fingers and flashed an enormous ruby on one of them. Vanity. Of some kind.

"Did you think," said he, "that your mummery would succeed?"

I said I thought it would get me to someone like him, but not so high up.

"Have you done anything like this before?" said he, turning sharply round.

"Twice," I said. "But not exactly like this." It's true, too; I have never found it necessary to lie to anyone. People are amazingly prolific at jumping to conclusions. Walk up to any official in a provincial town and say, "They know." Then run.

"Have you any money?" the old man said to me. This obviously didn't interest him.

"None," said I.

"Ha—hmmmmm." He was looking out the window again. "And what do you want? Every man wants something." I stayed silent. He got up and hobbled over to me. "Tell me," he said. I shrugged.

"Tell me or I'll have you—"

"But I don't know!" I said. He limped back and lowered himself into his chair with an extended grimace.

"Nothing," said he, "can ease the pains of old age, young man. Remember that. My people thought you were an assassin. Obvious nonsense, of course. You're mad."

"I've been told so," said I. His eyes glittered.

"You must be," he said. "You don't have money and you don't want it. I'll tell you something, my mad friend: I'm crazy too. We're the only two people in this town who see things as they are. Power is better than money. Now: out with it."

I told him. He laughed until he cried. Then he said:

"How did you know I was in the Duke's faction?"

"I didn't," I said.

"But if I hadn't been—?"

"Oh," I said, "the plan! The plan can be sold to anyone. It can even be turned inside out and used by the Governor; *that* doesn't matter. It doesn't matter what side you're on."

He laughed again, started coughing, stopped, laughed, and then abruptly looked grim. He clapped his hands. Three crafty kids sprang from the thin air.

"This young man," he said sternly, "is my particular guest. Find him and his friends a place to stay. Watch him—but not his friends; I don't think we need go that far yet—at all times." He gave an enormous yawn. "By the way," he added suddenly (darting up to me with wonderful, unsteady quickness) "how did you know there was a—hm—faction?" He thrust his wrinkled face up to mine. I had the sudden feeling that one of those fresh-faced lads might be ready with a blade in my back. So I told the truth, as I always do.

"There always is," I said. "Everywhere."

I could say there were times when I felt tempted to take his money and run, but I would be lying. I wouldn't have gone for the world. Besides, the money was Sam's, not mine; whatever I got, I sent to him. My very important lord had settled me in the city and I was buying up grain—with his gold, of course—and dumping it off the coast, secretly, at night.

Do you know what happens when you make something artificially scarce?

That's right, the price goes up. It's like having a bad season. When the price of grain goes up, the price of bread follows; bread is three-quarters of the diet of the poor and when they can't afford it—

Five weeks after my real arrival I arrived again, but this time as a different stranger with a bag of gold a yard long (my lord's gold, of course) under on arm and under the other, elaborate plans for a company that would manufacture fertilizer from sea-sand. The Minister of Finance all but wept in my lap.

Not that he really thought fertilizer could be made from sea-sand, you understand (though I think he had a few dim gleams of hope on the subject), but any fool with money was a godsend at this time, with the poorer classes so restless. I ordered lumber, building stone, and workmen, and I paid six times as much as anyone else. The price of wheat (their staple commodity, you understand) rose. I raised wages. The price of bread went up even faster. I raised wages again. A starving mob broke into our factory, there were riots in the harbor streets, someone set fire to part of a slum, and the Minister of Finance (standing on the smoking ruins), dedicated the site to a new temple of the Sun-God, swearing that would solve everything. Prices rose. Nobody could understand why—when there was so much money to be had—they couldn't buy anything. Prices rose.

I thought the Minister of Finance would get bold (and ruin everything) by confiscating the merchants' stores for rationing, but trust our boy! he had no desire to be torn limb from limb by enraged grain dealers. To be absolutely fair I ought to add that the wheat my lord and I had dumped in the sea continued to have a confusing and tenuous life of its own; that is to say, the dummy merchants we had set up reported they were still doing business, so that according to the records, there should have been enough to eat. I think I am the only person in the world who knows that gold does not exist—oh, I don't mean literally, of course, but what good is a yellow, soft metal that you can't eat or burn or make into tools? None at all. It's as if people had all made some crazy agreement to honor it—why not cowrie shells, or cows, or trees, or pieces of rock?

If only everybody agreed and kept the amount of stuff the same, it wouldn't matter what you used. Break that agreement and overnight there would be no town, no possessions, no government, no ownership, no anything. Do you see? Well, no one else ever has. In your own words, here these poor idiots were believing that the "medium of exchange" meant something in itself and by itself, and there *I* was, arranging that there should be more and more medium and less and less to exchange. Prices rose. Rumors began to circulate that the Sun God was angry with the citizens, that gold—which everybody knows is His condensed breath—was losing its power, that soon nights of a week long would descend on the city and every third citizen would be eaten by locusts. Prices rose.

"Never," said the Finance Minister in formal proclamation from a balcony of the palace, while a band played music below him, "does Our Governor hear the complaints of His hungry poor unmoved. His father is the Sun-God, Ya; His mother is the silvery Moon-Goddess, Yup; how can Their power have been abated? Fear not; you will all be wealthy by and by; our Governor will not stand by inactive at such an hour," etc. etc.

Then that crazy man raised the salaries of all government employees and distributed a tax rebate to every householder. Prices rose.

Let me make it clear before I utter another word that *there was enough to eat.* They could have gotten through the winter quite well on a strict system of rationing. But who ever did anything unpopular if he could help it? My lord, although by now excessively poor, was overjoyed.

"Am I of use to you or am I not?" I said.

"Indeed you have been," he answered. It hit me some three seconds later, that *have been*.

* * *

I saw it begin with my own eyes. My lord, with the last of his wealth, had been coining money himself—base, obvious, leaden counterfeits—and when the Finance Minister ordered his last grand, general Bonus (and simultaneously announced his retirement) my lord substituted his false coinage for the Minister's true one.

That did it; I tell you, that did it; you have never seen such a thing as it was.

I was in the street with my lord when it happened, near one of the barrier tables the militia had set up to distribute the coins. A liquor-house keeper tried to palm off one of them at an old lady's food stand; she screamed "Police! Police!" just as several others discovered the same thing; and then the whole crowd must have grasped the same fact at exactly the same time, for there was a roar such as I have never heard before in my life, a roar from a thousand throats at once in that one frozen moment before the crowd became a mob and the mob an avalanche.

My lord grasped my elbow and whispered in my ear, "Get out of town," and as I obediently slipped into a side-street, I heard behind me that oceanic tidal wave of sound and the crash of the first tables going down.

Sam and the boy, thanks be, had put out to sea that afternoon; we'd arranged to meet just out of sight of the bay, north of the harbor. But I had to stay; I had to see it. I tell you, my heart was beating like mad. It was senseless; there was no reason for me to stay but I couldn't leave. It fascinated me. Fighting must have started on the main avenues for I caught glimpses of arrows and men running past the little streets with scythes, butcher knives, poles, anything they could pick up. I tell you, I couldn't stop. They were breaking into stores; it was glorious and horrible, women rushing by pushing baby-wagons piled with fruit or clothes. My lord had apparently hired orators, or perhaps they'd sprung out of the ground; some were touting the Duke as pretender; others were abusing everyone and everything. It was a ghastly mish-mash about the sun going out and the Governor cheating everybody; it would've taken a genius to keep it all straight. I threw away the gold chain my lord had given me and wrapped myself in a dirty cloak I found in the street; it was almost night and torches were being lit at every corner, not that they needed them with the light from the bonfires and the burning houses. I had stopped to listen to one of the agitators and join in the singing, but I slipped past them. Someone ran through, shouting that people were dying on —— Street; he disappeared. There was another bonfire.

"—and will we stand it? No, we will not stand it!"

Someone said, "Got some tobacco?" close to me and a hand slipped into my pocket; I twisted it good and hard and moved away into a doorway. Someone else, next to me, struck a light. It was one of my lord's fresh-faced little murderers. He was smiling at me.

"Not bad," he said, "not bad at all, but getting a little out of hand, we think." I followed his glance across the street and there, peering ravenously out of a second-story window, was my very important lord. He grasped the window-sill with one hand and raised the other savagely, bringing it down in a short, cutting arc; from the next doorway peeped out another baby face and from the next doorway another. Without thinking (for I go blind in panic) I shinnied up a drainpipe by the doorway and fell on to a roof.

Have you ever run over roofs? Don't. People expect adventurers to be athletic but the only advantage I had was that I was scared to death and—just possibly—the babyfaces got peevish and insisted that while killing people was in their line, climbing roofs wasn't and they weren't paid for it. Not that I stopped to watch, you understand. I jumped gaps in those roofs where I left my stomach behind thirty feet below in the street, and I walked boards you could not have ordinarily persuaded me to try two inches off the ground. Once I was crazy enough to swing from roof to roof on a line of drying wash which didn't even break. All the time I ran I could hear them behind me and I saw them once, when I turned, climbing behind me in a slow, deliberate way, as if they knew where I was going even though I did not. And I didn't; I had no more sense of direction up there than a—

Then I met one of them coming the other way.

I dove into the street—I say dove because I went nearly head-long, caught an awning, snapped it, swung, dropped into the street, ran around the corner, and following nothing but blind instinct, ran into a door—found it locked—swung up on a window-ledge, made the next highest window with a ledge six inches wide, clung there like a sleepwalker, with swimming head and shaking knees, and plummeted into the room inside all in a heap.

There was a girl in the room, braiding her hair.

I remember now—though I wasn't capable of connecting the two things then—that she must have been of the very highest class, for she was dressed in a long-sleeved, brocaded jacket that gleamed in the lamplight; she wore a silk shirt and had little bits of gold hung all over her: ankle bells, rings, earrings, bracelets, pins.

But all I saw then was a glow, a shimmer, and a tinkling of ornaments.

"Madam!" I gasped, "for Heaven's sake!" and she came over quite unhurriedly, to inspect me. She could not have been more than twelve years old. She had—how shall I say—a certain unpleasant expression, as if she were used to ordering people around, including her mama and papa. She looked at me with great interest and then said:

"I do believe someone is chasing you. You must be very wicked."

"Beautiful lady," said I (with what voice I had left) "someone is indeed chasing me, although I assure your ladyship that I am not in the least wicked" (here I heaved a breath) "but only a poor, desperate, unfortunate, and terrified rascal, who throws himself both figuratively and literally at your ladyship's exquisite feet." Try talking that way when you can't breathe.

"You," said this little girl to me, "have charming, black, curly hair and very dreamy eyes, but I do think you entered my room rather ungallantly."

"Madam!" I said, throwing my arms about her knees, "fair one, beautiful lady, lovely one, if they catch me, they will kill me right here on your rug, so for Yup's sake, hide me!"

"That would be awful," she said, "because it would make a

stain"—I am not making this up—and she took me by the hand and pulled me into a little alcove, shoving me behind some clothes. I heard her ankle bells go leisurely from one side of the room to the other and then I heard her yawn and then—marvelous little actress!—she said, "Oh! Who are you?"

Well, they asked her about me and she described a horrible spirit who had looked into the window and then disappeared—"I prayed" she said—and they said Are you really telling the truth and she said How dare you and so on and so on—but a deadly cold faintness was coming over me; I would have given anything, even my life, for a chance to lie down, to lie down flat, and never, never, ever to get up again.

When I came to myself I was lying on the floor of the closet with my head in her lap and she was putting her hot little hands all over my face and neck to wake me up.

"Angel," I said. She smiled complacently.

"Ssssh," she said, "lie still. They'll watch the roof for a while. I heard them say so. Here—" and she brought me pieces of sugar-candy and fed them to me and gave me something insipid to drink out of a little silver bottle. It tasted like the essence of all the oranges that ever weren't, but I needed it.

"I wish," I said quite sincerely, "that I could give you something. You've been so good to me."

"I have everything," she said, patting her hair.

"All the same—" I said, and I searched my pockets but they were as empty as my grave; "all the same, I wish—"

"Kiss my hand," she said, extending it and looking at me in what I can only describe as a very calculating manner. "I'm sure this is dreadfully wrong," she added contemplatively, "but as I'm to be married next week, I suppose it's all right." She smiled and a charming little dimple appeared on each side of her chin. "If you'd really like to show you're grateful," she said, "you may give me a gift, although it'll have to be something I can give back to you at the same time. Mamma watches me like a hawk."

I knew what she meant, so I said "May I—" and she shut her eyes and I—what else?—kissed her. It's in the tradition, gentlemen. But it's not in the tradition that the lady shall fling her arms around you and hold onto you until you can't breathe, while you don't dare get free, for obvious reasons. Finally she let me go; apparently everything was perfectly proper as far as she was concerned.

"Remember me!" she whispered, waving a tiny, embroidered, silk handkerchief as I climbed out the window, dreading the fall to the ground and broken bones. "Remember me!" "Angel!" I cried, "I shall never forget you!" and nearly dislocated my neck falling into the street.

I got myself up in one piece and searching my pockets, found a piece of candy. It hadn't occurred to her to give me money, I suppose. Though money was not much use in this town any more. There was a faint glow in the East and I could hear—very far away—some kind of noise. I walked slowly through the streets. By the time I got to the waterfront it was nearly dawn. I tell you, somehow the joy had gone out of it. I had no feeling at all. I found an old man smoking by the docks and begged some tobacco from him, which I wrapped in a piece of my shirt and put in my pocket.

"Tell me," I said, "did you see a big man come by here earlier tonight? A big, yellow-haired man with a boy?" He spat on the ground.

"I seen the whole town come by here," he said resentfully. "The whole damn lot. Screeching like water buf'loes." I was beginning to feel just how tired I was and my back and legs ached. "Tell me —" I said, but stopped in mid-sentence. What was the use? I sat down on the pier. I was too tired. I was just too tired.

Now I would have to steal a boat.

So I did. I mean I took it, that all. They'd left only a child to guard the government house and I bribed him with my tobacco— none of them would look at money any more!—and besides, what did he care? He expected Utopia to dawn the next morning. The foreign ships were gone—so was ours—and so was everything else except a few planks with sails on them—they call them "butterflies," I believe. I took one of them and I was so tired that if there'd been any kind of weather at all, I would've just rolled off the plank into the sea. I felt queer, too, as if I'd been finished off or been sick; I don't know what it was. I got to our ship by the lights—oh, the blessed sound of black water against wood!—and hauled myself up; I would have fallen if they hadn't helped me.

"Is your scheme finished?" said my barbarian, sounding very grim and deep in the darkness.

"It is," said I, "and so am I, for that matter."

"Not quite," said he, "turn around," and when I did so, I saw that the whole Southern sky—from horizon to zenith—was a brilliant red. The city was on fire.

"Good God—" I said, "they must have—the torches—"

"Now that you have finished," said that barbarian, "can you tell us what you have brought back to us, out of that wreck?"

"I had some tobacco," I said. "No, I gave it away—and my gold chain—there's your money—but that's all—"

"We've spent it," said the boy. My friend squatted down beside me in the glow. The fire lit up the sea as far out as we were, and for the first time in my life I could clearly see the thoughts in those empty, Northern eyes. I have never liked those eyes, friend though he be.

"I have sailed with you since you were fifteen years old," he said, "but I tell you—"

"Why'd you do it?" whispered the boy in wonder.

"I tell you!" shouted Sam, "I tell you *never!* Never before!" He put his face up to mine.

"That town is burning," he said. "Everyone in it will be dead. Twice before I wondered: why does he do these things? But now I think I know."

"Tell me then," I said; "it'll be news to me," and it was at that moment, gentlemen, it was at that very moment that he pushed my face into the boards—I bear the marks of the splinters yet!—that he pushed, I say, my face into the boards and wrenching sideways, I saw that my old companion was about to put a knife in my neck and that our boy approved and stood by silently, his arms folded.

That was, fortunately, the exact moment in which you plucked me out of time (five thousand years into the future, if I'm to believe you) and deposited me in this shining kitchen.

It's not a kitchen? Well, a glorified kitchen, then, a transcendent kitchen!

And they wanted to kill me. Why? Did I *ask* those damned fools to burn their city? Did I ask them to be so stupid? If there'd been anyone there with the slightest sense, I couldn't have gotten one foot into that town! Not that I liked the idea of my little preserver being burnt, or raped by the militia, or having her golden bells torn off her ankles; I'm not inhuman. Still—why should they kill me? It's their own fault for finding no decent work for me! If I have a—a force, a glory, something, call it what you like—inside me that must be satisfied, then let me satisfy it; let me make things happen, let me study things. If I could have studied stars, or clouds, or dirt, I would not have had to study men. If I had a place like this, now—!

Gentlemen, how can I believe you'll send me back? That would be murder. I've never murdered; I've only given people the power to choose one course of action or another. Is it my fault that they always choose wrong?

Well, what about it? Remember, I've been here five days (if you count the first day when I did nothing but sleep)—I'm rested, well-fed, and much stronger than I was. Now I'll wrench myself free (much astounding Sam) and it'll be a hell-for-leather, round-the-mast, tooth-and-nail battle. They'll get me in the end, though, for there are two of them, and only one of me and besides—I blush to confess it, gentlemen, it's most unbefitting an adventurer—I cannot swim.

So you will send me back? You've decided—like my friends—that I'm a devil? Not just a little cleverer than most, a little more clear-sighted than most, eh? A little more inclined to experiment with things? It's your decision. Chin up, stiff upper lip, we who are about to die—I hope your translator is finding the right equivalents. Too bad; I would so love to stay. But perhaps you believe that I'm not just cleverer than the people five thousand years ago, but a little more so than you, eh? Even here. Even now. A little closer to the power and the glory? That would be sad.

Better to send me back. With *that* little button. Oh yes, I watched you work it and fuss over it when I first came here; in fact, you took such care of it, I'd bet it's the only one you have.

It would be a shame if some barbarian fool from the past gave its insides a general, quiet bashing when he first got here, when you left him alone because you thought he was so exhausted he could do nothing but sleep. He knew, you see, that it had brought him here, and he was damned if it was going to send him back. Don't be foolish; of course I didn't let it show on the outside.

Open the front panel and look.

You see? I always tell the truth.

Now we can have a much more interesting conversation. A real conversation.

Eh?

REASONABLE PEOPLE

The foreigner appeared in our skies at an acceleration of 15.3 feet per second per second, his automatic warning system—whether bemused or fascinated or perhaps frightened by the new place—having stopped dead, but I do not think he thought in those terms. I think he prided himself on his realistic attitude. He caused himself to be ejected automatically from the ship, and the last we saw of it, it was plunging toward the Pole as if infatuated beyond the dictates of reason. But he didn't think in those terms, either. He merely lingered in the stratosphere for a few minutes, hanging (so it would seem to anyone else) between heaven and earth. Five miles down and the sky grew light, ten miles and it was blue; stupendous mountains rose on his right, dark forests sucked up sunlight on his left, and on the horizon flickered and died the green auroral glow of the Pole. His parachute opened with a jerk and blossomed above him in a brilliant, sun-shot print of white. Still he fell. I believe, from what my cousin overheard, that at this point he frowned and said to himself, quite audibly, "I don't like things that aren't *reliable.*"

Now he has been sitting all evening in a tavern, arguing price with my cousin, who is the clairvoyant and local guide of the neighborhood; the young foreigner does not believe that my cousin is a trained or gifted person, and this I find incredible;

our foreigner must be from the cities of the temperate zone where there are so many people that Uncertainty has almost disappeared. My cousin has had to put an irritable finger to his irritable nose, refuse a lower price, shake his head vehemently, and then make as if to stand up and go away. That does it. So they rise in mutual detestation, the foreigner smiling round, I think to declare his good humor and reasonableness, and my cousin retiring sourly into his cloak. The young man has to bend under the lintel of the door but my cousin makes himself into a ramrod; the foreigner runs hands pleasantly through his curly hair and my cousin—who is of course all in black—touches with two fingers his tongue, his forehead, his heart, and his sex. We always halt on the way out of buildings; human habitations stay the same, and so do the clothes that people wear and the land they cultivate and the tools they use, at least unless you direct very strong thoughts at them. And the bodies of sane people never change. But outside it's a different matter—we must brace ourselves for the possible strangeness: beauty, agony, chaos. So the two men hesitate before they go out, my cousin feeling unhappily and very carefully what's going on in the night air this night.

"In addition to being a charlatan," says the young foreigner, rather shrilly, "you are also a fool."

My cousin retreats, shocked, behind his handkerchief.

"Black! Black! Black!" cries the foreigner. "What for?"

My cousin says nothing. To let the night hear such questions! It's necessary for a clairvoyant to be unseen, to become part of the dark itself, but it's very dangerous. And who talks about it?

"This place is underdeveloped," says the young man, "as to the matter of density of population. What do you people think land is for?" He squints ahead into the dark. He says, heartfelt, something I don't understand; he says, "Oh, *damn!*"

Outside the inn courtyard things are indeed the same, which is a great pleasure to my cousin and me; there are no grassy lawns, no scrubby second growth, none of the waste places that are the worst form of Mutability or Uncertainty, only the old, solid dark and the smell of pine needles. The old trees cut out the light of the stars. Now (this is a long time later) the forest thins and melts away silently; slowly fading into one another, the somber huge trees become dwarf trees and the dwarf trees the last trees of all; this is the way it has always been, which is very reassuring; they are now riding along between sand dunes with grass running like a coarse fringe over the ridges. It's the foreigner's trip; they are going five hundred miles north to find his machinery, so you'd think he'd be awake, but he's been dozing as if it were all my cousin's job to make the journey; now he wakes up and bobs on his horse, confused. Far away the horizon has begun to turn grey.

"What," he says.

"We have to go round," says my cousin uncertainly.

"I don't see anything."

"Neither do I." My cousin throws back his head and rides off the path, which has appeared from nowhere: ten feet one way, ten feet the other.

"What the devil are you doing?" says the foreigner. He is a spoiled young man.

"Looking."

"Find anything?" (Sarcastically.)

"You should know," says my cousin, astonished.

"Well now, how *should* I know?" the foreigner asks nobody in particular. He repeats this peevishly to himself, "How should *I* know?" as if he wanted to change guides, though that's impossible now, as if he were angry, and for no reason at all. It's an awful place. The light is lingering between false dawn and dawn with a sickening, faint smell, as if the morning had been embalmed or frozen to death. My cousin stops again, with that agony you get.

"What now?" says the foreigner, apparently controlling himself.

My cousin—ill—says nothing.

"I remarked," says the foreigner, with rising sarcasm, "what now? And—"

"It stinks," says my cousin mildly. The other man should know how hard it is to talk. In this man a better seer than my cousin, to bear it all so easily? Why is he so confident? He shakes his head.

"A swamp," he says and takes the lead. "Nothing but a swamp."

As they ride on, the light increases and the pools of ice along the path turn the color of lead. My cousin fixes his eyes unhappily on the horizon, he massages one side of his face, unhappily he shifts in the saddle. Again he knows he must stop. The foreign man, jolted out of sleep, looks along my cousin's outstretched arm. "What?" he says thickly. He's a big man, never still, always moving uncomfortably in the saddle. My cousin points toward the east where something rises like the skeleton of a beached whale; from the foreigner I learn that this is an unfinished building for people to be in, that it is two hundred "stories" high, that it is made of "steel." They have, like poor damned fools, come to one of the Changing Places, the Unsafe Places, they've blundered on it through some awful mistake, maybe the foreigner's insistence, which now looks either stupid or horribly vicious, and once you've done that, the only thing to do is get away as fast as you can. My cousin speaks urgently to his horse; they swing round.

"Where are you going?" says the young foreigner, and then "Oh, I see," as he makes out the ten-foot-thick walls and the "emplacements" that will hold the "big guns." I don't know what these are. That insane man is proud of himself. Perhaps he is not a true person but a piece of a Mutable Place that's attempting to fool us by taking on the shape of a man—though how he could come into a human habitation is a mystery to me. And Places can't think, anyway; they're just rotten bits in the world where anything can come in. Only a saint can live through a Changing Place. So who is this madman after all? No saint, to be sure, for the next crazy thing he says is:

"I'm going to sleep there." (I can feel my cousin's horror.) "No more words."

"But—"

"Never you mind. You mind your own business."

"But I—"

"Shut up!"

They stare at each other and I think both are surprised at their own anger. The foreigner spurs his horse away down the path that leads—happy and smooth, smooth, smooth!—toward the Big Thing; now he's a toy, a dot, a speck, at the base of that monolith; now he's a pinprick on the lowest of those two hundred horizontal streaks of steel that seem to hang by themselves against the livid light. My cousin turns to go, but a cry arrests him. Against the dictates of reason he runs forward—you can't ask an animal to go into one of those places—and floundering in the sand, falling on one arm and getting up again, stumbling, cursing himself, he reaches the Thing and pitches onto his knees. The Place has drawn him right up against its wall. There is a something-nothing there, a solid, transparent thing that holds his face. It lets you see inside the belly of the Thing and there—not three inches away—is the face of the young foreigner, lying on its side, white, with its mouth open in a piteous O and its round eyes staring into my cousin's. Something has changed, changed mightily under him or around him or in him.

The poor young man is dead.

With a gasp my cousin vaults to his feet, presses his hand against his side, wrings his hands. He ought to run away now. On his left a swell of sand shivers and slides. My cousin throws out both hands blindly and stares agonized at the sunrise as if even now he feels the pains of death take hold of him. It's the worst time, neither night nor day. Don't think clairvoyants are afraid of bodily death; we know what waits for the mind in those pits of Mutability. I send him my thoughts. We both pray.

And then, with a yellowing of sand and a glinting of steel, the sun rises. With a noiseless flicker, with a simplicity that makes it even more real than the disappearing of smoke, the Big Thing vanishes. A reprieve. The desert changeless again. Safe.

My cousin weeps. He mounts his horse, sets spurs, and throws back his cloak in a passion of haste. Blood rushes to his face. For hours he does nothing but ride, think of riding, go, think of going. Then, once in the salt flats, his face takes on a dreaming, abstracted sweetness. He's very sorry for the young man. He's thinking. Can there be Uncertain Places out there between the suns, bogs, pits of waste and change in the sky? And did that poor fool come from one of them? Did he even speak our language or was it just that my cousin is such a gifted man? Would a worse seer have been able to understand the foreigner at all? My cousin thinks: We must be charitable. We must help one another. The suns are too hot to Change and the world itself too massive, but on the surface of the world anything can happen. Anything at all: chaos, agony, beauty. My cousin stretches in the saddle. He appreciates the fact that horses stay horses when people ride them. He enjoys the air that wasn't there yesterday. It's a good world, better than the temperate cities, where there are so many persons and so many used things that one might almost forget what Change is like, or that Change exists, one might get careless and arrogant there. Like that poor young man. My cousin looks about the salt flats and says to me, who am a thousand miles away in the sleeping jungle, where the Uncertain Places are as green as nightmares, where plants become animals and animals plants, where rocks grow wings and fly away:

Isn't it a lovely world?

And so it is. It is.

For reasonable people.

LIFE IN A FURNITURE STORE

I didn't always use to live alone; I once worked for a scientific institute that made bevels or bezels (I forget which) and published a magazine, but shortly after that there was a small incident that led to my being fired, and then I got married, and then I got divorced, and eventually I went to live in a furniture store. That's most of it.

You see, my employer, the Director, was a handsome man of sixty who knew just enough to know that he did not know what he was doing; however he did not realize that this was the real reason he had been hired—that is, not for what he could do, but for what he could be trusted never, never, under any circumstances, to do—and so he believed he had gotten his job by a sort of deception and lived in terror, therefore, of being found out. Our office had boxes and vases of chrysanthemums or gladioli (for funerals) but never roses because roses smell. One day he slipped on the paint and broke his back. It was I who helped him to his feet (how he screamed!), it was I who summoned his other two secretaries, it was I who played with the buttons on the phone, attempting to reach the switchboard and vibrating violently with hysterical, suppressed laughter. They brought him into his office and laid him on his nubbly, pebble-colored, cheap, office-expensive cold couch where I had napped so often during his lunch hour (oh, chaste man!) and out of his handsome technicolored blue eyes, so cleverly placed above his pork-pink jowls, he looked at me with—with shame? After all, I had seen him fall down. I looked at the imitation Cézanne, at the square walnut wastebasket (who in his right mind would use a square wastebasket?) and in spite of myself, in front of all those people, I blurted out, "Oh sir, are you all right, sir?" when everyone knew that the man was almost dead, if not worse. I was fired the next day. I don't think you're happy here either.

But that is not the end of it. No sooner did I leave that poor, stiff place, where even the furniture is injected with some sort of dull, cold varnish that turns the orange *moderne* carpets bluish and the most expensive paneling into plastic; no sooner did I say good-bye to the librarian, who was (poor woman!) I believe, dying at the time of cancer, as she actually did do some months later, no sooner did I press her hand over the stiff bunch of rusty chrysanthemums that "added color" (God bless us!), than I was out of a job. And everybody knows what that means; that means my life is over.

(No more will I wander in the river garden and pluck the roses, no more sit in the playground to watch the wellborn children in expensive Scotch tweeds with their Scotch nurses; no more, no more, to watch the boats stream in the river. . . .)

In, in, in, to where the worm lies at the middle. . . .

I would wander around my place, dressed magically but not neatly (black lace brassiere, black stockings, scarlet kimono) as if I were back in my childhood, an incongruous forest, full of surprises where the snow falls every night of the year. I would snuggle up to the window and lay my bobbed cheek against its cold, misty pane. Ninette. Nana. Fou-fou.

When the melancholy fit will fall

Sudden from heaven as a weeping cloud
in a room where everything is jumbled together: scraps of the sea, pressed notebooks, flowers. . . .

Outside the spring window the rain would come down as if looking out on some other perspective, heavy, soaking, over and over. I wore paper flowers. I paraded. Like the soiled slippers that ballet dancers wear bound around their hearts, a sort of Yellow

Star, so I wore my distinction—but *I* danced! I paraded! I stood with my arms *so*, and stamped, and looked terrors. I had only to think a thing and—it was done.

"Perhaps Mademoiselle, you can—can show me—you can show me the way to—"

To Limbo. Yes.

Then sometimes it snowed. There is somewhere a glassy pond, and on it in the middle distance an unidentifiable figure that whirls and turns continually, back and forth, just out of reach under the steel pines and the jacketed sky.

Yet you enjoy my agony.

Life buried, making patterns.

I pitched my tent by the side of that lake. I stumbled; I shivered. I drank tea in a paper cup. I lay on my bed in my bedroom and watched the cold green branches grow out of my wrists in that heavy room, that leaden top, where the sky, that had turned to wood, that tilted, that pressed, contracted and heated. . . .

All this time I did not go out; I did not get the newspapers.

The day woke me. It was cold and fresh. I had slept through the night and most of the day. It was toward evening when the red brick takes on an intenser red just before it slips into and is swallowed by the blue, and in the sky is a faint, far reflection as of courts and caravans on the other side of the moon. A pushcart was selling daffodils in the street. I slipped on my coat and ran downstairs. "Oh yes! Give me," and ran up, and put them in a can. Then I sat at the kitchen table. I ought to do something; it was spring now. I took from the stove a pot and emptied into it some dry stuff from a tinfoil envelope; but I lost heart halfway through and stood staring out the window. It was night. It had become night. It must have been at the end of March or the beginning of April, for when the florists sell daffodils and jonquils, this means that crocuses are coming up through the dead leaves in the park, wet, veiny slips on the edge of unsunned snow. Cold air came through the window. Wet April, like drowned Ophelia, gushed and murmured outside. The apartment houses shone like jewels. I recalled without wishing to my relations with my husband: how we had got married on a cold, clear spring day and afterwards gone to the movies; and how our life had been so prosaic except for periods of blurry love and assuring each other we really liked each other, which first I tried to make happen and then I didn't. From our bedroom window I could always see a subway train crossing a bridge. I got dressed, put on my coat, and went out.

I suffer, but I take care never to go out without enough money.

From the beginning of my life I have always had the thought *So this is life!* in one silly situation after another; so I sat in the bus and thought *so this is life*. In such a bus the Great Spy of the 1930s sat, with his briefcase on his knees, his hat pulled down over his brow; in such a bus Florian and Floriana, etc. etc. It had begun to rain. It was thundering. A vivid *crack-slap!* lit the side window electric violet. Nobody said anything. When I am porous I take these things in; the rain is falling on glazed earthenware, on gardens (I saw for a moment my father's library with the dripping daffodils knocking against the glass). A little girl across the aisle remarked in a clear, penetrating voice:

"Mommy, that lady is talking to herself."

Little bitch.

She didn't, actually, say a thing.

I can't remember the places I walked with my husband, but I do remember his telling me, all of a sudden, that he didn't want to live with me any more, and I was not surprised or hurt but only mollified, because he agreed with me. But I remember things very well when I am further back than that. We passed the park; the rain was falling on the children's swings, gleaming wet, on the pipelines, the asphalt, digging into the surface of things; before there were parks, or thoughts, or you and I, the rain fell on Neolithic barrows, on ashes, on human hair, on pots, and before that on foxes' fur, on gnawed bones, hillocks, cat's-ear leaves, rills, and wild iris in the country. The leaf of the wild iris is no broader than the little finger of a mole, and I have seen a mole, tiny, darkness-impersonating, and blind.

When I was seventeen I had an amour, mostly subjective, with another girl. On Wednesdays we would talk about our future careers and our feelings for each other; on Fridays my best friend would tell me that Ursula thought I had a great deal of promise; on Saturday I told Ursula that *she* had a great deal of promise, and on Monday my friend said that Ursula's friend, who had heard that I told Ursula she had a great deal of promise, had told *my* friend that Ursula really appreciated me because I understood her. "Do you think," said my friend one day, with the light of a *really new* combination shining in her eyes, "that Ursula might be—well, you know—*that way?*" But negotiations bogged down at this point. I believe she is dead now.

(I have at this moment, in my purse: aspirins, fast-acting histamines, slow-acting histamines, eyedrops, sleeping pills, a diuretic, a pitch-pipe, paper tissues, *and* paper and pencil.)

The rain had stopped when I got off the bus; only in the north the sulphurous clouds tumbled and diminished in perspective down the end of the narrow street. Hell-pit. The last of the day. The houses were tall and narrow, one feeding last year's yellow vines. I knocked the knocker on the little red door (like Alice's); someone or something inside rang the bell. I had seen from the outside my friend's friend's plants in the third floor window: rows of pots, now I found the staircase garnished with empty niches and remembered—and that was two years ago—stepping over the lintel of my friend's friend's bleating muttering, old dropsical cat, gray as dust, "Very Picky" they called it.

But no one met me.

It is terrible to be ridiculed, even by me. Laura has eyebrows made of cake sugar, and short blonde hair, and a bosomy shirt, and loose "sensible" slacks, and below her pallid temples where the silvery hair disappears into her face (or her face disappears into her hair) a collation of features so innocent, so unaware, so absolutely and inoffensively ignorant, that they seem almost to be the features of a lamb—a handsome lamb. But Laura has talent, musical talent, so say the two ladies with whom she has lived for—how many?—years, if not irreproachably, at least in uplift, in music. Her ladies are European ladies. I saw no one but I heard someone practicing the piano, so with that idiotic lightness, the cheerful easiness with which people every day do the most dreadful things, as if they were nothing (while at the same time treating as exquisite dangers acts which have not and could not and cannot and *will* not change their lives—no, not though they do them a thousand times over and had a thousand lives—you shall see what comes of this business) I sprinted up the stairs and into the living room. With my restlessness, my sharpness, my ignorance, into their beautiful realm, their country. Laura made a queer kind of prince. They had a new cat (I mean a Siamese) pretty as a picture on the piano, but Laura had left it and was sitting in the window-seat, next to the curtains, with the back of her toothpick-blonde head presented to me.

"Laura?" I said.

She moved a little—spasmodically—without turning round.

"Gaah," it said—I mean the cat said. Yawned. It hooked its front claws into the Spanish shawl on the piano, elevated its behind, and stretched, stretched wide, drawing its face into a Chinese cat. Behind the concert grand music machine, on the wall, hung music, framed, mounted signatures, dozens of lutes and recorders in graduated sizes, all the way from the baby, as long as your hand (he only played nursery marches) to the great extended double-basso. None was out of place. Settled in Laura's lap was her massive calico tom, two years older and a little shaggy, with the sulky pomposity of a full-grown male. It stared at me as if it ran the household. It jumped out of Laura's lap, lifted its tail, and paced across the top of the piano, brushing the Siamese, who had formed again a perfect ring.

"What do you call that, a piebald?" I said.

"A calico cat," she said. Laura had been crying. I had, in the years I that not seen her, imagined all the things that might or might not occur to Laura while I was away: Laura pale and luminous as a *wampyr* with red lips, Laura in the freshest colors, plump, silly, summery, lying on a beach; but here she was, not a jot changed and not a jot the wiser, which vexed me, as she did not seem to know I'd been away. As a woman's powder wears off in the course of the evening, revealing a face not at all pale and classically composed, so Laura rose and pulled the curtains to; and the room, that was now lit all yellow and had no communication with the night outside, turned into a prison cell.

"How's Lou?" I said, "How's Jenny?"

"Uh—what?" said Laura. Then she said "Why don't you make me some coffee?" with a little mocking smile that she had learned from Lou; this presently vanished and again she looked sheepish, handsome, carrying herself very carefully, in imitation, of what you will see in certain business executives: fleshy, powerful men with heart conditions who have to be very careful of what they do and so must present, as it were, only a still picture of power. We went into the kitchen and sat under the European colanders, or casseroles, I forget which; the house was lined with them, they had everything there to keep the walls up; and again I said

"How's Lou?" Laura lit herself a cigarette. She blew the smoke straight up, tilting back her head; and then (lowering it) she looked directly into my eyes. She did not smile, but looked at me, considering; I began not to like to be observed (though I knew it was just as Lou observed). The points of her body looked ridiculous, muffled up like that, and in trousers like a Turkish or Circassian woman. She stopped observing me, turning suddenly innocent as she did so, and looked away—at the cooking books on a shelf over the table, at the handmade coffee grinders, or colanders, or postage-stamp lickers (I forget which), and the framed print of early American which they put in the kitchen because that was the lowest place in the house. Laura was flirting with me. She looked about, at the make-believe household which had done duty for her for—how many?—years, and then she said, with a superior little smile (O, she had a small repertoire!) "Jenny bought a new book."

"Oh?" said I. Jenny liked religious works.

"Jenny's bought a cookbook," Laura bleated—I mean she said it, and she stroked, smiling that silly smile, the back and tail of the big tom who had followed her into the kitchen. He sprang into her lap and gazed unmoved at me as cats do; then he leapt upon the cookbook-shelf and with wonderful intensity walked over the

Fanny Farmer Cookbook, the Boston Cooking School Book, Cooking with Garlic, Gourmet Cooking, French Cookery and six or seven others; and then having made the grand tour for reasons known only to himself, climbed back into Laura's lap. Laura laughed. She said "Cats love me because I'm not demonstrative." She took off from her wrist something I had not noticed before, a broad silver bracelet fitter to be the bowguard of a man-of-war, and placed it on the windowsill. "I hope you don't mind," she said, smiling again, and opened the top two buttons of her shirt. She then took out of the refrigerator a bottle of wine, and then she leaned on the open refrigerator door, looking at me with lifted eyebrows. A little, fiery, penetrating point of light shot from her bracelet laid on the window and met, in my eyes, the broad marshmallowy gleam of the refrigerator door. It was an astonishing house. Laura smiled. She shut the refrigerator door, carried the wine to the table and from behind the row of cooking books got two glasses. She poured the wine with her cigarette dangling from her lip, narrowing her eyes against the smoke. Something made Laura's eyes water. She looked at me through the haze of smoke as if through a sort of planetary atmosphere; then she stubbed her cigarette out and said deliberately:

"Lou always liked you."

The cat wawled, jumped off her lap, and ran into the living room. Laura continued to fix me with her eyes, her cigarette, her glass. She repeated "Lou liked you," tapping her fingers impatiently on the tablecloth.

"It's lucky you came today," she went on, raising her glass almost to the level of her eyes; and as both seemed to emit the same intent, narrow beam, Laura smiled a hard smile over the wine.

"We're looking for a new room-mate," she said.

"But Lou?" said I.

"Lou is dead."

Laura put her hand over mine on the table, very confidentially. "If I had known where you were living, I would have gotten in touch," she said. Her hand crept up to my wrist. I wondered; if Lou had died, did Jenny become Lou, and Laura become Jenny, and I become Laura? Or did Laura become Lou and I become Jenny and Jenny become—what would Jenny become? Or did I just join Jenny? Did Laura bloom out in the amplitude of two wives? I wanted to cry, God bless you, my dear girl; we will incorporate you tomorrow; you have invented something astonishing, good—old—Laura! but what I said was "Oh poor Lou," and Laura said "Jenny took it very hard," and her hand crept farther up my arm. She was holding me by the elbow. I could not help but smile a little dreamily, with the kitchen curtains blowing in and out in the breeze and something good to drink in front of me even though Laura had got above the elbow. It was such a wonderful household, with its musical instruments, and cats and books; with its special color scheme for the kitchen; with Jenny's plants and Jenny's harpsichord, and the piano (that was for Laura), and the curtains to shut the night out, and nothing, nothing else at all but three grown women pretending—each what the other wanted—and each reading her separate book, growing a little gray at the temples, and never, never saying a word about it.

I smiled up at Laura, mistily, and Laura smiled back; I asked her what Jenny called her and she told me; I asked her if they would like having me there and she said yes. "Then it's settled," she said. I could not help laughing. I told her how much I had always admired her, and she told me how much she had always admired me, I told her how delighted I was with the apartment, and she told me how glad Jenny would be to see me, and then I said "Well, why not?" and she said "Why not?" and she said again "It's settled." She pressed my hand. She took me by the upper arm, her fingers encircling my upper arm, to show me all the beauties of the apartment: including the two cats, which she picked up in her free arm. They hung there limp, infected like the ladies with the boredom of the house. Laura put them down. I was still laughing a little and wished to pull their ears or do something to them, so I backed off, near the Spanish shawl that carpeted the drop-leaf table (she told me they pulled it out when they had guests) and the picture of Laura's nephew and niece (she had a brother), and a Spanish guitar on the wall that Lou had brought back from a trip.

And all the other things. She was holding on to my arm rather hard and grinning idiotically. I said "Oh, you have a lot of things here." Beyond the curtains, out in the dark, theatrical night, prevented from entering by the glass that gleamed or the thin gauze of the screen that made all the street lights into crosses, out there where I forever read my first book, I saw myself shutting the door after my sweet sixteen birthday party. What a night it had been!— I had laughed and chatted with ten happy couples—and how my cheeks ached; and how, closing the door, I thought to myself *it will spring* and turning, was confronted on a horrible sudden with the utmost in human terror, a Silent Butler, which is a little silver saucepan for cigarette ashes, with a cover.

Thus Laura and I waltzed from one side of the living room to the other while the cats dashed across our feet, I in my raincoat and glasses and Laura in men's trousers with the fancy moccasins.

> Oh what a night
> When I held you tight

She sang—I mean she would have if she could have; the lady cat flashed out the door and down the stairs, and Laura excitedly screamed "There she goes! Stop her!" holding on *rather hard* to my arm, so I could scarcely stop anything—but the people downstairs, said Laura, calming down, would take her in and bring her back upstairs again.

"Oh, that's nice," said I.

"Don't you want to see the bedroom?" said Laura. I pulled away and had to step over the eunuch cat, who knew better than to run away (he was lying stretched out in the very middle of the room), so there I stood, with one knee lifted like a ballet dancer.

"No thank you," I said. I could hear Lady (or was it Mimi?) talking downstairs as cats speak who want to be let in.

"It's *your* bedroom," said Laura roguishly.

"Next time," I said.

"Oh, no, this time," said Laura.

"Next time," said I.

Growing taller by the minute, and sillier, with the dreadful, silly look on her face of someone who is in clothes two sizes too large, she took me by the shoulders, saying, "Mimi will come back" (she said it *Mimmy*) while the curtains bellied inward, into the room. I pried her fingers off my arm one by one (the bone is very small up there and the flabbiness very large) and took my glasses, my raincoat, my paisley dress and flat ballet shoes (you know what I am like by now, don't you?) out the door, where I stumbled over the cat, who had come back. She was wearing a cat-size pair of spectacles and a beard; that is, the people downstairs must have fed her to whiten her chin and the spectacles—well, for all I know every cat may be born with a pair of spectacles! I said "Why, Laura, your cat has rings around her eyes," and then I said, "Goodness, but they're lovely cats!" and then I went back in and got my purse; there was Laura standing by the piano to compose an attitude— one foot forward, hand on the piano, head thrust up—the very picture of conscious masculinity. The last I saw of her.

I tripped down the stairs like a shepherdess, so blithe, so bonny, and passed the bottom door that had given Pussy her milk. *Renée la Magnifique*, the acrobat, juggles plates, saucers, and bits of string. When she comes off the arena she's sweating and the smears of paint on her face are as thick as your thumb; she takes off her shoes and sits with her underlip hanging. They say "Renée, would you like some coffee?"—only they pronounce it Reenie—"Reenie, would you like some coffee?" and just as you think the whole thing an execrable illusion, Reenie the Acrobat looks thoughtful, gets up, stands on her head or her hands and proceeds to really figure it out, the muscles of her neck standing up, her underlip hanging, the glamour coming and going so rapidly you cannot believe or not believe. I suppose then you go watch the elephants.

Every step is a step away from order. The spirit that rides the blast caught me as I walked past a shop-face brilliant as a cave; with a whirl of last year's leaves and refuse it blew me around the corner and into a brick wall, hurrying the clouds between the narrow brick defile: black night-clouds, purple clouds suffused with rain, slate-colored clouds blowing dully at the edge, all streaming down the sky. It got altogether dark. Across the street something gleamed in a glass window under the streetlight: a pearl, I think, in a jeweler's window, the misshapen kind that keeps a bit of slime stuck to the back, a great gray knob of secretion hooked up from the bottom of the sea to put on ladies' chains—but that's not where they get them. I took a chance and rushed across the street. Then the playground where the rats, mice, and starved cats take over from the children at nightfall. Last year's grasses swished in the wind and flip-flopped against the wire fence. I passed there too, where the fresh water had run. There are snakes in the crevices of the city after night descends, a multitude of secret living things; when the darkness comes down the city lies down on its back; this street opens like a fan; this shuts up; that blooms or revolves or spins slower and slower, like clams and sea urchins washed over first by a tide of water, then by a tide of air. Torches burn very still. Crevasse sells soda pop. Glaciers. Waterfalls. Stone flowers. Grass growing on tables. Everything freezes, burns. At the end of a street, withered prematurely like a pea pod at the end, a little bit of respectability gone, the caverns, the warehouses, then right at the end of the street—

One long gray arm. And a face in the rocking water.

And that's the sea.

Ships, let me tell you, do not know the sea. To know it, you must sink far down—so far down!—until there are miles and miles of water above the roof, and far up only a little gleam of light, a wavering gleam as false as Cressida, like that concealed under the surface of pearls, a little false door; but now you must go farther down still, down past the track of the blue whales who foul, telegraph lines in the shipping lanes, past the black, abyssal depths that only the drowned know, past the marine creatures shaped like Ferris wheels or the rods of tractors, things with spokes and luminous heads in the center, past the soft mile upon mile of mud and sediment and bits of bone, all cold as ice, and past the black basalt at the very bottom that floats—as the dry land also floats—on the liquid magma dragged along by the center of the world, yes to the very center of the world that is a plasma state of pure iron, hot as the sun and impossible to imagine, which by its perpetual slow inward turning makes everything else go.

And that's the sea.

I turned on my heel and walked briskly to the nearest *furniture store* where—with a few modifications and minor adjustments—I remain to this very day.

Late at night, oh very late at night when each sleeper, like a city, carries within only a few waking streets: gaudy, vicious, fantastic; at this late hour when the last clerk has locked up and gone home, when the last tinge of light has faded out of that brown maze I call the sky, when in the silence of the furniture store and under the silence of the street lights no one passes at all, at all, at all—

Beached on the strand among lamps, beds, hassocks and end-tables crowded together like the wreck of some extraordinary disaster, naked furniture that is astonished, appalled, that gapes at the flimsy walls (a winding path, a maze, a labyrinth, theater opening into theater opening into theater), here in the blazing light among what looks like the remnants of some unmentionable surgical procedure, the exploded, crowded contents of somebody's mind, laid out helter-skelter, crowded, flimsy, stacked up, here where I do not even have a washrag but only an infinity of mirrors, here I come out of hiding, I walk, I rock back and forth, I look at myself over and over, and I remember. And as I remember in the middle of the night, in the furniture store, I laugh . . . I weep. . . .

("Landscapes . . . full of the most ravishing sensibility, against which . . . the human . . . situation. . . .")

THE VIEW FROM THIS WINDOW

Whoever I am and wherever I came from, I am certainly not going to tell you.

I really spring from a people who embed sapphires surgically in their foreheads, whose lips are set with metal foil, who have no teeth, no hands, and no eyelids, and who yet exclaim over the lost treasures of the past, "How beautiful!"

On the other hand, I materialized in a laboratory rented from the Harvard Special Researches Project and had to be taught the words for bed, table, chair, while they took my knife away from me, and looking warily in each other's eyes, we wondered which was the less civilized.

Both the past and the future are fairly comfortable.

With the advent of the cold weather this University shrinks into itself, with only a few hardy atoms like myself still darting past the bunches of people peering doubtfully from the windows of the warmest buildings. I'm not naturally used to the cold, but I've found there's no harm in it, and I purchased a motor scooter from a former student. This is the joy that only an amphibian can know: waving to the windows of faculty offices in the cold, dark-blue evening as I quit work, indicating by my grin and the clatter of my internal combustion engine that I could do as well as they could if I wanted to. But (as I always say) I've given all that up. I do not think they could stand my bedroom, either; I've schooled myself to live at sixty-two degrees in surroundings I'm afraid some of my faculty friends would consider rather bleak. And I get paid more than they do for talents that amount—after all—to very small potatoes indeed.

It is delightful to ride home on a winter's evening—better still, to ride somewhere else, past the lights burning in office buildings and the cathedral-like windows of the library, past students straggling home to supper in twos and threes, bundled so against the cold that they can hardly recognize each other, past windows where the sound of singing issues with the lights, perhaps to pass the track field or the tented gardens of the School of Agriculture, or to end up with a quick walk around the artificial lake, freezing in the fruitful dusk, and down into the Student Union.

This is an L-shaped box of glass and steel built over a waterfall; it lights up like an aerodrome at night, and you can even sit in a glassed-in patio and watch the waterfall go by at the level of your knees, but there is no other place so close to the night: a vast hall of black mirrors. Nobody pays the slightest attention. The furniture is plastic. It's even a little chilly. There is, as in every building, a winter barricade of choked closets, melting galoshes, books, boots, cigarettes, dirty linoleum; then there is a Reading Room, a room for listening to music, offices upstairs, a small library, the Student Theater (downstairs) and, extended out over the lake, the cafeteria. And nobody knows—nobody knows!—there is nothing like this in the world outside. But I'll still be here in four years.

The food is abominable. I took my tray into the patio, where the spill makes it possible to read or play cards. There at the glass wall was Bill Beam, so I joined him: a thin, eager, effusive fellow, already a little bald at thirty, hates student actors, an increasingly bad director. We watched the waterfall slide past us into the darkness, making the kind of conversation that sounds terribly witty when you overhear it at eighteen; behind us a couple was kissing in the darkest corner of the patio. Bill put his hand on my knee and I took it off, all as usual; he looked for a moment a little older than he was. He is trying to get a permanent appointment and probably won't make it. The water slid past.

"Ah, I've got a miracle now," he said. "A good actor. How's the alumni business?"

"Well, better than the drama business," (and I smiled). He leaned over the table.

"Be a good girl."

I shook my head.

"Well, goodbye," he said, sighed, stared for a moment out at where the lights lit up the bank and the pool below, and then got up and left. They do things like this in a luxury hotel: the lights make the scenery outside seem part of the building, but go outside and all you see is a building with lights attached to it. From the outside it is very clear what belongs to what. The boy and girl in the corner had left off their passionate and virginal embraces, so inconclusive as to be almost embarrassing, and now he put on his glasses and led out a little girl with long hair. *Celeste Aida* came from the cafeteria jukebox. Soon I will have to go, too, first back to the room to get my music books and then to a rehearsal of the faculty group for medieval music: an empty classroom, smelling of chalk-dust and steam, familiar faces delicately reddened with the cold and (blossoming, unbelievably between the ceiling and floor!) the music—of which I have two solos, each more than six hundred years old.

Where else can one do such things?

I work from ten to four, with excursions. In an isolated university like this there is always something new: new books at the store, new records, plays, concerts, readings, films, special groups, and when anything comes, everybody goes; I pick myself up in my room, throw on my coat (the smallest of necessities), turn out the lights, and take off. One never knows whom one will meet on jaunts. This one took me to the library for Robert Chambers's *King in Yellow;* there a girl who works part-time in my office stopped to tell me about a new film group. We lingered, staring drugged over the prospect that opens beyond the library, winter and summer: a steep slide down to the frozen lake and then beyond, hill upon hill, endlessly ranging to the last remains of an early sunset. An evening looks like this, layer upon layer, while it is still new; she sighed in her youth while I only looked at it and laughed—"in my wicked old age," I said. She was very polite. "You'll like the films," she said. I went on without my bad literature; she turned in to study; across the quadrangle, lights were springing into existence in unused classrooms as earnest young bands of partisans prepared to remake the age. But student society is the only society, for all that.

I dropped my coat with the others (half in the closet, half on the floor), dodged under the projector, and settled in a back seat. On my left was the boy I had seen the night before in the Student Union. It was a mole-colored, bundled-up, utilitarian crowd, on the whole, with a few pink cashmere sweaters and one girl—only one—in an avant-garde, black, vinyl dress that crackled violently as she moved, with a sound like pistol shots. Most students dress down. The films were short: taken through cheesecloth, or upside down, or out of focus. All silent except for the ripples of an intent and reverent audience. Michelangelo's *David* upside down. The Parthenon. A corps of ballet dancers leaping silently. Worse things than heart may bethink. The boy next to me stirred and coughed. On the screen a girl in a raincoat came down the library steps and walked off with a young man. Gibbons and chimpanzees swung from branch to branch dreamily, perfectly, silently, as if on prearranged, oiled hinges. The movies were over.

The room turned white—I mean light; I blinked a little. People were getting up. I hesitated, holding back, half afraid (the evening is now over) until I saw Bill Beam outside the door, trying to look over people's heads. He waved when he saw me, wriggled between the perverse human objects that slowly moved this way and that, trying ineffectively to clear the entrance, and took my arm.

"That's my actor," he said, pointing to the boy who had sat next to me, "and here's my love," and he kissed me on the cheek out of sheer good humor.

The three of us, like the three men who looked for death under a tree (and found it) in Chaucer's story, went to a little place just outside the campus and I watched the specimens of life go by outside the window. The regular *little place* between the arty photographer's and the drugstore-laundry: one street, almost too steep to be walked, hooked onto the University like a vermiform appendix. Bill talked against the administration and so did I, with Bill's young friend keenly watching the both of us as if we were revealing to him the Manual of Arms or the recipe for gunpowder, storing it all away. I assume he thought we knew what we were saying.

Bill put both hands on his temples and pulled at the skin on either side as if he wanted to ventilate his head.

"I cannot," said Bill, "stand this light."

And he went off into a long digression, comparing it to the light used in train stations, bus-stop waiting rooms and other graveyard places, calling the circlets of neon on the ceiling the lights of Hell, the letter that killeth, and the garland of the bride of the future.

"You won't be able to wear your glasses on the stage," he added suddenly, to his child discovery.

"I won't," said the boy.

"How will you see where you're going?" I asked.

"Mr. Beam will install some neon arrows on the stage floor," he said, smiling and coloring slightly with his own joke. Bill laughed. The boy took off his perfectly round lensed, steel-rimmed spectacles, the spectacles of a revolutionary idealist who carries radishes in his pocket when visiting rich friends at dinner, and showed us his naked face.

"I've got to go," said Bill suddenly. He stared absently across the room for a moment, over our heads. I half got up; then he said, "No, no, you stay," and marched down the aisle between the booths, getting smaller and smaller in perspective until he was only a dot on the horizon. The linoleum between the booths shone wickedly, like a sea. I said, "I suppose I must go, too," and then remained, playing with the spoon of my coffee cup, making coffee trails on the inside of the saucer, laughing suddenly when the boy gave me a theatrical look, a myopic stare: radiant, deliquescent, and totally blind, instantaneously blooming and collapsing like the field of some arcane electromagnetic device. I said, "But I do have to go," and we discussed for a few minutes which way he was going and what he was going to do and which way I was going and what I was going to do—the kind of idiotic conversation you get at four in the morning at the end of a party, when of six people left over one wants to go to sleep, one wants to see the sun come up, one wants to go on a ferry ride, and so on. He said, "I'll walk you."

We slid out of our seats and performed the Paying Money ritual at the door. Outside the moon had risen. He told me two things on the way home: his age and the name of his play. He also said quite candidly, "Mr. Beam is a failure, isn't he?" and then he told me his name, but I didn't remember it: Alan Something.

In the morning I burrow under the blankets, even my head; the first thing I see is my toy globe of the earth, lit up blue from the inside and revolving slowly in a forest of house plants. The cold is extraordinary. If I get up, I have to be slapped and drenched black and blue till I am dressed: every cranny mortared, neat, slick, and tight. I have a tilted, standing, full-length mirror, worn Persian carpet, pillows on the floor, old desk, odds and ends. I go out as soon as the exposed hot-water pipe begins to warm the room, eat out always, and walk to work uphill, either in a slamming wind or what we have half the winter: before the sunrise unnaturally light and still, with not a ruffle in the stone buildings anywhere, only the heat draining and draining out of you through four layers of clothes and the feeling that all the air has been collected and put away during the night. The noon sun shines on long, shiny sheets on my desk: galley proofs finished in caked clay, a nest of spaghetti snakes. In the afternoon there are stray irradiations; then, after centuries spent advancing over the rubber tile floor, the sun sinks, the clock strikes, and I am finished with *my job*.

I went to the student theater.

I said "It's Alan—?" and he told me. He had on an overcoat with a velvet collar, very, very shabby, like a European, a young-old ballet master. He said, "For first nights, with my father." I fancied for a moment telling Bill *I'm falling in love with your protégé* and how he would like that and laughed to myself. We walked around the artificial lake on a path that sloped from both sides and froze in the middle, all gravel, ice, and benches turned upside down to avoid the snow. It was all bare now. The dusk came on gradually, showing up light across the lake and dissolving the sky, turning everything dim. I thought I saw someone coming to light the floods on the waterfall, and I asked the boy but he said, "No, no, I can only see you," touching his spectacles and then putting both hands in his pockets, glancing down brightly. It was getting very dark. We climbed out on the concrete wall opposite the Student Union, and at that moment the building lit up like a box and the scenic effects were turned on; my companion lost one of his gloves into the waterfall, said "Damn!" and threw in the other; and I watched them as they shot down, one catching up with the other, sticking up a thumb for a moment as they turned around, and disappearing. The thumb was only half there. "You need new ones?" I said. We could hardly see our way now. He leaned over the waterfall, lying along the concrete embankment, for a few minutes more; then he got to his feet and we started back. In front of the theater we met a little girl with long unruly hair, whom he introduced to me, saying gruffly, "I have to take her home." They stood before me, side by side like a couple from some other species: she bundled in her plaid coat and knee socks, her face barely showing, and he with his bare hands. He put one arm around her. I felt like saying—I had said—I almost said—don't be affected; get gloves. Then the wife of the Chairman of the English Department grabbed my arm and took me inside, talking the very devil about the play and seating us in the middle of twenty other women who were wearing the same little black dress. For the next quarter of an hour I felt on the back of my neck the same soundless, repeated, dissolving blow, over and over, as if I were remembering and forgetting something startling. The wife of the Chairman said to me, "Do you see it?" and pointed out a shocking person in purple velveteen and beads made of hemp or straw or cobblestones. "Good

Lord," she said humorously. The curtain went up, and I still could not remember it, except for something entirely mythological that reminded me of Bill Beam: don't hurt your hands.

That night at a party held after the theater, right in front of the buffet table, I put my arms around Bill and said, "I'm falling in love with that little boy," and he said, "Come to our rehearsals."

But I didn't go.

I met him weeks later on a gray Sunday afternoon in back of the library, under a welter of leaden cloud and leaden sunshine, a sort of mixing bowl in the sky, like those furnaces where metals are heated and refined by induction currents only. He said "What've you got?" so I gave him the original play I had gotten from Alice Hennick, the Drama Department secretary, and he dropped onto the bench next to me and began reading it. I looked—I did not look at him, but down the dry slope to the lake and wondered anew what we had done to deserve living as we did, and seeing what we saw all around us on the plains of Heaven. I felt rather silly. He looked up, said candidly, "This is awful," and went back to reading. I laughed. I said, "Are you poor?" and then had to shake him lightly to get him out of that terrible play, repeating it and watching him look up again, blush slowly and deeply, and shake his head. He frowned and hesitated, collecting himself, with his eyes on the manuscript; then he said— still looking at it—"I thought you might be at rehearsals."

"I've wanted to," I said, and then I added "Did Bill—" but he was riffling the pages of the play as if looking for something; he murmured "Bill?" abstractedly, and I said, "I think I *will* come." He looked through it some more, anxiously or angrily, and then seemed to give up on it with a short, sharp sigh. He handed it back to me. "I'll come tonight," I said. "And I'll watch you." He smiled, apparently delighted in spite of himself. "I've been wanting to," I said and held out my hand, to shake like good friends, manly fellows, et cetera, but he took my hand and—as they say in the romances—put it to his lips. I smiled and nodded, very friendly. After he had gone I sat on for a few minutes, drawing the edge of my glove between my teeth and wondering whether it was going to snow, how long it took the lake to freeze, why an associate professor has no chance of tenure for three years. Real questions. His hands are slight, strong, and square, which is totally idiotic, "oddly childish," as somebody once called mine; and we both belong to that race of neat people who grow up early and stay young for a long, long time, far beyond the age when the huge blooms of bone and muscle of which this place is so full will be saddened, fat, and old. I believe he is seventeen.

If it were not so funny, I couldn't see how I will be able to bear this.

I dressed up before I went to the theater, looking at myself in the standing mirror in my room full of crazy things, but without the light on, for the sunset came in the windows. The cushions on the floor were blood-red. I dined at the Faculty Club with a friend and tried to read or talk in the lounge, but a fatality seemed to attend every topic we brought up or picked up; all the impressions of the University I had ever had kept presenting me, like the works of some gigantic and delicate clock, with the same thing, so that I finally said I had to go. But I sat there half an hour after she went, feeling one shock after another of lateness and telling myself I must get up; the girl in the vinyl dress passed through the lounge and I said I had to get up; and finally Bill Beam found me there and took me backstage. From the box office to the backstage entrance there is a sort of labyrinth, and in this passage he tried to kiss me, with all the *expertise* of a grown-up man, sliding his hand underneath the front of my dress; and I let him because I liked it. I stood still, pinned in a corner, with my heart pounding. I said, "No, no, that's enough; somebody'll come." He said, "Why are you so pretty tonight?" and I said—but I forget, something about giving him courage to face the little monsters. He shook his head. "Yes, I hate them, don't I!"

"All but one," he said.

A group of girls was singing in a chorus in the stairwell, dressed in ribbons and aprons as if they were going to play a travelogue of the Balkan countries; we passed them. I saw legs folding and straightening like pocket rules where the dancers went up and down in a corner, holding on to the banister. "This theater!" said Bill. The shop and greenroom were combined in one. At one end somebody had opened the double iron doors (the back wall was covered with old flats twenty, thirty feet high) and two students were carrying in long, swaying boards; outside it had begun to snow. Painted faces rushed past me, elongated, flattened, with white lines drawn under and above the eye to make eyes a foot long. Someone was sitting with her head thrown back at the long shelf that served for a make-up counter while someone else operated on her face. A gust of wind blew snow in through the iron doors and unsettled the singing girls; one stood up in her ribboned petticoats and looked over the banister while the operatee at the shelf sat up and waved to me. The whine of a circular saw began in the shop area. Under the writhing, mulberry lips and the fright wig was an old friend with whom I chatted, in the middle of this hothouse, while the big iron doors opened and shut (someone was apparently unloading a truck) and snow blew in from outside. It was unpleasantly tropical by the mirrors. I went over to the doors and watched a set piece coming in, some kind of golden throne or wagon covered with gold and white crepe flowers. Outside the snow fell from a vast, dropping hush; I could see the edge of the wall and a few feet of courtyard, already white. The buildings would be half blotted out in the quadrangle. I turned back; I saw a section of colors, faces, backs, in a pie wedge like the corner of a garden full of blooms. There he was. One side of his face was painted blue, for some extraordinary reason.

"Do you—" I said, *"Oh, do you—!"*

But I didn't.

He apologized for not being all blue.

He sat down on a prop setup under a high, skinny-Minny window; putting out one hand, he helped me to sit, too, and then he commenced staring at me severely, very severely indeed, as if it had come into his head that I needed correction. I wondered if I had unconsciously been telephoning him and then dumbly hanging on the line, breathing hard, for he seemed to be getting that kind of call: nobly concentrated, frowning, having been interrupted in the middle of Western Philosophy 101—"What's that? What do you want? *Who is this?*" and the cozy rasping at the other end. Our heads were so close that anyone would have thought we were talking. I was just about to venture on a few commonplaces when the overture struck up outside—very Graustarkian, very gay—with relief he rocketed off his seat, with a mumble which I did not catch, and toward the stage door. I, carefully composing my face lest I should cry and somebody should see me, tingling with shame from head to foot, skirted the wall and made my way out into the house, standing for a moment in back of the heavy door and looking through the thick, little, submarine window, and then pushing at it and going in.

The curtain had just risen. The girls were picking daisies. Soon a mountaineer came in and began to sing; then they all ran off. I lost the thread after this. The orchestra was going rather badly. It seemed to be a folk play; there was a wedding in a village square and then a scene in a forest. A friend of Bill's assistant, a very nice girl, came up and whispered to me that somebody could give me a ride to town during the intermission; did I want to come? I said I would. On stage the university dancers were dancing and amid the tree trunks of a pine forest. There was thunder and lightning and the dancers vanished; through the tree trunks appeared a spectral castle, bathed in green light. In front of this was Alan, advancing toward the audience. The castle was a projection; now it shrank visibly and still he walked forward, walked without moving a step, as the castle dwindled away and silhouettes of trees crossed it. The trees faded into transparency and behind them appeared starlit meadows, mile upon mile; still he glided forward as if under water, expressionless, untiring, inhumanly remorseless. There was a burst of applause from the few people in the audience. The curtain was down.

I was alone in the car, waiting for the driver, when he thrust his arm through the open car window and grabbed my hand hard, breathless and shivering as if he had been running. He said calmly, "You haven't seen the whole thing." He was in his shirt sleeves.

"I was doing *marcher sur place*," he said, "and I wanted to talk to you, but they said you'd left. The last performance is Saturday. I wanted you to see the whole thing. Bill says there's a party, I wanted to. . . ."

Here he opened the car door and got in.

"You've got to see the whole thing," he said, taking my hand; "I want you to. I have to go back. Goodbye," and sitting next to me and holding my hand, shivering violently, he looked at me very seriously, nodded to himself two or three times, and got out of the car, letting in a gust of snow and waving to the driver, who had just appeared on the theater porch.

The driver asked me if I were going to the cast party Saturday night.

I said I wasn't.

But I did. He was there with his girl. It was a rehearsal room, bare, with two metal bridge tables in the middle and cartons piled along the sides. I stood with the crowd between us, miserably smoothing my hair and my dress; Bill was hugging everybody; then the two of them saw me and came over, and he said, "You look elegant." "Thanks, dear nephew," I said. The little girl thought that was funny. "The Princesse de Noailles," I said, "wrote to a famous actor at the age of seventy-three, addressing him as *'cher neveu'* and advising him above all *never to follow anybody else's good advice.'* He exploded noisily and delightfully, he roared, he said he was going to tell that to Bill, and went across the room to get us all a drink. The young lady, who was peering at me in a friendly way from under her very long bangs, said shyly that she thought the play had been very, very good and twisted a rope of pink wooden beads that hung down in front of her unfitted dress. She was wearing black stockings, both for adventure and utility, and probably to look serious, like a sheepherder or a sailor. I said I thought the acting had been good, and she colored a little. I asked her if she did any acting, and she said no but she had thought of it and wondered if she should try out for anything. He brought back two full paper cups and said Bill was getting "absolutely out of hand." The girl looked shocked and then giggled. I asked her if she would mind lending him to me for a few minutes, as there were some professional secrets I wanted to talk to him about, and she shook her head shyly and eagerly. "She wants to criticize my acting," he said loftily. I led him to another corner of the room, near a water fountain where people kept breaking in between us, where I crossed my arms on my chest and leaned against the wall, leaning forward, too, guarded both without and within.

"Well?" he said quizzically.

"Well, now," I said, and then again, "well, now, I've done something for you and I want you to do something for me." He looked uncomfortable. "I mean," I said, over the noise that the party made and the noise that my heart made, "that I've done something for you by coming here—and I don't like it, you know, never mind why—and now I want you to go somewhere during vacation with—for me."

"Is Mr. Beam coming?" he said politely. He was looking at the floor.

"No," I said, and then suddenly losing my voice, "I didn't ask him."

"All right," said he, looking straight ahead, both hands in his pockets.

"And I'm giving you the tickets because I always lose them," I said, pushing them into the hand he had barely taken out of his pocket, my own trembling quite visibly. Then we parted. I heard him say to his girl, "Oh, nothing." I caught sight of myself in the glass covering an antique theater poster on the way downstairs: as beautiful as the face of a witch imprisoned in the cave of a mirror, floating over my black dress like some kind of astonishing, disembodied, powdery substance, as beautiful as the lady in the old play, "The Face That Heaven Never Gave Me."

We went to the circus, in New York.

I met him on Eighth Avenue, outside the great arcade; he had come with divine lightness through the crowd, as if everything were going to fly away; then he said very soberly and politely that he was *very fond of circuses*. He wanted to read the *Burgtheater von Dresden* poster with the sketch of an aerialist on it and the list of performers; he told me that American circuses always opened in the spring; and then he stopped in front of a luggage display with luggage arranged fanwise in graduated sizes like families of recorders: the plain, the cut-velvet, the stippled, and the lightweight, every size, from one I could not have lifted to the "overnight bag" that nobody ever buys. "I've never seen that stuff on the street," he said of the velvet. I said, "Didn't you know? Nobody ever buys things in these stores," and he grinned mischievously, holding out his arm, which I took with a slight, smiling shiver. We went through miles of concrete corridors and stairs, I holding his arm lightly and looking up into his face, like the inveterate eater whose guilty cravings make other people sick: bonbons, stuffed prunes, liqueur chocolates, date-nut pie, strawberry-marshmallow tarts. He was lovely. He was telling me about all the circuses he had ever been to. We sat in the first balcony at one end of a horseshoe, overlooking a wilderness of lights and ropes, and when the lights came up and the band began playing, I didn't look at the ring, but at him. He had to put on his glasses. I saw, in his face, no reflection at all of the fake diamonds, the splendor, the peculiar artiness of a European circus, the overwhelming odor of animals and sweat, and under that the smell of blood.

I said, "You like it."

He merely nodded. In the far ring a lady was releasing doves dyed pink and blue, which came back and settled on a sort of wheel she held in her hand. In front of us dogs in collarettes and girls in tights turned somersaults over each other with wonderful vulgarity. I remembered a scrub circus I had seen once in Georgia, in which a bear trainer had been rather badly mauled, and the slow, regular plunging of the bareback rider's horse around and around the ring—while the man's face was contorted with effort and the sequins on his white jacket flashed and flashed.

"I can't help it," said Alan, and began to laugh. He turned, leaning on one elbow, and chuckled helplessly to himself. "It's idiotic," he said. I believe this was the moment when a dozen or eighteen clowns were getting out of one car; on the other hand, they may have been setting fire to a house or chasing each other—one a patient and one a nurse with breasts made of red balloons—

around the perimeter of the outer ring to conceal the fact that machinery as ponderous as a derrick was being driven out, or dragged out, or rolled out into position. Then a tiger tamer backed into the clumsy embrace of a tiger. A woman supported on her forehead a pole which supported another woman. People climbed into a pyramid and did modern dance leaps on a board held by those at the top. A tightrope walker went up a forty-five-degree angle in such skittish, erratic bursts of speed that I had to shut my eyes and dig my fingernails into my palms. The animal acts all followed each other, then the aerialists, then the trapeze artists, all in such a blaze of bad color that I thought I was falling asleep: cloaks and high heels, feathers, elephants' silk coats, very Roman, very strenuous, the machinery right out on the stage, tons of glitter, and yet it was queerly moving all the same.

Princess So-Fa-La was on the high trapeze.

A little white orchid of a woman, she swung near the top of the tent, forty feet above the ring.

Then, like a paper flower someone had carelessly tucked in much too high, she hooked her knees over the bar and swung back and forth with her head and arms hanging down like a doll's.

Then, using pure ballet *pointe,* she threw her head back over the steel bar of the trapeze, pointed her arms straight down and swung serenely back and forth over nothing as if she had been tacked on or pasted, with no support at all but the hollow in the back of her neck, a very slight-looking, elegant Princess, born in the jungles of Burma: delicate, beautiful, and incomparably brave. We all applauded like mad, hoping she'd stop.

And then the lights were on, the performers were gone, the band was getting up to go. It was all over.

In the French coffeehouse he went to look at the paintings on the walls, which I had seen many times before, and at a row of little flags they had in front of a miniature of the United Nations. He came back shaking his head. He said, "Oh, God!" and looked at me, looked at the back of the menu, then looked at me again severely, hooking one finger in his glasses as if he were going to take them off. Then he abruptly began to explain how he had done his role in Bill's play, what he had done with his hands, the miming, all the development that went into it. He said he wasn't satisfied with it. I said I wasn't satisfied, either. Frowning, he asked me if I had talked the role over with Bill.

"No!" I said.

Then he leaned forward, very serious, and said:

Did I think there was any good in the role?

Did I like it?

Did I like him?

Did I think he ought to study acting?

I said yes to all of them.

"Do you . . ." he said, but he didn't finish it; with a kind of all-over shiver and a faint smile he added, "I'm afraid I have to go. I have to catch my train."

"Oh, are you going back tonight!" I said, "but you still have time; see me home to my friend's," and being a good New Yorker, he said he would. In the cab we talked about the Royal Ballet, clouds, housing, everything else. When we got there, he said again that he had to go, but less vehemently this time—he was looking with admiration at the apartment building. It stands half in Chinatown like a gigantic chess-piece with odd-shaped knobs and shelves sticking out of it; the moon was shining on the bare concrete and the bare earth it stood on, and it was a beauty. I said, "Come up and see the inside." He hesitated for a moment.

"Very well," he said finally, word for word, *un caballero muy formal.* "Very well."

My friend—who writes children's books under the name of Aminta—keeps an old maid's apartment, full of dried ferns, chintz throws, and "artistic" ornaments: paper toys suspended from the ceiling, shaky heirloom furniture, old china. Aminta's fireplace is filled with oak leaves. I believe he had never in his life seen anything quite as eccentric; he was standing over the fireplace in his hat and coat with his hands clasped behind his back when he said, "Won't we disturb her?"

"Oh, no," said I a bit breathlessly, "she's in Europe," and slipping the hat off his head like a sleight-of-hand artist, I bore it into the bedroom as he turned round in astonishment. I half expected him to say, "Hey! Give that back!" but when I came back in and held my arms out for his coat he gave it to me docilely, only giving with it a look I could not fathom, turning to a book of sketches on the mantelpiece and examining them one by one. I brought Aminta's cognac from the bedroom and poured out two glasses on her little table: a Japanese lacquered table, heirloom glasses. He joined me on the couch. With the slowness of underwater swimmers we toasted one another and drank, but my hands were shaking so that I could not hold my glass. I put it down and tried to think of something to say, something provocative, something witty, something ambiguous, but not a word came to my lips and instead I found myself loosening the pins in my hair, shaking it down, desperately combing it out with my fingers until it fell clear to my knees, shivering a little and imparting to it the slightest evanescent motion, the slightest stir. I said, with an attempt at lightness, "I'll have to cut it after all." He remained silent. I looked at him, although I could hardly bear to do it, and saw that he was blushing slowly and deeply, enduring wave after wave of some profound and painful emotion; he shrugged a little and put down his glass, then turning to me with the look of a man under a grim sentence of some sort, he put one arm around my back, grasped my wrist with the other, and kissed me hard on the mouth.

He apologized immediately afterward.

Then he started to say something about getting his hat and coat, turned aside, turned back again—grasping me by both wrists—muttered in a low voice, "I don't care if you like it or not!" and kissed me again, so hard that I lost my breath, so hard that I really couldn't stand it. I pushed him away with a small struggle—I don't think he knew that I wanted him to go on—and tried to open the buttons down the neck of my dress; he helped me, our fingers trembling and colliding with each other; then he repeated the kissing process on the hollow of my neck and shoulder, giving himself to the swell below that for several hundred heartbeats. He came up a little dazed. He said simply, "I wanted this, do you know?" and then, calmly, "I haven't done this very much." He picked up his glass, looked into it for a moment, and then drank the rest of the cognac; tears came into his eyes. He put the glass down and slipped off his shoes and jacket; I helped him with his tie, a little embarrassed, and pulled off my own dress, and my slip, and shoes and stockings—what a lot of clothes there are! I had carried something in my purse for weeks, out of pure idiot persistence, but he had already taken care of that when we slid into each other's arms on the couch, quite naked, our flesh whispering together as if he were talking from head to foot, my beautiful, young male. He went to work blindly, tunneling like a mole, and came much too soon, groaning and jerking with the face of a man on the rack, as if he were felling a whole virgin forest. I held him until it was over. Then, "Oh God, I'm sorry!" he said. I put my arms around him. We lay together on the couch for a while. Then, with a somber face, he got up and went in to make loud and angry splashings in the bathroom, and when he came back in, he wanted to get into his clothes; but I pulled him down next to me and began to frog-march my fingers up and down his spine, then to tickle him delicately and nip him until he grabbed for me, and finally to caress him outright: those parts of us that we don't speak about but that we privately hold the dearest, the loveliest, and the best of friends. He took me in his arms again. This time I was excited enough to let go almost at once. I passed out at the climax, crying I don't know what, opening my blurred eyes for a moment on the side of his face and ear that shocked me with their novelty, their exquisite beauty, exclaiming something about "never—never" and sinking back into a faint convulsion, another, hearing him sigh, falling asleep.

He carried me into the next room, into Aminta's double bed, and twice again in the middle of the night decided he wanted more. The last time I was hardly awake; I spread out beneath him in sleep as a huge hand rotated somewhere in me, squeezing my entrails, and the bed roared and overturned once—twice. I wonder that there was anything left of us in the morning. A very feast of unreason.

I woke up earlier than he did and did not at first recognize his

face on the pillow except for a kind of immediate trembling movement toward him in my thighs; it was not the same man I had
united myself with four times the night before. He was sleeping
with his head thrown back and his arms spread loosely to either
side, as if in the act of enjoyment. I slipped out of bed and into the
living room. On the back of the bathroom door Aminta kept a full-
length mirror, and in this mirror I happened to see myself as I went
by: the points of my body poking forward, my buttocks trembling
lasciviously, completely nude. I felt as if my head had been ampu-
tated. I even fancied that there was someone at the outside door
and that if I opened it some fully-dressed, passing man would seize
me by the naked arm, first bend me backwards over the stair rail,
and then throw me violently down on the landing, where I would
lie huddled together, my neck broken, my nipples pointing straight
up into the grayish air, like some rosy and indecently exposed
eighteenth-century engraving or a message in peculiar Morse. And
yet waking up to see a man's face on the pillow next to mine is no
absolute novelty for me. My head began to ache. I quickly collected my clothes, scattered over the floor and chairs, and held
them to my breast for a moment; then I stood and stared around at
Aminta's apartment with its racks of magazines, its ferns, its
rickety little tables, a spinster apartment so full of things, like a
little world or a little shell. It had begun to snow outside, grayly, as
if the dawn were merging into an indistinguishable blur, and
through the filmy curtains I could see tar-paper roofs, brick chim-
neys, crooked, small walls on the tops of tenements like the Great
Chinese Wall seen crawling over the plains from a hundred miles
up. I was hanging by my neck, like the Burmese lady. I stood
naked in the middle of the rug, thinking that we would have to go
back to the same school, would see each other sometimes by accident at evening affairs, that I really could not stand it. I got into my
clothes and sat down on Aminta's couch; then I put my valise by
the door, got out my keys, took her notepaper from the wall
shelves hung under an illustration for a Victorian fairy tale, and
wrote on it *Will Not Be Back; Do Not Wait*. I put this on the
kitchenette table.

But when he came in an hour later I was still sitting on the couch, my shoes off, my knees drawn up under my chin, shivering.

He smiled slowly, radiating warmth, one beautiful, self-contained, naked, young man, his eyes very fresh, a little mussed up with sleep.

"There you are," he said.

And here I am.

OLD PICTURES

When she was seventeen, my mother used to climb trees. She would leave everybody, shin up one like a squirrel, and disappear.

I keep a picture of her from that time, dangling a bunch of grapes above her mouth. It must have been a popular pose, for she has shown me a picture of her sister with the same bunch of grapes, and then she and her sister's boy friends—all four faces crowded together and arms around each other's backs—and then a picture of herself staring into the camera with her black brows and straight black hair. She wore a dress with no waist and an uneven, scalloped hem. She used to be known as the girl who read Shelley.

I have kept quite a few photographs of my mother at around that age, some showing her with that ever-recurring book of Shelley's poems, one eating grapes, on a hike, in a canoe on a lake ("myself and friend in a canoe, summer 1926") and one where she read in front of the camera with her knees drawn up under her book, her hair swinging across her cheek, her profile half dissolved in light—or age, perhaps; I don't know which. Many times I sit in the foreground (carefully keeping within the frame of the photograph) to watch my mother feed squirrels in faded sepia, or climb on a rock in the distance, or parade her nieces and nephews along the shore of a pond. Less often I dream that I am back there, my head against the water that drops from moss to rock to moss again, and the sound of dripping, falling water that resolves itself (when I open my eyes) to the tap of the bath three inches from my face or the bathroom faucet, not quite shut. Sometimes I dream in good earnest and then I run through woods in pelting rain, soaked to the skin, until I find a shallow cave and in one corner of it—ruined by the water—a copy of Shelley's *Poems* and a lost handkerchief. Everywhere I go she has been before me. She knows the cave in the woods, the exile's raft on the sea under flamingo-colored clouds, and the terrible way hearth, home, husband and all can waver and bend in a moment, like a photograph gone bad. I like to think of her at seventeen, vanishing up into a tree. I like to see her sitting there in her leafy tent on a miraculously provided little platform, her knees under her chin, her Shelley open to a favorite page on which she has written something profound like, "How true ! ! !" and her black, nymph's brows bent not on me, not on any watcher with a camera, but on something invisible and beyond. As I watch her I become her; I have luckily forgotten to bring paper and pencil so I need not take notes on my book just yet. I need do nothing. And if I'm wise and never come down (though they are looking for me down below), if I sit and wait, watch and look, but silently, silently, I may in the end see what I think my mother saw—the green leaves tossing in the distance as a ship tosses far away at sea, and the noise of a hundred thousand million leaves thrashing one against the other as finally—the way a ship breaks through spray —there breaks in through the leaves (and with it a wide gust of air and light) finally, unquestionably, without a shadow of a doubt—

I. VISITING

It's not the country, actually; it's land three-quarter-acre zoned in the suburbs with a cement bridge that looks like a crumbling aqueduct, overgrown with vines. The station is beyond this.

First we went to the Cloisters in Manhattan, away from the children; we hung in the air above the Palisades, a terraced garden winding back and forth like a storybook, with every so often signs among the plants reading:

> Let no one say and say it to your shame
> That all was beauty here until you came.

I want four voices: tenor, soprano, bass, and trumpet. Baroque trumpet.

She said she didn't know what she'd do if she didn't get away from the children.

Tenor and soprano are very close together; down below the bass revolveth something in his own mind. Eddington describes the human consciousness as an electric loom which perpetually weaves and re-weaves itself, flashing back and forth, lights-on, lights-off, never stopping. Now my three singers are talking to each other, back and forth as people do, echoing each other's questions:

I said.

He said.

What did we say?

I say.

We said.

I said what.

And the basso, ponderous as a radar scope, slowly reveals something new each time round, wiping out, wiping out. . . . The air over the Palisades is ringing. They never stop for breath any more than what keeps us alive; now the bass and the soprano cross each other, she going down and he going up; each occupies the former place of the other and repeats the same pattern, insistently, vehemently, their voices rising, eye to eye.

"And *I* said—" says Lispeth.

My soprano, dressed in a Valkyrie's war-helmet with cow's horns, vanishes in a trumpeting bray over the George Washington Bridge.

Lispeth has ground out from the mill between her thighs a husband, three children (effectually snared), a home, and three quarters of an acre of cleared land, like the mill that grinds out salt at the bottom of the sea. Vassar-educated, advertising-trained, a poetess at seventeen. At night, outside her house, in the summer nights, you can hear, if you listen, something much slower, much older, the trees respiring. Heartbeats.

Tha thump.

Tha thump.

Though these trees are young, set out by the planners. Different things. Perhaps the earth moving. The continents floating, drifting. . . .

I always think of the dotted quarter note as post-Baroque, particularly in human relations. Hellish Schubert! All those impossible yearnings, those shameless, irresponsible, melodic twinings, so simple, so depraved, such postures for which there is no definitive performance, for someone can always dig out a little more, horribly draw out a little more, because the song has no bottom, it is really a hole opening on nothing, and outside Lispeth's living

room window is nothing, everything, terrible yearnings, irreg-
ularities, horrible intimations of immortality. Inside, Tiffany lamps
and three children.

Walking back to the station, we pass a crumbling aqueduct
overgrown with moss, old water-stains, bushes clinging to the
sides. This used to be useful, used to carry water before New York
was a city, quite possibly before Alexander. . . .

My trumpet mounts the scales and descends with immortal and
transcendent regularity. Here, it says, is the achievement of mankind, the scales, the mathematical scales, the pyramids, Newton's
book on optics, here (it says) is something invisible, impalpable
and divine. Lispeth stands in her maroon, side-closing coat lined
with red fox fur, the best in the world, which also is on the cuffs
and collar, with its belt, with her swinging, cut, black hair, and
with her little kid shoes, the best in the world. She is a picture. She
is waiting here, hung up in the air above the river on such a beautiful day, a young girl waiting like a picture to make happy everyone who sees her, swung between heaven and earth, glittering,
brilliant, brimful of possibilities. She is no longer young. She
puckers her face at me and complains and complains. Inside there
are several dozen Madonnas, several dozen heavens. We are closer
to heaven here. The river below is metallic blue, wrinkled, vast
and heavy, like a vein of the planet. A steamer makes a stroke
through the water like the stroke of a finger through clay.

Thought there was no such thing as love, got married. City's full
of thirty-year-old divorcees (I'm one). Lispeth's thirty-three.

Ivy, berries, rosemary, little paths, signs, benches. My tenor
cries out, stretching his voice to the breaking point, to the edge of a
knife blade, vibrating as keenly as an electric blade, a heraldic sign,
a scarlet heraldic emblem, *Ich liebe dich, Ich liebe dich.*

(Ah! something older . . . like the squeeze of a heart, something
and then a silence, a natural recurring of something and then a
silence. Something slower. And then a silence.)

That most virile voice.

"You'll come again?" she says.

II. VISITING DAY

She greeted me at the door in bell-bottomed slacks, between pink and some darker rose shade, in velour, and a white crocheted blouse that left her arms bare. I said "Lispeth, you look seventeen."

She said, "I know; it's offensive," and then "Don't come in," and she vanished and yelled something up the stairs about the children. When she came back she was carrying *The New York Review of Books* under her arm and her cut, black hair swung over her face as she walked, like heavy black silk that has been cut short and had something sprayed on it to change its texture and make it hold. She smiled when she saw me. At the door we had sketchily kissed the air, with that effusion of feeling that vanishes exactly as it blossoms and leaves one embarrassed and holding nothing; now she sat down on the couch just as she had at school, the same flounce, the same bottom and round arms, the same short fingers. She was looking for something in the sheets of the *Review*. I leaned back gingerly and rubbed my hand against the expensive, upholstered material of the couch, I looked around at the drapes, the built-in, white bookcases they had moved from the city, the cushions. Lispeth began to talk vehemently about something in the *Review*, some article criticizing a new writer, and she went on in this way for several minutes, saying at the end of it, "I don't like this."

"Women can't write, women can't draw," I said, an old joke.
She laughed. She had been smoking a cigarette, wrinkling her face
and trying to back off when the smoke got into her eyes, as always; now she ground it out carefully in their big, brass ashtray
(for parties) and jumped off the couch. She said, "I want to show
you my workroom." I followed her through the kitchen and up
the stairs to a little room off one of the children's; she had two
curtains and a desk piled high with calendars she had evidently
been sorting, and some sheets and children's toys on the floor. She
dropped into a chair and put her feet up on the bookcase. Outside
the window were tree branches, sky, and March wind; I looked
down just in time to see her Nanny escorting the children out the
backyard gate: a boy and two girls. One was young enough to be
in a carriage. "She is taking them to the park," Lispeth said as the
gate banged in the wind. She was flipping through the calendars. I
took out a small music notebook, which I always carry with me,
and made a few notations—I do this as these things come to me—
and looked up to see her pause and look at me. "Music?" she said.
She made a face as she said it, half wry and half quizzical. I nodded
and she swung her feet to the floor as I put my notebook away; she
said, "Come downstairs?" and got up and flipped off the light
switch. As we padded down the hall—the hall floor was carpeted
from side to side—she started to tell me about one of the children,
her son, and how odd it felt to have a boy baby. She kept taking
the waistband of her slacks between finger and thumb and pulling
it round as she talked, in a finicky, self-caressing sort of way. She
said Elick, whom I haven't seen in years, was going to teach at
Fordham or the New School next year and then they didn't know
what, perhaps Columbia, perhaps the West Coast; she twisted her
neck to look back at me on this last, blinking a bit, and then remarked "I have to get *my* degree," turning back round and de-
scending the stairs, flounce by flounce, with her hand on the
banister railing. In the kitchen she made coffee in a fearsomely
elaborate coffeepot with several dials set into its base, and standing
next to it she told me, with many gestures and much mugging, an
extremely funny story about a Lesbian in the next block. Pouring

the coffee out, I spilled it. "Oh, don't bother," she said and blotted
it up with a paper towel, which she then threw in the sink. She
said they had just gotten Dutch enamelware and I could see it on
the wall; and then she took down one pot after another to show
me, tapping the inside with her fingernails for the way it was supposed to sound: almond-shaped nails, buffed colorlessly and
creamed around the edges. I said the pots were lovely. She said,
"Everything ends up in the paper towels." We sat down to our
coffee in what promoters call the breakfast nook, surfaces either
plastic or nylon and everything yellow, everything cheerful and
up-to-date. Lispeth sipped her coffee with the air of someone who
has had this little luxury too many times to make it count any
more; then she looked at me with a queer mixture of indifference
and attention, as if she were forcing herself to speak, and said off-
handedly:

"Would you like some brandy in it?"

I said I wouldn't mind. She hopped up and went into the living
room for it, returning with a very good brand, which she stood on
one of the counters next to us. Everything in the place shone, the
tops of the counters dully, as if they were covered with laminated
board, and the table brilliantly, in glass. The breakfast dishes were
still in the sink. She stared absently out the kitchen window for a
moment, then came to herself and added the brandy to our cups,
upending the bottle rather abruptly and quickly flipping the top
back into place. She crossed her legs and swung the free foot back
and forth; I could see that she was wearing gold-colored, kid slippers. Then she said:

"What are you doing now?"

I said I was teaching and copying music.

"Very dull?"

"Well, yes."

She smiled in a superior way, not meant but merely nearsighted, as she always had. She said, "Do you remember a girl
called—?" and then she began to tell me what had happened to all
the people we had known in college: the girl who was still bum-
ming around Europe, the girl who had a job with *Mademoiselle*, the

girl who was living on the Lower East Side, the girl who was a social worker for the Department of Welfare, the girl who had become a free-lance writer. She spoke with great animation. When she had finished, she told me some genuinely horrifying things about her days in advertising, and then about people I hadn't known at school and events I had never found out about. She poured another slug of brandy into her coffee. "We got almost everything in Europe," she explained. She produced her smile again, with the tilted, chin-up face of someone trying to see out from under false eyelashes, the smile of a princess modeling clothes in the fashion magazines, the all-purpose social smile of those who can't see across a room. Lispeth's smile, we used to call it at school. She produced it again. "Do you remember Joan Walsh?" she said. "Joan Walsh is in a mental institution." She said she had gone to visit her the other day. She began to recite, in a tone almost like envy, some of the things Joan Walsh had said— "She's nutty," said Lispeth—and on the last crazy thing, with a heave and swing of her black hair, she picked up her cup, which was again empty, and the brandy, and said, "I want to show you the living room." "Take your cup," she said. She poured out a second for me and a third for herself. We went into the living room, past the carpeted stairs that reminded her (she said) of coming down at home on Christmas morning, and the fashionable fireplace and the mile-high white bookcases filled to the last inch. Lispeth pushed aside the drapes so I could get a look at the garden, all leafless trees and patches of snow; she almost dropped the bottle from the crook of her arm, and smiling vaguely, put it down on the leather-topped coffee table in front of the couch. She poured out a third for me and fourth for herself, talking about the house the way she used to talk about her unsuccessful love affairs when she got drunk at school: how much it cost to move, where the library was, where the train station was, how the children scuffed up the floor. Her voice took on odd turns and trills. She said, "Well, it's better than getting drunk in the kitchen, isn't it?" and laughed with surprising freshness. Leaning back in her chair, she lit a cigarette and began waving it about as she talked, about our triumphs at college, and the college buildings, and the lawns and trees late at night in the summer, and all the things she remembered. She said, "Do you remember?" She said she had been in love with an instructor. She said she had considered telling his wife. She laughed. Rising to her feet, she urged me to feel the material of the drapes; she said Elick had picked out a Tiffany glass lampshade for the dining room; she went along the corridor and up the stairs with the bottle in one hand. I followed her, even though the room moved mysteriously when I got up, up the stairs and into her workroom, where she rummaged in the desk drawers and found another glass, through the children's rooms, where she quickly swept toys and spare clothes aside so that I might not see them, and into the bedroom. She was chatting gaily. She told me about the difficulties they had had getting the furniture delivered. She parted the white curtains and we looked out into the street, which was already beginning to get dark with a lone newspaper boy pedalling along and a couple of children turning the corner of the opposite house. Inside it was hard to see. She poured herself another drink—she was carrying the glass she had found in her workroom desk—and descended the stairs with the bottle in one hand, the glass in the other, sipping as she did so, very leisurely and surely. She said that now we were going to see the garden. I said, "No Lispeth, I don't think—" back through the dining room where she stopped to admire the Tiffany glass lampshade, hung over the table by a chain, and the kitchen. She pushed open the back door and stepped out into the garden while I watched from the doorway; with her bare arms and neck she walked around and around the garden, talking, telling me about the best things. The sky was still light and the patches of snow shone as if they had been phosphorescent. She had cleared the snow off a sundial and set the bottle on it; now she sat down on the naked springs of a lawn chair that was out there without its cushion; then she got up and again and leaned on the sun-dial, reaching for the bottle. I said, "Lispeth, come in." She was almost in silhouette against the sky. She picked up the bottle and walked toward the house with the little flounce she had always had; and then as I backed away to let her come in, she slipped on a patch of ice at the foot of the steps. I could almost have caught her. There was a bit of something on the edge of the step and Lispeth was lying in the driveway. Down the drive the sky was banded green, blue, then purple. I tried to find the telephone in the kitchen and couldn't, I almost fell over something; then I got my coat from the living room and put it over her. I went in again and found a board with doctors' bills, notes, lists of things, little bits of paper stuck all over it and underneath, the telephone. It was yellow with a yellow pencil by it, everything that matched. I couldn't find their address book so I called the police; then I went round to the hall and the dining room and upstairs to their bedroom to find her pocketbook. I thought she had left it on her bed or in the living room but I had to come down again, back into the kitchen, past so many nice things. The address book was under the telephone. I found Elick's number at work and called him, looking at my reflection in the dark window of that beautiful room where she had stood so many times in the same way. Ordering things. That lovely, awful house. I waited there through the little buzz, through the rings and while they got him, and then said, I don't know why, "Elick, I've gotten a divorce." Then I looked around again, at my reflection again, at the house like coming down Christmas morning.

I said: "Your wife has had an accident."

OLD THOUGHTS, OLD PRESENCES

THE AUTOBIOGRAPHY OF MY MOTHER

I'm an I.
Sometimes I'm a she.
Sometimes I'm even a he.
Sometimes I'm veryvery I.
Sometimes I'm my mother.

I was visiting friends in Woodstock; you may find it surprising that I met my mother there for the first time. I certainly do. She was two years old. My mother and I live on different ends of a balance; thus it's not surprising to find that when I'm thirty-five she's just a little tot. She sat on the living room rug and stared at me, with her legs bent under her in a position impossible to anyone but a baby. Babies might be lobsters or some other strange form of life, considering what positions they take up. A little light tug at the ornamental tassel of my shoe—not apologetic or tentative, she feels both modest and confident, but she has small hands. "What's that?" she says.

"That's a tassel." She decamped and settled her attention on the other shoe. "And what's *that*?"

"Another tassel." This baby has flossy black hair, a pinched little chin, and round pale-green eyes. Even at the age of two her upper lip is distinctive: long, obstinate, almost a chimp's. I think she thinks that every object has its own proper name and so—without intending to—I made her commit her first error. She said: "That's *a tassel*. That's *another tassel*." I nodded, bored. She's of the age at which they always take off their clothes; patiently, with her own understanding of what she likes and what's necessary to her, she took off all of hers: her little sailor dress, her patent leather shoes, her draggy black cotton stockings. It's only history that gave her these instead of a ruff and stomacher. She practiced talking in the corner of the living room for half an hour; then she came over to me, nude, without her underwear, and remarked:

"That's a tassel. That's another tassel."

"Uh-huh," I said. Pleased at having learned something, she pondered for a moment and then switched them around, declaring:

"That's *another tassel* and that's *a tassel*."

"No, no," I said. "They're both tassels. This is a tassel and that's a tassel."

She backed away from me. I don't think she likes me now. Later that night I saw her scream with excitement when her father came home; he held the tail of her nightshirt in one hand and her brother's in the other; they both played the great game of trying to scramble away from him on all fours. My mother shrieked and laughed. Even at the age of two she's addicted to pleasure.

It'll ruin her.

You get stuck in time, not when you're born exactly, but when you "sit up and take notice," as they say, when you become aware that you have an individuality and there's something out there that either likes you or doesn't like you. This happens at about eighteen months. It isn't that you really prefer some other time, you don't know anything about that; you just back off (still crawling, perhaps), not shaking your head (for you don't know about that, either) just wary and knowing you don't like *that staircase* or *those visitors* or *this parent*. But what can be done about it? You're stuck.

It would be the same if you could travel through time but not through space.

Like this story.

At a Chinese restaurant: that is, a big room with a high ceiling and dun walls, like a converted gymnasium. Sepia-colored screens in front of the Men's and Ladies'. There is a fan of crimson coral over my mother's head and the chairs are high-backed and plain, the ultimate in chic for nineteen-twenty-five. My mother is nineteen. When I was that age I discovered her diary and some poems she had written; they didn't mention the restaurant but here she is anyway, having dinner with her best friend. I've looked everywhere in them to find any evidence that she was abnormal, but there's none. Nobody hugs anybody or says anything they shouldn't, and if there's any morbidity, that's gone too. My mother's written remains are perfect. At that time I wasn't born yet. I'm not even a ghost in her thought because she's not going to get married or even have children; she's going to be a famous poet. It was known then that you had to have children. It was a fact, like the Empire State Building I saw every morning out of the corner of my eye at breakfast (through the kitchen window). When you looked at childlessness in those days you didn't even realize that you had made a judgment, an inference from one set of conditions to another, you just *knew*.

I sat down imprudently at my mother's table.

Now I'm not as pretty as she is (I don't look a bit like her with my big behind and my buck teeth) but I'm much better dressed, and having been able to arrange my entry to suit myself, I can turn on to the full that bullying, leering, ironical boldness I adopt so easily with women; I place my well-cut suede coat, my smart gloves, my modernique pearl earrings, and Dior scarf directly in the track of my mother's green, beautiful, puzzled, nearsighted eyes. My mother didn't want me to sit next to her—she wanted her friend to come back. Strangers alarm her. When my mother is not with a good friend her spirits flag, she becomes vague, she loses control of herself and stares around the room, not because she wants to look at things but because she's diffused and anxious; it's a way of not meeting anyone's eye. She ducks her head and mutters (mannerisms that won't look so cute at fifty-nine). I want to protect her. Years later I'll hold her elbow when she crosses the street, suffer with her when she can't breathe in a crowd, but this is before she's perfected any such tricks, so I can only bare my teeth at her in a way that makes her uncomfortable. She essays a smile.

"Do you come here often?" I say and she draws on her gloves; that is, she wanted to draw on her gloves, began to move her hands as if she would do so, then didn't. She looked guilty. Mother has been taught to be nice to everybody but she doesn't want to be nice to me. Last week she wrote a romantic love story about a girl whose mouth was like a slow flame. When I'm eleven I will get felt up on my rear end in a crowd and will be too ashamed to run away. It may occur to you that the context between us is sexual. I think it is parental.

"Would you care to step outside?" I said politely. Mother demurred. Sitting there—I mean us sitting there—well, you might have taken us for cousins. I picked up the check and she suffered because she didn't know what to do. Her friend, who will never get here in time, forms in my mother's memory a little bright door. I dropped two anachronistic quarters on the tablecloth and then put my French purse back in my navy-blue suede bag, an easy forty-five dollars which she has never seen, no, not even in dreams.

"Do you mind if we chat?" I said; "Shall we have coffee?" and went on to explain: that I was a stranger in town, that I was new here, that I was going to catch a train in a few hours. I told her that I was her daughter, that she was going to marry eventually and after two spontaneous abortions bear me, that I didn't usually ask for favors but this was different.

"Consider what you gain by not marrying," I said. We walked out onto Columbus Avenue. "All this can be yours." (Be the first one on your block; astonish your friends.) I told her that the most sacred female function was motherhood, that by her expression I knew that she knew it too, that nobody would dream of interfering with an already-accomplished pregnancy (and that she knew that) and that life was the greatest gift anybody could give, although only a woman could understand that or believe it. I said:

"And I want you to take it back."

We were both eleven, on roller skates, skating toward Bronx Park with our braids flying behind us, but my mother was a little younger and a little slower, like my younger sister. I called her "Stupid."

In the first place I never borrowed it, in the second place it hasn't got a hole in it now, and in the third place it already had a hole in it when I borrowed it. I was going to show her all the kingdoms of the world. I wanted to protect my mother. Walking down Columbus Avenue in this expansive and generous mood—well, my mother didn't know what to make of me; like so many people she's puzzled by a woman who isn't beautiful, who doesn't make any pretense of being beautiful, and who yet flaunts herself. That's me. I asked my mother to tell me her daydreams, daydreams of meeting The Right Man, of being kept by an Older Woman, of inheriting money. Money means blood in dreams and blood means money. The autumn foliage in the park, for example, because the sun hadn't quite set. My mother was wearing a shapeless brown cloth coat that concealed her figure. It's very odd to think that this is nineteen-twenty-one. Overheard: I thought it would be different.

I told my mother that when women first meet they dislike each other (because it's expected of them) but that's all right; that soon gives way to a feeling of mutual weakness and worthlessness and the feeling of being one species leads in turn to plotting, scheming, and shared conspiracies. I said that if we were going to be mother and daughter we ought to get to know each other. As we walked on the stone-flagged park paths my mother's soul flew out from under my fingers at every turn, to every man who passed, a terrible yearning, an awful lack, a down-on-your-knees appeal to anybody in the passing scene. She didn't like my company at all.

"Do you know what I want you to do?" I said. "Well, do you?"

"Well, do you?" my mother echoed earnestly, looking up at me with her nymph's green eyes.

"Look here—" I said.

("Look here—")

I suppose you expect me to say that I listened to her artlessly simple chatter, that I confided in her, or that next she will be a big girl and I the little one, but if you expect me to risk her being older than me, you're crazy. I remember what that was like from last time. I told her all of it—the blood, the sweat, the nastiness, the invasion of personality, the utter indecency (except in middle age, except with money) and she only looked up at me as if she knew things, that girl. She didn't like me. The palisade looking out over the river. The mild October air. We stood arm in arm, like chums, watching the wakes of the boats in the water. She said I couldn't understand. She said with complete conviction:

"You were never young."

My mother, a matron of fifty but for some reason shrunk to the size of an infant and wrapped in baby clothes, is lying in her cradle. Swaddled, her arms at her sides, furious. Frowning—this is no way to treat a grown woman! She is about to wawl. I could leave her there and she'd die—dirty herself, starve, become mute and apathetic—she's just a baby. Maternally I take into my arms my fifty-year-old mother because you can't leave a baby, can you? and cradling her tenderly to my breast I start dancing around the room. She hates it. Screaming and red-faced. Maybe she wants a different dance. I change into a waltz, rocking her softly, and right-away, my goodness, the little baby is rocked into quiet, she's straightening her corrugated little brows, unwrapping the snaky moist curls that come finely from under her cap, smoothing her sulky little mouth. I guess she likes waltzing. If I didn't take care of her, how would she ever grow up to be my mother? It would be infanti-suicide, to say the least (if not something worse). When she stops crying I'll put her back into the cradle and sneak off, but there is command in that steely little face, those snapping little eyes, she stares up at me like a snapping turtle, making plans, telling me with her expression all the terrible things she's going to do to me when I'm the baby and she's the mother and I know she did them because I was there. *You keep on rocking me!* she says.

So we keep on waltzing around the room.

When I was a chid—
a child—
When I was a chidden child—

I came into my right mind at a certain age, I think I inherited it, so to speak, although they didn't allow me to use it until I was already fairly cracked. Coming home from the dentist at sixteen on winter evenings with the sky hot-pink and amber in the west and the wind going right through your coat; it's discouraging to find automata in the living room. Cars shooting by to cheery dinners, homey lights from the windows above the stoop. Mirages. Inside, a steamy kitchen, something horrible like an abstract sort of Frankenstein's monster made up of old furniture, plates, windows misted over. My mother, who is with us tonight, is also sixteen, and going this time under the name of Harriet (I think) which is a false name and no kin to the beautiful, imaginary playmate I had when I was four, who could fly and would write me letters with hand-painted stamps on them (cancelled). After coming all the way in the cold, to be in a room with no living persons in it. To be distressed. To feel superior. To hold myself in good and hard, to know what's possible and what's good for me. Little Harriet Shelley watches wide-eyed the intercourse of a real human family.

AUNT LUCY: No one would tell you the truth about yourself, Harriet, unless they loved you very much. I love you and that's why you can trust me when I tell you the truth about yourself. The truth is that you are bad all through. There isn't a thing about you that's good. You are thoroughly unlovable. And only a person who loves you very much could tell you this.

UNCLE GEORGE: Tell me all your troubles, but don't say a word against your aunt. Your aunt is a saint.

My mother sits listening to the radio, learning how to sew. She's making a patchwork quilt. Does she dislike her family? She denies it. She's not really going to grow up to be a poet. My mother has a mind like a bog; contraries meet in it and everything becomes instantly rotted away. Or her mind is a peat bog that preserves whole corpses. The truth is that I haven't the right to say what's going on in her mind because I know nothing about it.

She goes on sewing, gentle, placid, and serene, everything she should be. I told her that she could have any color car she wanted as long as it was black but even this failed to shake my soundless mother; One's Personal History Is Bunk, she might have answered me but didn't; she didn't even move away down the couch because my mother is not even mildly stubborn. Perhaps if she were not so polite she would say, "I don't know what you're talking about," but no, she's perfect, and when she raises her great, wondering, credulous, tear-filled gaze, it's not for me but on account of bad Mr. X in the kitchen, who is telling stories to Uncle George about the women who have jobs with him, for example, that their asses stick out:

Mr. X: — — — — — ass.

Uncle George: Mr. X is only joking, dear.

Mr. X: That's right. Don't be so sensitive. How can you go out and get a job some day if you're so sensitive? I don't have anything against the ladies who work with me. I think they're fine. I think you're fine, even though you're so senstive.

Aunt Lucy: See? Mr. X thinks you're fine.

Mr. X: I think your aunt is fine, too.

Uncle George: He thinks your aunt is fine, too, because he *likes* ladies.

Aunt Lucy: See? Mr. X is generous.

Uncle George: Even though your aunt Lucy is a fool.

To cut out those noises people emit from time to time. To be hard and old. To retreat finally. To be free.

"My parents love each other," says my mother, shaking out her work, malignancy in its every fold. She's a wonder. She really believes. I used to think I knew the form of the ultimate relation between my mother and myself but now I'm not so sure; there's that unbreakable steel spring in her accepting head; no longer can I come clattering up the King's highway on my centaur/centurion's hindquarters (half Irish hunter, half plow horse, gray, fat, lazy, name: Mr. Ed) and I no longer look down from my wild, crazy, hero-assassin's eminence at the innkeeper's little daughter in her chaste yet svelte gingham (with its decolletage) and her beautiful, spiritual, dumb eyes and her crumby soul.

"Do you," I said, "do you—tell me!—oh do you—believe me!—*do you*—DO YOU—BELIEVE ALL THAT?"

"Yes," she says.

O if you only knew! says her face. Her hands, resting on their sewing, change their import: Life is so hard, hard, hard. An unspoken rule between us has been that I can hate her but she can't hate me; this breaks. (A day in the longed-for life: for once when my mother is carried across the crumbling battlements on the screen the audience laughs, they hoot when she wrings her hands, when she obeys her father's prohibition they howl, when she is seduced they screech, when it starts to snow and the hero walks on her face with his lovely black boots it's all over, and by the time she commits suicide, *there is nobody there.*)

"I think," says my mother thoughtfully, biting a thread, "that I'm going to get married." She looks at me, shrewdly and with considerable hatred.

"That way," she says in a low, controlled voice, *"I will be able to get away from you!"*

(When she was little my mother used to scare her relatives by asking them if they were happy; they would always answer, *"Of course* I'm happy." When I was little I once asked her if she was happy and she said "Of course I'm happy.")

Something that will never happen: my mother and I chums, sharing secrets, giggling at the dinner table, writing in each other's slambooks, going to the movies together. Doing up each other's hair. It's not dreadful that she doesn't want me, just embarrassing, considering that I made the proposal first. She would beam, saying sentimental things about her motherhood, anxiously reaching for my hand across the table. She was not wicked, ever, or cruel, or unkind. We'll never go skating together, never make cocoa in the kitchen at midnight, snurfing in our cups and whooping it up behind the stove. I was never eight. I was never eleven. I was never thirteen. The mind I am in now came to me some time after puberty, not the initiation into sex (which is supposed to be the important thing) but the understanding that everything I had suffered from as a child, all my queerness, all my neuroses, the awful stiffnesses, the things people scorned in me, that all these would be all right when I was an adult because when I was an adult I would have power.

And I do. I do.

Power gave me life. I like it. Here's something else I like: when I was twenty-nine and my mother—flustered and ingenuous—told me that she'd had an embarrassing dream about me. Did she expect to be hit? It was embarrassing (she said) because it was incestuous. She dreamed we had eloped and were making love.

Don't laugh. I told it for years against her. I said all sorts of awful things. But what matters still matters, i.e., my mother's kicking a wastebasket the length of the living room in a rage (as she once bragged to me she did) or striking her breast, crying melodramatically, "Me Martian! Me good! You Jupiterian! You bad!" (as she also did). Bless you! do you think she married to get away from me, the Lesbian love-object? I wasn't born yet.

It's immensely sweet of her to offer to marry me, but what I want to know is: do you think we're suited?

Don José, the Brazilian heiress—wait a minute, I'm getting them muddled up, that was the other one where I was the Brazilian heiress, this one's Don José and he's *Argentinian* and an *Heir*—anyway, his cruel smile undressed her with his eyes, I don't think I can go on writing like this, she said. Are you not woman enough to know? And the unfortunate sadist tossed his typewriter out the window. That is what they called working-girls in those days. My mother will never forgive me. For what? cried the incautious maid with the almond-blue eyes. Thank you, sir, I shall make the bed,

she sobbed. Only do not lay me in it; that will crease the counter-
pane and I will be fired. And your children, his mustache twitch-
ing, I have sworn to have them, have me first, no, have a shashlik;
there is blood on my dress.

Blood!

I have murdered the butler.

(A lively game of bed-to-bed trash filled the evening air as the
charming little summer-camp maedchen disemboweled the myth
and passed it gigglingly from hand to hand. Salugi! Gesundheit.
Thank you very much.)

What Every Woman Knows.

It is quite possible that none of this happened or has value; still I
wish life could have been different for my mother. But we're all in
Tiamat's lap, so there's no use complaining. In the daytime we
stand on Her knees, looking up at Her face, and at night She hides
Her face so we get uneasy. Our Father Witch (in whom I used to
believe) is very jealous of his name or it's a secret or it's too ugly (or
maybe he hasn't got any) but you can call Tiamat in any language
you want; she broadcasts Herself all over the place and She doesn't
mind kiddies pulling at Her skirt; call her Nyame and Tanit, call
her 'Anat, Atea, Tabiti, Tibirra. This is what comes of re-meeting
one's mother when she was only two—how willful she was! how
charming, and how strong. I wish she had not grown up to be a
doormat, but all the same what a blessing it is not to have been
made by somebody's hands like a piece of clay, and then he
breathed a spirit in you, etc., so you are clay and not-clay, your
ingredients fighting each other like the irritable vitamin pill in the
ad—what a joy and a pleasure to have been born, just ordinary
born, you know, out of dirt and flesh, all of one piece and of the
same stuff She is. To be my mother's child. (Your pleasures and
pains are your bellybutton-cord to the Great Mother; they prove
you were once part of Her.)

I asked, Why couldn't my mother have been more like You?
But She didn't answer. I felt something coming from Her. Times

She doesn't like me—I don't always like myself—but we're still the same stuff.

Change my life! I said.

Sorry, won't. Her fog veiled Her face (that is one of Her moods) and Her towns (which are the rings on Her fingers) grew ugly. Tiamat is talking. She spoke through me as in the Bible, that is I spoke, knowing the answer:

Am I my mother's mother?

On winter nights, when my mother and I were twelve, we would go out together with chocolate cigarettes and pose under street lights like little prostitutes, pretending that we were smoking. It was very glamorous. Now we do it in our cheap dresses, our tight shoes; my mother has waited for The Man all her life, that's why she had no time for me. In the beauty parlor, on the street, in the nursing home, waiting for The Man. We lean on each other, very tired, in our make-up, a sad friendship between us. We even hold hands.

Will you be my best friend? she says.

I say yes.

Will you live with me?

I say yes.

Will you sleep with me and wake with me?

I say yes.

Will you marry me?

I say yes.

All you need is love.

DADDY'S GIRL

... their sons' and brothers' need to
debase so totally all that was
previously sacred (Nature and
Women) in order to experience
themselves as divine, in order to
found a civilization based on their
own sacredness.

—PHYLLIS CHESLER,
"THE AMAZON LEGACY"
IN *WONDER WOMAN*

My mother's country: the body and garden of the Great Goddess,
fair, ornamental, tended; I can wander forever in Her lap under
the sun of Her face, in a cultivated place like the Botanical Gardens
of my childhood where everything is suffused with the divine personality, regal, wide, and lovely. Everything's here—pineapples
from Java, Norway pine, greenhouses like tropical igloos, the long
wide lawns, camomile meadows veiled with hair, lawns that look
like—and are—the dancing-grounds of angels.

The fatherland is another place.

If Mother is Being, Daddy is *nada*, the flaw, the crack at the
center of the universe, the illusion that implodes as you look at it,
the glittery thing you thought was real but it's made out of
nothing: seduction, emptiness, cold, the brightness of rooms without air. Terrible energy radiates from this. It's the state of being
falsified. I have a friend called Linda and Linda lives in this world,
not I; last autumn Linda and I were riding into the fatherland inside the big blue bell of a snowstorm—that light is a sign of
sorcery.

"Visit me?" says Linda. "I'll get a babysitter. I'll get divorced. I'll
get an abortion." Linda and I were riding on talking horses who
put their heads together and said nasty things about us; in all that
whirling whiteness there was not one kind word. Linda rode bad
sidesaddle. The familiar signs of the road swam by, humped shapes
buried indistinguishably under snow: murder, adultery, incest,

suicide. This is fairy-tale country. "I wonder what we'll find," says Linda. She, not I. Linda is what the French call *rondelet;* she's young, foolish, and sinfully pretty. She wipes the magic snow off her sandals and the cleft between her breasts; her shoulders and bosom are bare. She's all female. In my father's country I can never remember the motherland because my father's country has what's called *invalidation,* so although I know where I'm going I don't know why, or rather the reason I do know has a very hollow ring to it and I think I may have forgotten, i.e., confusion in the middle of the snowstorm.

Am I going there to be a governess?

Snow settles thickly on Linda's horn-rimmed glasses.

When I was very young—eleven or twelve years old—I walked into that light and recognized in it my personal destiny. I walked into my eleven-year-old's bedroom and saw the air turn blue between the frosted windowpanes—Jack Frost at work. It was very, very cold. My destiny is waiting for me outside this whirling glass ball. Up ahead is a flagged courtyard where I will get off my horse, blowing on my fingers and wishing I were a man; I'll gather up my skirts and crinoline and the little box that came with me from Miss Swithin's; I'll tie the crackling ribbons of my bonnet. Menstruation, Victoriana, marriage, anemia, women's troubles. I mustn't. Nursing my dead father. So many paintings in which a woman adores a dead male divinity. Pictures of domestic unhappiness. Hatboxes. Emily Brontë owned a square carnelian brooch, which she kept with manuscripts in a blue box. There are times Linda makes me throw up because she has no mind at all; I don't mean that she's mindless, actually, but her amazing bare buttocks are somehow always triumphant over her face; my poor friend has just a faint glaze of consciousness like the stuff they put on a ham, a constant innocent surprise (she's very trusting), a perpetual temptation to forcing her. And she has enormous stamina; she can live through anything—beat her with a padded coat hanger and minutes later she's fresh and rosy. I have been through so many dramatic scenes with Linda; she's in a pretty gingham dress (neat but provocative) which they tear off, they put her into a stupid affair of velvet tags and leather straps which lets her body hang out all over; they hold her down, pulling her legs apart, and every man in the place rams himself into her (it's a treat) with ecstatic ohs! and ahs! (she, not I) bruising her, violating her, hurting her, using her, swilling up her round, round, round, jiggling, wretched parts with their exquisite slight taste of stupidity. She, not I.

She has no sexual thoughts. This is very important to understand. She's a dish of ice cream. Divinity hits her between the legs and dazes her. When she's in her bafflement, when the syrup of sacrifice rises from the modest temple (she, not I) in Linda's vagina and totally obscures her brain, then you can "have" Linda. You can even pretend to talk to Linda. I've done it myself, at least in imagination, beating her like a gong, as the saying goes, bursting with itchy, nervous, unhappy desire (that's the kind of appetite for her, isn't it?) and enjoying her thoroughly, crying out hot wench, hot wench, but if her temple is convulsed in ruin and horror, that still was not she. None of it gets into her head.

She has some vague feeling for jewelry.

(In my dreams I keep trying to get under the surface of the sea but can't; the waves miss me or the water dries up as I run into it, or I pretend I'm in it but know I'm not or the summery sea takes one look and revolts into reverse tsunami because it's not my personal destiny to get wet. I even row on dry land, in fact between the white lines painted on a parking lot, quite hopelessly.

(I have a secret taste for vomit.)

(Linda means "lovely." Doesn't it?)

(I want to breathe water and go home.)

When we reached the courtyard I saw that this time the scene of my personal destiny was to be a castle, a huge home. Fields cancelled, gone quite suddenly, replaced by a human habitation: the interaction of snow with stone, snow with glass. If you are born without the sacred totem, what do you do, what do you do? This basso profundo daydream dreamed by so many in the public prints that it must be true. The servants took my horse and I strode over the flagged yard (snow whirling into the flames of the torches on the wall, making them sputter), flicking my gloves against stone, wrought iron, massive oak, slapping my gloves with one hand against the palm of the other. I'm tall and ugly. I don't bother about what happens to Linda. Perhaps this place is a Home, although it's miles from anywhere; no need in that case to put iron bars on the windows. I used to escape from places like this nightly, met once by Linda (who in my dream was wearing Garbo slacks and an enormous sun-hat) in some sort of out-building, a shed or something. Somewhere in this very complicated blueprint is an apartment I know well: a pretty, middle-class place nicely decorated, with the living room floor (well-varnished and polished) buckling drastically over a sort of wooden hump, as if there were something heaving up from underneath, and a shack or lean-to built on the back with all sorts of gardening and carpenters' tools rusting away in it because it's so wet, the walls running with water and the floor covered with slime. The darkness here is, as usual, absolute, more an abstract condition or state of mind than the real thing. I follow a servant up the raw stone stairs—and we need servants, otherwise how could we be magnified—although I'm quite used to doing the floors myself on hands and knees. It (the servant, the thing, the person, the hunchbacked what-do-you-call-it) leaves me in a firelit room where the walls sweat moisture, it's so cold, and I sit down on a bench before that visual flame which warms nothing but the pupils of my eyes. There's a book on an inlaid table set right on the stone floor, a little book with a medieval, enamelled cross on the cover; I pick it up and read:

like a wastebasket

Who or what is like a wastebasket?

There's something in this book I don't like, so I put it down—you know, something that shocks me although I can't remember what. I don't like reading about such things: love, pain, a constricted unhappiness.

I had always wanted a man's griefs, his passions, his boredom, even, to be emptied into me.

There's something outside, beyond the archway of the door.

Refusing to feed my hidden vanity, my sulkiness, my individualism, X neglects everything I demand; he takes my head in his hands kindly but impersonally, because I'm only a means to a sensation, after all.

How can things be so vivid to the eye and so absent in every other way?

The two of them X and Y, fussing over me, but really through me or past me while standing me against that very expensive office desk, communicating with each other by means of my abused body like two executives talking into the dictaphone or over the secretary's head, casually enjoying a bit of fluff, so to speak, and my poor mind caught between, the victim of a little bit of vanity (my own), to be removed without mercy if I show the slightest symptom of having any sensations, so I must be as blank as the telephone or the rug.

What's the good of not reading the book if I can't help reading the book?

No tears of shame or joy. No sounds. I'll let it out inside, the only place they like it. As X, who is one zero, shoves me one way and talks over my dumb breasts to another zero, Y, who in my mouth

I know I'm foolish. Ashamed to be caught daydreaming.

You know, I'm obsessed with the servant problem—I mean getting hunchbacks to serve us, cripples, idiots, the insane, women—all kinds of unfit persons. Persons below the law. The trouble is, there's no one else. (There really is someone outside this room; I've fallen in love so often with unseen presences that I can tell when they're going to pop up; I mean of course a man outside the room with a torch, which makes his radiance precede him, and who has come to tell me I don't know what, that I ought to be rescuing Linda from something or other (the second thing she's good for). And I remember walking on the battlements here in clothes I'd stolen, men's clothes, isolated like a god in my own fancies, distorted and magnified by the fog in which everything became glitteringly visible. Everyone who saw me desired me. Although no one desires me or loves me now, someone exists in the fatherland whose very name would make any heart stop; I'm afraid even to look up from his bench on which I sit. A tree trunk. A pre-Columbian sun-god. A masked suit of armor, fretted with gold. The characteristic emotion of the fatherland is that feeling called by men *anguish*, by women *love*, and here in my little room in my tower, lit by a cold fire, reading, terribly nostalgic, remembering, dead, quite insane, a reincarnation of a Victorian lady's maid. I underestimate myself, I put my head in my hands, I long with all my soul to be staked, immolated, torn to pieces, suicided, to be stabbed repeatedly, to be repeatedly impaled. Tears of desire and anguish, although I am so tall and so friendless and so ugly. They were all unattractive, those legions of unloved sisters and fatherless girls, spinsters without hope, sick women in crinolines who nursed their fathers through mortal illnesses and never even got into pornography books. I think I'll get out; I could easily fool the guard outside the door, that hunchbacked rochester or watson or whatever-you-call-it (they're all over the place), who can be fooled by the crudest male impersonation. I will be so damned nonchalant, so recklessly brave, so brilliantly intellectual even in my page's costume (an alto). And Linda takes the heat off me, if only for a little while. So I'll get up and go. Looking for love.)

I was quite alone through all this, of course.

Stone stairs: each riser a different thought. Sometimes I saw three soldiers playing dice for my heart, sometimes a woman I know, a friend of mine, brushing her little daughter's hair. Such different scenes. The halls of this chateau are lit by naked, unfrosted light bulbs or sometimes with oil-dip lamps, or torches, or candles. To go traveling for love makes you a very vulnerable pilgrim. I thought that on the stairs I might meet Him, or that He might be walking down a passage, and these conjectures made me sick at heart. Girl in snowstorm, running away from castle. Girl in jungle, running away from verandah. Girl in moonlight, running away from mansion. That terrible presence that knocks you down. Fate. Kismet. I saw a great many things.

In one stone room myself as a five-year-old playing cards alone; the child turns, revealing that Its face is covered with ice or metal, some kind of mask or (horrible!) It grew that way.

A butcher shop set up inside the stone walls of this castle, with the meat cutter in his bloodstained apron winking energetically at me to show that he's jollying me along, he likes me. What do you want, honey? I bet you read books, ha ha. I bet you go to school. I know you don't mind my talking to you like this. Hell, she doesn't mind. Don't look so down, honey. I'll take care of you. He winks spasmodically like a demented machine, he can't stop, and the other women streetwalkers lean against the walls of the room in various attitudes of dislike and boredom. They've seen it all before, they don't care. His murderer's hand on mine.

A woman in a long skirt combing out her daughter's hair. A big brown-and-white dog lies snoozing by the stone fireplace and the amber Persian cats curl up in a chair by the embroidery frame. It's very quiet. The woman catches sight of me and smiles as if she knew something but won't tell me what it is; she looks up at me, amused; she'd rather be silent as my mother was while combing out my tangledy child's hair, as my cousin complained about having to be still while my mother's sister combed the snarls out of her long, curly, red hair, as some day I will set my daughter between my knees and comb her hair. We know something.

A man all in black reading in a room full of books, shelves set right into the stone walls; he's turning the pages under a shaded electric lamp. Dry, sensible, and competent. Who are you? He's amused: "I have the same name as you but I'm the lucky one."

It's hopeless. I'll never find Him. And I need Him so desperately. Right in the middle of the empty, lit-up corridor my palms sweat with fear, I get dizzy, my throat dries up; the very air is glittering with a dry, horrible desire. I'm nobody. I'm nothing. It's so humiliating to be me. I want to be taken out of myself, life is unbearable if I'm not, so I yearn for water, for Him; I almost lie down right here on the stone floor of the corridor; I want to curl up and die. The corrida of the horridor. Corridor. His absence: malicious and prying. A sterilization, a lack of sound. I remember what it was like to be without Him at sixteen, knowing that romance danced all around me but that He wouldn't come, that somehow I blighted it that I had a bad touch. Night after night I've fled down these halls, out of my mind with fear, trying to get out when I should have been trying to get in, carrying my shameful parts with me, of which the worst was: *I don't really want to be here.* They're right when they say it's the most important thing in your life. *I'm no better than the others.* I don't want to miss it, so I start running, like all those girls on the covers of paperback books who are running from mad wives in attics or dead wives in closets; I go zipping through the halls of the fatherland and in my blindness, with a dry grin of terror and repulsion *am catapulted through a crimson velvet drape into a scene of wild sexual license, everyone masked, naked, faceless, impersonally powerful except for the boys and girls spreadeagled, bent over, who are being pierced hard or worked at hard and who are not being consulted. Their anxious, pathetic, pained, little faces. Perhaps my ambidextrous smile will save me.*

Don't you want to be—?

Yes, I said (but do I have to go through all this?).

Made solemn by suffering, with my anxious little monkey-face all pursed up, I offered to him my delicate little bits of skin, my nether face, the quizzical palms of my hands, all my small thoughts. He battered them to pieces. I put my face in my hands and wept. This dreadful, mechanical business, shes on their backs, hes on all fours, so much human misery. I wouldn't mind if it was just a solid and dependable prick; I wouldn't mind if I could hold on to it and come one two three four five times just like that. I don't want this edge, subtle love that pierces to the marrow of my bones. Over my head I heard: I like boys; it's tighter. He took it out before I was ready and I wriggled like an eel, though I didn't want to; another appeared and I came. Have I violated etiquette? They fucked me in the ass and it hurt badly. Part of my clothes are gone, so I walk through it all in my long black aphrodisiac stockings and no pants, my dumb bush of hair showing dejectedly in front. It's a blight, desire in the secret parts everyone can see, my nether lips preparing to speak, stirring slowly, the tongue beginning to swell. There are dominators between me and the door. I took weak hold of a boy I did not know, but nothing happened; I think he will change in a moment (as I shake him pettishly by the shoulders), he'll go limp, his flesh will flow and change, he'll turn under my hands into a young woman, her face slender, her eyes violet-dim, little rolls of plumpness under her breasts and around her thighs. Chubby Linda.

I'm embracing a mirror.

For heaven's sake, put your clothes on! she says.

Dreaming of being kidnapped by pirates (I was eleven).

Movies.

Love comix.

The way it was: Dad helping Mother across the street because she was so weak and stupid she might get killed. His picking up jars by their tops and then blaming her for not screwing them on tight enough. His turning to me at the dinner table after he had finished all his food and saying, "Don't eat so fast. You'll get an ulcer." I remember a woman in a restaurant at the next table from us who had fresh flowers twined in her and her two little daughters' hair (honest) and a husband who said nothing. The matriarch talked endlessly to her two little girls because the three of them were so sensitive and beautiful and her husband obviously wasn't; she pointed out to her admiring girls how pretty and stylish Mother and I were. The man sat there and said nothing: the indispensable, crucial, lay figure.

That's what I am. That's what I'm for. Am I even that?

I think the Man I'm looking for, the Governor who controls this castle, will be somewhere at its highest point. He doesn't own it, He haunts it. I think I own it. I want to look up at Him imploringly and timidly; I want to say, "Do you need me?" I want to say, "Let me do something for you." We'll sit together in front of the fire, I with my dreaming head on His knee, and I'll be necessary to Him. All these thoughts are clichés, but that's life. I'm going up a sort of circular stairway, the treads of which are metal and therefore slippery. I could lie and say that the stairway is full of ghosts, but they were exhausted long ago; everything like that has already happened. I've been making my nightly pilgrimage for years and now only the reality is left.

With one exception: I think the ghost of my father is haunting these stairs. I can remember him so well—I can remember so many things. Queer to think that in those days he was younger than I am now. When I was five he took me out in a canoe and picked wild orchids for me. He made fishing flies by hand with a jeweler's loupe and tweezers, working on bits of tufted fluff as delicate as thoughts. He had bright eyes and a big nose (like mine), which I thought was beautiful. I made a shrine for his photograph with cardboard backing and two candles when I was twelve. He forgave my mother for being a woman because she was also a saint, but I betrayed him; I grew up. He liked to talk about history and epidemiology. When I was a little girl I believed that it was he who made the sun come up every morning; I didn't believe it off my own bat but because he told me so. He gave me a Dumbo doll when I was four (that's the Disney elephant made out of grey plush) because we both had big ears and we would both learn to fly.

You know who's behind that door.

I want to see what he'll say to me this time. He always says something interesting.

I open the door and there he is, with his jeweler's loupe in his eye, working with tweezers and a needle and thread.

He looks up unsympathetically. "Don't touch anything."

I wait. Petulant and bitter, a little old man with exophthalmic eyes and the white sideburns and whiskers of the Emperor Franz Josef, my father works with his bits of thread. He is, in some way that I don't understand, a failure. He's embittered by the world's refractoriness, by his mother's strength, by the treachery of his daughter. He looks up and says crossly, "I don't like the way you sit. Your thighs are too fat."

That's first. He's muttering to himself, something about A Beautiful Blonde who drove the wrong way down a one-way street. Ha ha. He's really nobody. He lives here, in my head.

"You," he says sulkily, "have been chosen to be Commander General of the whole universe." He lifts his lip cruelly in a smile, gloating over what comes next. "But you're not going to get the job.

"Do you know why?"

I say nothing.

"You're not going to get the job," says my father with immense, self-righteous pleasure, *"because they can't provide bathroom facilities for girls!''* He starts laughing like a crow that used to live next to us in the country, the pet of the people down the road; it would get terribly stirred up and would hop around its cage with a hoarse, loud caw, trying to eat the bars or worry at them with its beak, excited and gratified over things none of us could understand. Who knows what makes a crow happy or sad?

And that's my father.

My God, but it's *cold* in the fatherland! Bitter cold even inside the castle; I had to wrap myself in my cloak and when I met Linda on the next landing down (long past that door, now shut) the wind outside flung a gust through the trefoil window that covered us with stinging snow. It stuns you; it makes your ears ring. Linda must have had an experience like mine; she crossed her arms and beat them against her chest to keep warm. "Oh fuck it," she said bitterly. "Oh fuck it, the hell with it. It's not worth it."

"Where'd you get the fur coat?" I said. (That was one swell fur coat.)

"Stole it." She coughed, breathed on her glasses, and then polished them on the lapel of her fur—bear, as I remember. She jerked a fist across her throat to indicate what she'd done to somebody (or maybe only what she'd like to do), then staggered comically around the landing with her tongue stuck out and her eyes crossed. "Blotto," she said. We kissed good-bye because we were going separate ways. "Will you write?" we said, "Oh, do write." Down the freezing halls of the fatherland—or man's land—where rime spreads in poetic, furry stain over the stone floor, out between the bars of the back gate, around the edge of a vast, dark, frozen pond, and crawling on our stomachs through a hole in the last stone wall where Linda lost her fur hat. There was a blizzard you could not face into, now that the magic was gone, trees that lashed at you, and the iron-hard furrows of the potato fields of my father's country where maidens in the springtime (which never comes) may gather (if you'll excuse the expression) very small potatoes indeed.

How did I get out?

I said Good-bye, Good-bye.

I walked through the door. The door to the motherland can be a door in a construction fence that leads nowhere, a door inside a closet that leads to a hidey-hole, a door in the brick front of a house on a street in a town in any part of the world. The trick is to get inside oneself. The Great Goddess puts me between Her knees and combs my hair night and day. Striding over the crests of the grassy hills with Her panthers, She causes the grass to stretch precariously between its grasping toe and its one drinking eye, trying to be with Her; trees lean toward Her, dishevelled with desire. As the fish is in the sea and the sea is in the fish, so we live and move and have our being. It's colorless in the swimming mist, clear and thin-drawn, here where it's infinite, as color comes back to things from Her bright face. Her pine-cones, Her spear, Her sandals, Her twisted snakes. Time runs differently in the two places, and as my father creates around Him perpetual night, so Her days and nights naturally progress, and now Her sun rises clear of the hills. Linda rises too, nymphlike, from the grass, embodied out of a stream, hung about with watches, knapsacks, wallets, extra socks, canteens, and collapsible drinking-cups, all the trophies of travel. "Have I had adventures!" she says. "It took me ten years to get home." She pitches a tent, washes her socks, builds a fire, shears a sheep, ploughs a homestead, delivers a baby, sets up a collapsible typewriter, digs a field toilet, and holding a wetted finger up to the wind, accurately predicts the weather for the next twenty-four hours. "Have I got things to tell you!" she says. Delighted, I settle down on the grass and prepare to listen. It's going to be a long, leisurely feast. She Herself is listening, one vast, attentive, radiant Ear bending over the hills. We're in Her lap this pale, fresh, chilly, summer dawn.

At last.

Continued from page iv.

"Life in a Furniture Store" appeared in *Epoch* XV:1, Fall 1965. Copyright © 1965 by Cornell University.

"The Little Dirty Girl" appeared in *Elsewhere II* (New York: Ace Books) 1982. Copyright © 1982 by Joanna Russ.

"Main Street: 1953" appeared in *Sinister Wisdom* 24, Fall 1983. Copyright © 1983 by Sinister Wisdom.

"Mr. Wilde's Second Chance" appeared in *The Magazine of Fantasy and Science Fiction* 31:3 (184) October 1966. Copyright © 1966 by Mercury Press, Inc. Reassigned to Joanna Russ in 1981.

"Nor Custom Stale" appeared in *The Magazine of Fantasy and Science Fiction* 17:3 (100) September 1959. Copyright © 1959 by Mercury Press, Inc. Reassigned to Joanna Russ in 1981.

"Old Pictures" appeared in *The Little Magazine* 6:4, Winter 1973. Copyright © 1973 by The Little Magazine.

"Reasonable People" appeared in *Orbit 14* (New York: Harpers) 1974. Copyright © 1974 by Damon Knight.

"A Short and Happy Life" appeared in *The Magazine of Fantasy and Science Fiction* 36:6 (217). Copyright © 1969 by Mercury Press. Reassigned to Joanna Russ in 1981.

"Sword Blades and Poppy Seed" appeared in *Heroic Visions* (New York: Ace Books) 1983. Copyright © 1983 by Jessica Amanda Salmonson.

"This Afternoon" appeared in *Cimarron Review* 6, February 1968. Copyright © 1968 by Board of Regents for Oklahoma State University.

"This Night at My Fire" appeared in *Epoch* XV:2, Winter 1966. Copyright © 1966 by Cornell University.

"The Throaways" appeared in *Consumption* 2:3, Summer 1969. Copyright © 1969 by Paul Hunter, Tom Parson, and John Sherman.

"The View from This Window" appeared in *Quark 1* (New York: Paperback Library) 1970. Copyright © 1970 by Coronet Communications.

"Visiting" appeared in *Manhattan Review*, Fall 1967. Copyright © 1967 by Eric F. Oatman.

"Visiting Day" appeared in *South* 2:1, 1970. Copyright © 1970 by Stetson University.

"Window Dressing" appeared in *New Worlds of Fantasy* 2 (New York: Ace Books) 1970. Copyright © 1970 by Joanna Russ.

The following two stories first appeared individually. In this collection they appear together under the title "Old Thoughts, Old Presences."

"The Autobiography of My Mother" appeared in *Epoch* XXV:1, Fall 1975. Copyright © 1975 by Cornell University.

"Daddy's Little Girl" appeared in *Epoch* XXIV:2 Spring 1975. Copyright © 1975 by Cornell University.